THE DAY HE SAID HELLO

HAWTHORNE HARBOR SECOND CHANCE
ROMANCE BOOK 3

ELANA JOHNSON

AEJ
CREATIVE WORKS

ISBN-13: 978-1-953506-06-1

1

"Hey, Uno." Bennett Patterson took a moment to bend down and pat the Dalmatian that greeted all the firefighters when they came into work. The dog had been a gift from Fire House Two to Fire House One when their previous dog had passed away.

Bennett had spent a fair bit of time training Uno how to jump into the fire truck, where to ride, and what to do on the job.

Not that they had many of those in Hawthorne Harbor. But hey, Bennett and all the other firefighters were prepared, right down to their canine mascot.

He sighed as he straightened, not quite sure if he was ready for his overnight shift. He did like sleeping at the station, because at least then he wasn't home alone.

Not alone, he thought as he went to put his food in the

fridge. Charles was on tonight too, so he'd cook dinner, and Bennett's mouth was already watering.

And he wasn't really alone at home. He had Gemma, the big, black Labrador retriever to keep him company. He'd gotten the dog when she was a puppy, right after his marriage had dissolved.

Bennett pushed away the thoughts and took a deep breath. This, right here. Fire House One. This was where he belonged, and where he wanted to be, even if the possibility of getting a job more interesting than saving a cat from a hot tin roof was slim to none.

Heck, he probably wouldn't even get to save the cat.

Normally, he didn't mind. He'd work out, and read a little to Uno. The Dalmatian didn't care that Bennett took a little longer on some words as he tried to get his dyslexia to cooperate with his brain. He'd maybe call Jason, his best friend, over at the police station and see if they could go out on a patrol. Something.

Somehow, Bennett would find a way to fill the hours.

"There you are." Charles Hiatt appeared in the kitchen too. "You ready for tonight? I brought ribs and brisket."

Bennett grinned at his fellow firefighter. "Totally ready. Did Melinda make any of that potato salad?"

"As a matter of fact." Charles lifted a blue bowl the size of a watermelon, and Bennett grinned.

Charles opened the fridge and started moving things around inside it to make room of the vat of potato salad. "Did you see the note from the chief?"

"Nope, I just got here." Bennett wasn't going to let Charles know about his internal pep talk, or the fact that he was bored out of his mind in this job.

It was a job, and one Bennett wanted, despite certain drawbacks.

"Inspection by Monday." Charles shoved the bowl inside and closed the fridge in a hurry, grinning like he'd just solved the problem of childhood hunger.

Bennett groaned. "Inspection?" That meant hours of cleaning the station. Not so much as a single dog hair should be found, and wow, Uno lost *a lot* of hair.

"Oh, come on." Charles grinned and clapped one giant hand on Bennett's shoulder. "It'll give us something to do, at least."

Bennett nodded, already mourning the loss of a lazy afternoon ride in the police cruiser, maybe with enough time to stop down at the beach for a snack.

"You didn't bring Gemma?" Charles looked around as if the dog was simply playing hide and seek.

"I let Nelly have her this time." Bennett turned away from Charles and opened the cupboard where the cleaning supplies were kept.

"That kid." Charles chuckled as he took the broom from its spot in the corner. "You're going to spoil her, and then you'll be sorry."

Bennett shrugged, not really caring if he spoiled the cute five-year-old who lived next door. Her parents loved Gemma too, and this way, everyone got to enjoy the dog and only Bennett had to take care of her. Sort of. The Yardley's would certainly care for Gemma for the next two days until Bennett returned home. It was like they'd come to a joint custody arrangement for the black lab. So what if it had all come about because Nelly-the-five-year-old had the biggest blue eyes on the planet? Blue eyes Bennett hadn't been able to say no to. Her parents either, apparently.

As he wiped and scrubbed, dusted and swept, he listened to Charles hum and then sing. Uno followed them everywhere they went, and Bennett's bad mood quickly moved into something more positive.

"Hey, are you still handy with a hammer?" Charles asked after they'd sat down to lunch.

"Sometimes," Bennett said, looking at his friend. Charles seemed made of shades of brown. His eyes were the darkest, just a step or two below his hair. His skin sat a shade above that.

"Melinda wants to expand our back deck. I told her you might be able to do it."

The prospect of another carpentry project brought a tingle of excitement to Bennett's fingertips. He tried to ignore how *a deck* had lifted his blood pressure.

"I can come look," he said casually. "When we get off tomorrow." He really wanted to go right now. If a call came in—he wasn't holding his breath—it would forward to their cell phones.

"Great."

Chief Harvey walked in, sniffing like he was part bloodhound. "Place smells great, guys. You must've gotten my note."

"Yes, sir," Charles said, practically saluting with his barking voice.

Bennett rolled his eyes and took another bite of potato salad, reasoning that he had a job, friends, a dog, and this delicious salad. He didn't need anything else.

But the void he'd felt in his life these past few months simply wouldn't budge, even when he stuffed himself full of potato salad and then, later, ribs.

THE WHITE LIGHT WOKE HIM A SPLIT SECOND BEFORE THE shrill ring of the telephone. Bennett sat up, all his senses on high alert as that blinding light continued to flash and the phone got covered with the sound of an alarm.

"Finally," he said, pulling on his pants, then his fire suit and boots. He grabbed his hat and made it into the truck bay four steps ahead of Charles.

"What's the call?" he asked. "Come on, Uno. Load up."

The Dalmatian jumped into the truck and Bennett followed.

Charles read a meaningless address to Bennett, who though he now lived in Hawthorne Harbor had grown up in Bell Hill. Besides, he didn't know every residential address.

"Neighbor reported flames," Charles said, starting the truck, which roared to life and sent vibrations down Bennett's spine.

The alarm sounded one more time, and then quieted. Charles put the siren on, and they picked up speed as they moved down Main Street toward the north end of town.

Hawthorne Harbor wasn't that big, but it took several turns to get to the address. Bennett's hopes fell when they pulled up and found several people standing on the lawn.

There were no flames to be seen.

No fire.

Bennett got out of the truck anyway, his suit suddenly heavy and ridiculous. Charles took the lead, as he was the senior firefighter on duty that night, and Bennett waited with Uno.

"I saw smoke," a woman said. "And then the bright flash of flames. I didn't know if anyone was home. She just moved in."

"Who lives here?" Charles asked.

"I can't remember her name." The woman's hands clawed at themselves. "I don't see her car, and she hasn't come out."

Just then, the front door to the quaint little cottage opened, and a female figure appeared in the rectangle of light.

Charles said, "Thank you," and moved toward the woman, Bennett in tow.

"Ma'am," he called. "Are you okay?"

"I got the fire out," she said, her voice not quite as appreciative as Bennett would've liked.

He also recognized the voice, from somewhere in his far distant past. He couldn't quite place it immediately, and it seemed like she had a spotlight framing her, because he couldn't see her either.

"Well, we need to check it out," Charles said in his best fatherly tone. Not too condescending. Not too demanding. Just like, *Oh, it's not big deal, but we're here so we'll take a look.*

Bennett needed to work on his tone, as most of what he said ended up sounding like a bark.

"Fine." The woman turned, her long hair swishing in the light, and went back in the house without inviting them in.

Another memory stirred inside Bennett's mind. He'd seen hair like that. Touched it....

"Can't be," he muttered to himself. Jennie Zimmerman had left Hawthorne Harbor two decades ago, vowing never to come back.

He followed Charles into the house, which admittedly, didn't seem like it was even remotely on fire.

"Something just sparked in my kiln," she said irritably. "It was nothing. A few flames for a few seconds. I honestly don't know how anyone saw it."

She folded her arms and stood outside of a doorway. "You can't touch anything."

Charles walked right past her, and she turned her face toward Bennett's.

His breath stuck somewhere behind his lungs, making a choking sound gargle from his throat.

It *was* Jennie Zimmerman, and she was just as blonde, just as blue-eyed, and just as beautiful as she'd been in high school.

She glared at him as if they hadn't gone out several times, as if he hadn't taken her to his senior prom, as if he hadn't been her first kiss.

"Hello, Jennie," he managed to say. He wanted to shout, *Do you remember me? Why are you looking at me like that?*

"Bennett?" Her expression didn't soften. If anything, she cinched her arms tighter around herself.

"Bennett," Charles called, and Bennett held her gaze for one more moment before stepping into the art studio.

It looked less like a place someone could create beautiful work and more like a paint bomb had gone off.

Or a plaster bomb. Probably both. Multiple times.

He couldn't glance from surface to surface fast enough, couldn't absorb all the different mediums in the room—or place the smell that hit him like a sucker punch.

"I mean it," Jennie said, squeezing in behind him. "I'm in the middle of four commissioned pieces, and you can't touch anything."

Charles had bent over a huge contraption in the

corner, and Bennett stepped through the chaos of brushes, wire, boxes of clay, paint, and dozens of other supplies to get to him.

His suit was so bulky, he couldn't help touching the tiniest corner of some things, and Jennie sighed heavily behind him.

He wanted to round on her and let her have it. This place was a fire waiting to happen. One spark from the kiln...she was lucky it hadn't ignited some cleaning fluid or any of the dozens of parchments she had stacked on a table.

"This outlet," Charles indicated it, and Bennett immediately saw the black singe marks.

"Shorted," he said.

"Sparked," Charles confirmed. "Ma'am, you'll have to replace this outlet."

Jennie crammed herself into the tight space with Charles and Bennett, her weight pressing against Bennett's side. He told himself not to take a deep breath of her, not to try to find that underlying scent of flowers and fruit she always had. But he did it anyway.

And beneath the scorching smell, and the industrial powder smell of art supplies, he found it.

A sigh passed through his body, and Bennett wondered if maybe he had room for one more thing in his life.

Then Jennie said, "Still bald, I see," and backed up.

Bennett gave Charles a bit more room too, retreating and blinking at Jennie as he tried to make his brain work.

"I don't know how one goes about becoming un-bald," he said. At least it wasn't a bark. He stroked one gloved hand down his very full beard, which he took great pride in as he couldn't seem to get the top of his head to grow hair.

"Still unhappy to be in Hawthorne Harbor, I see." Bennett saw the punch his words carried as Jennie flinched, her face contorting for a moment before she smoothed it back to normal.

She opened her mouth to say something—another insult, no doubt—and burst into tears instead.

2

Jennie Zimmerman was in fact, not happy to be back in Hawthorne Harbor. And to have Bennett Patterson right there in front of her? A witness to her creative madness. Judging how she'd plugged in her appliances.

And now watching her cry like a fool.

She tried to school her emotions but they'd been on a yo-yo for weeks now.

Months, she thought. Six months, to be exact. Six months *today* since her fiancé had not shown up at the altar, leaving Jennie standing at the end of the aisle, her hand clutching her father's arm, desperately hoping he'd come out any moment.

Well, he hadn't. And Jennie hadn't seen him again at all.

"You really can't plug six things into an outlet meant

for two," the older of the two firemen said. Jennie knew his name; she just couldn't think of it.

He held up the surge protector she'd been using. "That kiln is way more than any of these can take. It needs a special outlet with the right voltage." He wore a very serious look, and when Bennett joined him as a united front against her, Jennie finally seized onto her anger enough to ebb the flow of tears.

"Fine," she said.

"Charles," Bennett said, putting his ridiculously huge hand on his partner's.

The two men exchanged a glance and Charles left with the ruined surge protector. Was he going to bag it for evidence?

She'd gotten the fire out herself. Nothing had been too damaged, and there had been no public threat.

"He'll cut the electricity to your studio until you fix the outlet," Bennett said. He seemed sorry. Sort of. Jennie couldn't really tell. He'd always worn his emotions behind a mask, never letting anyone see how he felt.

But Jennie had figured out how to get him to take that mask off. Say all kinds of things. Reveal how he truly felt, what he thought, all of it.

Yeah, she thought, staring at him. And then you left without even saying goodbye.

Her biggest regret so far.

"I don't know how to fix it."

"You call an electrician," he said, starting to step past her.

"Wait." She put her hand on his arm, but the fire suit was way too thick. Still, he paused, looking at her hand and then into her face.

A surge of power seemed to jump from him to her. Or her to him. She again wasn't sure. Jennie was unsure of almost everything these days.

"What?" he asked, his voice soft but teeming against his impatience. At least that hadn't changed about him.

Everything else had, though. He'd grown at least three more inches, and firefighting obviously did a body good, because his shoulders filled out his fire suit spectacularly.

She'd always liked that he was bald, and with the thick, black beard he wore with it? Jennie had trouble swallowing, blinking, breathing.

"Are you okay?" He peered closer at her. "I can call an ambulance."

"I don't need an ambulance."

"There isn't a car out front."

"I don't own a car."

"Did you inhale any smoke?"

She shook her head. "I told you, I got the fire out in seconds. The window was open."

He gave one nod and dropped his gaze to her hand, which still sat on his forearm.

"Aren't you an electrician?" she asked.

Those eyes—dark and dreamy and dangerous to her health—turned sharp and hard.

"I never finished," he said. "Excuse me."

Jennie turned and watched him stride out of her art studio, never looking back once.

Everything inside her caved in, and she slumped against the nearest table. What a night this had turned into.

She'd just come into the studio to get her piece into the kiln. Then she'd been planning to maybe do a little bit of the painting Mabel had asked for.

A huge project, the painting was almost a mural, and Mabel wanted it to fill an entire wall in the west wing she was renovating.

Jennie had been grateful for the work. She'd left her studio in San Francisco after the failed wedding, because Kyle the fiancé was the manager of her space.

She simply couldn't come face-to-face with him every day and stay sane. So while she hadn't wanted to return to her hometown, without a studio, or any other job prospects, she hadn't had much choice.

She left her art behind and went back through the house to the front porch, where the firefighters stood talking to one another.

The crowd on the lawn had dispersed, thankfully, and Jennie asked, "So is there anything else I need to do?"

Both men trained their eyes on her, and Jennie wilted

under Charles's and wanted to bask in the heat from Bennett's.

Heat?

She startled at the thought. She was in no position to start another relationship, and certainly not with the high school flame she'd abandoned over twenty years ago.

Nope. Not happening.

"I've cut power to your studio for now," Charles said. "We can give you the names of some great electricians. They'll get you back up and running once everything is in compliance."

Jennie cringed at the last word. She didn't want to be compliant. Not anymore.

Charles walked away, leaving Bennett to stare at her.

"And you might want to clean that place up a little," he said. "Honestly, Jennie, it looks like a crime scene."

She expected him to laugh, but he didn't. She tried to find a tease in the words, but there wasn't one.

"Oh, I forgot," she said, a measure of sarcasm in her voice. "You're Mister Organized."

He shook his head, finally a small smile gracing that powerful mouth. She willed herself not to think about kissing him, but her memories were too huge, too powerful, to hold back.

"One of us had to be, sweetheart." With those as parting words, he left her standing on the front porch. Her heart dangled from a string inside her chest, nowhere near ready to take on another man. Especially one as gorgeous, as stubborn, and as broken as Bennett Patterson.

"WHAT DO YOU MEAN, YOUR STUDIO IS SHUT DOWN?" Pepper Howard slid a cup of tea across the table to Jennie, then set another one in front of an empty seat. So Callie would be coming.

Pepper ran her fingers through her short, mohawked hair before lifting her coffee to her lips. How anyone drank that stuff, Jennie didn't know.

"By order of the fire marshal," she said. "Or something." She actually had no idea what Charles was. All she knew was that he was powerful enough to shut her down. Bennett wasn't a marshal. She didn't have power in her studio, but her house and Internet worked just fine. So she'd spent some time looking him up.

She knew more about him than she probably should, and she was going to keep that to herself during this impromptu breakfast initiated by Pepper.

"What are you going to do about the pieces?"

"I'll get them done." Jennie waved her hand like she could conjure up a new outlet as easily. "So what are we doing here, Pepper? It's barely eight."

The rest of the crowd seemed to swell in and rush right back out, like waves against the shore. People with nine-to-five jobs, something neither she nor Pepper had.

Callie did, though, and as she huffed and sat, she said, "Whew. There is nowhere to park out there." She glanced at Jennie and then Pepper, a smile lighting up her pretty face. "Is this for me?" She wrapped her fingers around the teacup as if it were winter in Hawthorne Harbor and not the height of the hottest time of the year.

"We're here this early, because I have some news." Pepper fiddled with her hair again, prolonging the moment.

Jennie deliberately didn't take another sip of her tea.

"Oh, go on," Callie said. "You're killing us." She nudged Jennie with her elbow and Jennie nodded solemnly.

She couldn't hold the look long, and broke into a grin. "It's about Hunter, right?"

"We went ring shopping on Wedding Row last night!" Pepper practically yelled the last couple of words, drawing the attention of a couple of men wearing suits and gripping coffee cups like their very lives depended on the caffeine inside.

Callie squealed like a stuck pig, and while Jennie congratulated her friend and laughed and smiled and acted interested in the pictures on Pepper's phone, all she could think was, *Good luck getting down the aisle.*

She settled down first, taking another careful sip of her tea though it was already too cool for her taste.

The door behind her opened, and she glanced toward the men that entered. She almost spit out her tea at the sight of Charles and Bennett—*oh, my Bennett*—walking toward the counter to order.

He wore a pair of jeans that disappeared into a heavy-duty pair of work boots and a T-shirt that said *Hawthorne Harbor Fire Department* splashed across the chest.

The arms needed to be taken out, because wow, the man had biceps for days.

"Are you okay?" Callie's question cut through Jennie's stupor, and she hastily reached for the napkin Pepper had extended toward her.

She wiped the drips of tea from her lips, wondering why her heart had started rapid-firing in her chest in such a strange way.

"Is that Bennett Patterson?" Callie asked, pushing her hair over her shoulder.

"He's off-limits," Pepper said quickly, her eyes landing on Jennie's for a moment.

"Oh?" Callie looked away from the two men putting in their order. "Why? We don't like him?"

Pepper nodded toward Jennie. "One of her exes."

Callie hadn't grown up in town, and she'd had no trouble getting a date—at least according to Pepper, who'd been friends with her for a few years.

Jennie was just barely back in town, and it had been hard enough reopening her friendship with Pepper. She hadn't warmed to Callie as easily as she might have if she'd been more functional, but Jennie knew she definitely didn't want Bennett and Callie to go out.

"Oh, was it bad?" Callie's bright blue eyes searched Jennie's.

"She's still interested in him," Pepper said, making Jennie suck in a tight breath. "So he's off-limits until she figures things out."

"I'm not still interested in him," Jennie hissed as he turned, his to-go cup of coffee clutched in one hand while a large slab of banana bread balanced in the other.

"You've never said as much, but you don't date," Pepper said.

Jennie had a reason for that. Just because she hadn't told anyone—not a single soul—in Hawthorne Harbor what it was didn't make it any less valid.

Bennett's eye caught hers, and he lifted the banana bread as if that meant hello.

Jennie's eyebrows shot up, especially when he started navigating through the tables toward her instead of just going toward the exit after Charles.

"Hey," he said, positioning himself next to her. "Did you get that email I sent over?"

"I haven't had time to look," she said coolly, wondering how she could ever truly look him in the face again. After what she'd done all those years ago, and then after bursting into tears last night.

He didn't seem to carry any of the awkwardness with him that he'd had last night, and his gaze flickered to Pepper and then Callie.

"Well, check when you can," he said. "It's got all the

electrician information." His eyes settled on her again, and the weight of them felt like a load of lead.

"Thanks," she said, barely glancing up. Not enough to truly lock her gaze onto his. If she did...everyone in the coffee shop would knew that yes, she was still interested in him.

"See you later. Hey, Pepper."

"Bennett."

The man walked away, and finally Jennie was able to take a decent breath. The lingering scent of his cologne filled her nostrils, and she wished she'd had the willpower to hold out a little longer.

She lifted her teacup to her lips, ignoring Callie when she said, "I see what you mean, Pepper." She cleared her throat and tossed her hair. "So he's off-limits. Who else looks interesting?"

3

Bennett couldn't stop thinking about Jennie Zimmerman. She'd turned up twice in his life in the past twenty-four hours, and he wondered if maybe it was a sign.

Or something.

He didn't really believe in signs. Didn't spend a lot of time in church, or thinking too hard about things.

When Jennie had left town two days after her high school graduation, Bennett had been...upset. That word seemed to fit as well as any others he could think of.

He and Jennie hadn't been terribly serious, though he was a couple of years older than her and had dated her even after he'd left high school and started into some trade professions.

He hadn't finished his electrician training, but he had

become a master carpenter and a firefighter after she'd left town.

He knew she hadn't liked the small town lifestyle, but he'd been hoping some of their last conversations—about marriage and family and a beach house down the lane from her parents—would turn into reality.

His reality had taken him down a completely different road, and it sounded like Jennie didn't know anything about it.

Why he wanted to get together with her and tell her all about it, he couldn't fathom. She hadn't even been nice last night.

But the tears were a dead giveaway of her stress—her *dis*tress. For the Jennie Zimmerman he'd known growing up never cried. Never.

She disliked coffee, and as he followed the chief around as he inspected every shelf and each tiny space for dust or lint, Bennett liked that at least that hadn't changed about Jennie.

Little had, actually. She still had those aquamarine eyes that pulled at him to come closer, hold tighter, kiss longer. That same long, blonde hair that swished around her waistline. Her love of tea. And Pepper Howard at her side.

He hadn't recognized the other woman at the table, but he didn't much care who she was. Bennett seemed to only have eyes for Jennie—again.

"Looks good, boys," Chief Harvey finally said, and

Bennett breathed a sigh of relief. The ribs had been magnificent last night, and then there was the brief fire scare at Jennie's. And with the cleaning, Bennett's long shift for the month had actually gone quickly.

"Someone here for you," Charles said, and the chief turned. "Oh, for Bennett." Charles ducked back out the door toward the front of the firehouse, while Bennett's imagination went nuts.

Maybe it was Jennie, stopping by to profess how she'd never gotten over him, even after all these years.

He shook his head to clear it. He wasn't even looking for a relationship at the moment. In fact, he'd turned down the last three women who'd asked him out. Best thing about a small town? Word had gotten around that he wouldn't say yes, and the girls had stopped asking completely.

He didn't need a girlfriend. He had Gemma. And Uno. And his friends at the station, one of whom happened to be his boss and was staring at him.

"Are you going to go see who it is?" Chief Harvey asked.

"Yes." Bennett sprang toward the door. "Yes, I am." He stepped into the outer lobby to find old Mabel Magleby standing there.

"Mabel?" he asked, glancing around as if Jennie might be hiding behind the petite woman who had to be close to ninety years old.

"There you are," she said with a definite hint of grumpiness in her tone. "Thought you might be napping."

He chuckled and came around the counter where Charles sat filling out some paperwork from last night's adventure.

"Nope, not napping. What can I help you with?"

"You said you'd come help demolish the west wing."

Demolition of a house or project was almost better than rebuilding it. "Of course. Are you ready for that already? I thought you needed to meet with...someone." He couldn't really remember the details. The older woman had stopped him at the Lavender Festival last month to ask him about doing some work on the Mansion she owned and operated.

He'd had his sights set on the winning lavender brownies and had agreed with her quickly so he could slip away before the treat was all gone.

"I'm ready," she said in a sure voice. Her hands shook the slightest bit. "What's your schedule like?"

"I'm off for the next couple of days," he said, shooting a glance at Charles. "Should I come out tomorrow?"

"Tomorrow's fine." Mabel wore a frown but she patted his hand and shuffled toward the door. "Not too early. I'm old these days and need my beauty sleep." She opened the door and stepped into the evening. Once the door snapped closed again, Bennett let his laugh fly free.

"She's a character," he said to Charles, who laughed with him.

"Yeah." He watched the door for a moment. "Wonder what'll happen to Magleby Mansion when she passes."

Bennett fell silent with the sobering thought. "I don't know. I hadn't thought about it."

"She has no kids," Charles said. "Maybe a neice or nephew will take it over."

"Maybe." Bennett went to get his bag and get ready to go home. "I'm taking Uno for a couple of days, remember?"

"Yep. Got it." Charles didn't look up from his work.

Bennett leashed Uno and grabbed his stuff, loading everyone and everything up in his truck. "Want to run today, boy?" He glanced at the dog like he would answer back.

"No? You're young. Gemma will go, and she's starting to go gray around her mouth." He continued his one-sided conversation with Uno as he drove out of town and toward Bell Hill. He didn't live in town anymore, but on the outskirts of Hawthorne Harbor.

The road held six houses, all on the same side of the street, all facing inland with the lush forests of Washington in front of them.

He pulled into his driveway and let Uno out. The dog sniffed around the front yard, took care of his business, and trotted after Bennett as he went next door to collect Gemma.

A booming bark sounded from the back yard, and

Bennett changed his course to go through the gate instead of to the front door.

Splashing and the sweet scent of sugar filled the air as he unlatched the gate and called, "Nelly? It's Bennett."

In the next three seconds, the little girl appeared, soaked from head to toe with a huge smile on her face. "Bennett! Come see Gemma swim."

"Gemma can't—" But Nelly had run off before Bennett could finish. He grinned and chuckled, not overly enthused about his dog being wet the way Nelly was. Uno hovered at Bennett's side, somehow sensing that if he let Nelly too close, he could end up in the pool too.

Because the Yardley's had a huge swimming pool in their backyard—the above ground kind that required Nelly to navigate a ladder to get in and out—and Gemma was currently paddling her way around it, a huge Labrador smile on her face.

"Oh, wow," Bennett said, stepping up to the pool. "Look at you, Gemma. Look at you swimming."

So maybe his voice strayed into a higher octave. So he loved his dog. Big deal.

Gemma swam over to him and lunged at him to lick his face. Bennett laughed but fell back, not needing sixty pounds of muscly dog splashing him with water.

"Do you have to take him?" Nelly asked.

"It's a her," Bennett said for at least the hundredth time. "And yes, you've had her for two whole days." He bent down to look right into Nelly's blue eyes. "I brought

Uno. You can come play with them in the fields, if you want."

Her whole face lit up. "Can I? I'll ask my mom right now!" She turned to race into the house, but Montana Yardley said, "Not today, Nelly. Remember we're going to Nana's?" before she'd taken more than two steps.

Bennett straightened and waved to Montana. "Hey, there," he said. "Thanks for having Gemma."

"Oh, we love her." Montana wore a big smile to go with the statement, but her clothes said she would not be coming down off the deck. She wore a ribbed black sweater with pearls around her neck, and a pair of black slacks. With heels. Apparently visiting Nana was a *very* serious occasion.

Montana extended her hand to Nelly. "Come on, Nels. You need a bath. We have to leave in an hour."

"I'll get—" Before Bennett could finish, Gemma heaved herself out of the pool, bringing at least twenty gallons of water with her—most of it splashing and soaking Bennett's shoes and pants.

He did not want to shower and change for the second time that day, but his only choice was to laugh and say, "Well, that's one way to get out of the pool."

THE FOLLOWING MORNING—NOT TOO EARLY—BENNETT loaded up the dogs and drove toward the beach and

Magleby Mansion. Uno whined, but if Bennett had wanted to run along the sand with the dalmatian, he should've come a lot earlier. The breeze coming off the water probably would've kept him cool enough, but Bennett liked to run before the sun made it's full appearance for the day, craving that feeling of being the only person in Hawthorne Harbor that was awake.

"We'll go tomorrow," he told Uno. He had to be to work for the afternoon shift, so he'd be able to get in his pre-dawn run then.

Uno gave one last whine and put his front paws on the dashboard as Gemma was hogging the passenger window, her whole body almost hanging outside of the truck.

He pulled into the long driveway that led up to the Mansion, his mind automatically flowing back to the time he'd driven this way, his bride-to-be at his side.

He really thought he'd be with Cynthia forever. They got along great, and she laughed at all his corny jokes, and the first couple of years of their marriage had been fantastic.

He pushed the memories away and pulled right up to the front door, which several ancient hawthorn trees shaded.

The stones looked centuries old, with vines climbing them. Every flower and bush grew exactly right, and Bennett wondered how many gardeners Mabel employed.

She used to take care of the grounds herself, he knew

that. He'd visited the Hawthorne Harbor town museum more times than he wanted to admit.

He let the dogs out and said, "Stay," as he indicated the huge gardens and grassy areas surrounding them. Gemma ran off with Uno, and Bennett turned to face the Mansion. A bicycle leaned against the wall behind the stairs, but it almost looked like it belonged there, sort of a vintage piece.

He climbed the steps and tried the door, finding it open. "Hello?" he called, his voice echoing against the stones inside too.

The Mansion stood three stories tall, and Bennett could see all the way up to the top floor from the magnificent stairwell in the middle of the room.

"Mabel," he tried next, and somewhere within the Mansion a door closed.

"Back here." Her voice reached him, and Bennett moved across the stone floor to find her hurrying from an office.

She smiled at him—an actual smile—and Bennett returned it. "I hope it's not too early."

"Oh, pish posh. I've been up for hours."

Of course she had. Bennett simply kept his smile in place and tucked his hands in his pockets while he waited for her to tell him what to do.

"So I'm doing a major renovation on the west wing on the second and third floors." Mabel moved toward the staircase, getting a very firm hold on the banister before she lifted her foot to climb.

Bennett wanted to grab onto her to keep her steady, but he wasn't sure she'd appreciate it. He'd heard her say "I'm old, not dead," to more than one person who'd offered their help during festivals and around town.

So he simply positioned himself behind her so he could catch her should she fall.

Painstaking step by painstaking step, they finally reached the second floor.

Mabel wheezed a bit and said, "So my artist is here, taking some measurements, but she'll be out of the way in no time."

Bennett had enough time to think *Artist?* before Mabel moved through a doorway and into a section of the Mansion that had certainly seen better days.

"This is Jennifer Zimmerman. I'm sure you guys know each other. Her family lives just down the beach a bit." Mabel looked at Bennett expectantly, but he had no idea what she wanted him to do.

Jennie indeed stood in the room, across from the large windows, a measuring tape in her hand. She wore a pair of cutoff shorts that showed her long, tan legs, and Bennett forgot his own name for a moment.

"Of course I know Bennett," Jennie said, a slip of disdain in her voice. None of it showed on her face, which also didn't hold even a hint of makeup. He loved this natural look of hers, as he'd always thought he'd seen the real her when she didn't cover up her imperfections.

"We dated a bit in high school," she said, her gaze skimming past him again. He really didn't like that she hadn't fully looked at him once since she'd been reintroduced into his life.

"You did?" Mabel's acting skills could certainly use some work as well.

Jennie smiled and shook her head, her long hair wisping a bit out of the topknot she'd tied at the back of her skull. Her shirt was the color of bright lemon rinds, and had little lemons all over it, making her seem like the sun illuminated her face.

"I'm almost done," she said, shaking out the tape measure. "I just can't seem to get the length. I'm not sure my tape measure is long enough."

"Bennett can help you," Mabel said, and Bennett sprang into action. He wondered how long he'd been standing there staring, wondering if he could somehow get Jennie to stay while he worked, talk to him the way she used to, and then take her to dinner.

Not going to happen, he told himself. After all, she wouldn't even *look* at him. She wouldn't hang around and chat him up. And going out?

Not going to happen.

But he did hold the end of her tape measure, and move it where she wanted him to, watched her make notes on a clipboard, and let her direct him through a couple more rooms as she took measurements.

"Thanks, Bennett." She bent over a backpack as she slid the clipboard into it. "You really helped speed the process up." She straightened and pushed out her breath, bracing her hands against her back and stretching. Her gaze flicked to his, and he nodded his acknowledgement that she'd thanked him.

"So, what are you doing here?" she asked.

Bennett once again felt like he'd lost an unknown amount of time as he stared at this beautiful woman he thought he'd never see again.

"Oh, Mabel's hired me to do the construction here."

Another woman walked into the room, a tool belt hanging off her hips. Bennett backpedaled quickly. "Well, she's obviously hired Lauren Michaels to do the construction. Hey, Lauren." He practically yelled to the brunette, who smiled and veered toward them.

She was a transplant to Hawthorne Harbor, but she did really fine work, and she'd been the lead general contractor on the new subdivision going in on the northeast edge of town.

Jennie didn't seem like she cared, but she shook Lauren's hand and then finally, *finally*, looked at Bennett.

"So if she's the general contractor, what are you doing here?"

"Demo," he said, wondering where Mabel had gotten to. She'd never said anything about a contract or pay, and he'd need to get those things in line before he just started knocking things down.

"He does a lot more than demo," Lauren said, glancing between the two of them. "He's the best master carpenter in the state."

Pride swelled within Bennett, but he waved his hand at Lauren. "An exaggeration."

Lauren smiled but looked at him evenly. "It's true. My guess is he's here to do the fireplace mantles. All the cabinetry. Anything that Mabel wants crafted from wood." She flipped a few pages on the clipboard she carried. "Yep. She didn't hire me for any of that."

Bennett lifted one shoulder as if to say, *Yep, that's why I'm here.*

Honestly? He hadn't signed or negotiated anything yet. But his fingers practically itched to get working on this beautiful piece of property, and bring new life to it through wood and craft.

"I've been commissioned for five art pieces," Jennie said, and Bennett's smile practically moved into a beam.

"That's great," he said.

Lauren's phone rang and she said, "Excuse me," before moving away and answering it.

Bennett looked at Jennie, glad to find her watching him back. "Carpentry, huh?"

"I guess it's what electrician drop-outs do."

Jennie grinned and shook her head. "And a firefighter. Wow."

He didn't mention the almost-pro baseball career. No need to. No one cared about the almosts in professional sports. "One pays all the bills. The other is just something I really enjoy."

"You always were good with your hands." Jennie gave him a sly smile, and Bennett's heart started jumping around like it had been shocked with electricity.

Was that flirting? Was she *flirting* with him?

"Here's your contract," Mabel said, entering the room, her face slightly flushed. "Wow, there are more stairs here than I remember." She wiped the back of her hand across her forehead and looked at Jennie, who stood there with one hand on her cocked hip.

"Did you get your measurements, dear?"

Jennie startled, tearing her eyes from Bennett. "Yes, ma'am. I'll bring you a sketch of the first piece soon." She started to move away, but Mabel called her back.

"I heard your studio is closed," the older woman said. "Perhaps you'd like to stay and help Bennett with the demolition today. I have a feeling he's going to need all the help he can get."

Bennett may have argued if it was anyone besides Jennie who would be staying. He smiled and looked at Jennie, hoping she'd stay—and thinking he'd somehow gone insane in the past couple of days to even think he had half a chance to try things with her again.

4

J ennie's pulse skipped around her system like it was trying to win a jump roping contest. "Stay?" squeaked from her lips. She steadfastly refused to look at Bennett. Just what she could see in her peripheral vision was enough.

Dark. Dreamy. Dangerous.

Handsome. Honest. Hardworking.

She could probably keep going, but Mabel said, "I'll pay you fifteen dollars an hour," and moved over to Bennett to go over his contract with him.

A war started in Jennie's mind. She'd looked at Bennett's email about the electricians, but she hadn't hired anyone yet. Mostly because they couldn't just drop everything and come take care of her job. But also, because the quote she'd managed to get over the phone from one of them was well outside of her budget.

So maybe a day working for actual money would be worthwhile. And if "helping" Bennett while he used those muscles to rip apart walls came with it?

Well, Jennie couldn't see a downside.

Mabel finished with Bennett and turned back to her. "Well?"

"I'm not wearing the right shoes." She lifted her right foot to show Mabel the flimsy, yellow sandals.

"Run home and change."

Jennie cleared her throat, wishing she were having this conversation with Mabel in private. But Bennett stood right there, not even trying to hide that he was hanging on every word.

"I, uh, don't own a car," she said. In fact, the sale of her very fancy sports coupe in San Francisco had allowed her to move here and live these past few months without many sales.

"I rode my bike."

"Oh, well." Mabel waved her hand. "Bennett can take you real quick. By then, Lauren will have everything marked, and the demolition can begin."

Jennie had no idea how demolition worked, but she nodded anyway. She really didn't like that her ability to take the job relied on Bennett's willingness to drive her home real quick to get proper footwear.

She didn't like depending on anyone. Not anymore. She didn't want to bend to what anyone else wanted her to do, or be who they wanted her to be.

She'd learned that when she'd stood in the bathroom in the church where she and Kyle were supposed to be married. She'd stared into her own face and had no idea who the woman looking back was.

And she'd vowed she'd be herself. Do her own thing. Figure out who she was and *be that person.*

"I can take her," Bennett said. "She doesn't live far from here."

Mabel nodded. "I'll go find Lauren. We'll be ready when you get back." She hobbled off, leaving Jennie alone with Bennett again.

He indicated that she should leave the room in front of him, and she did. "I didn't peg you for a bike-rider," he said. "Seems like I remember you *not* liking the outdoors all that much."

Jennie scoffed, though he'd hit the nail on the head. "Yes, well, sometimes we do things we don't want to do." She started down the steps, keeping one hand on the banister because she'd tripped in these sandals before.

"Like coming back to Hawthorne Harbor?" he asked. "I never thought I'd see you again."

She reached the bottom of the steps and spun to give him a piece of her mind. But he wore a look of pure guile on his face. He wasn't goading her. Wasn't teasing.

The fight went out of her, just like it always had when she came face-to-face with Bennett. "Yes, well, things change."

"I'd love to hear about it," he said.

Jennie groaned. "I think I'll pass."

His fingers brushed hers as they walked through the cavernous lobby toward the front door. An innocent gesture—or so she thought. But on the next step, he took her hand in his.

"Bennett."

He slid his fingers right out of hers. "Sorry."

She didn't like the level of foolishness she heard in the quiet murmur. She increased her pace and reached the door a half-step ahead of him, pausing to face him again.

"Look, I'll be honest." She'd promised herself to be brutally honest moving forward. She hadn't thought she'd have to do it with Bennett Patterson, just herself.

"My fiancé left me at the wrong end of the aisle only six months ago," she said, all the fury, fire, and fight she'd been living with for half a year returning. "So I'm not really ready to be doing...that." She gestured to his hand.

He blinked, his eyes turning soft. Compassionate. "Jennie, I'm so sorry." He stepped right into her and gathered her into his arms.

Her first instinct was to shove him back, tell him that was *exactly* the kind of thing she *didn't* want. But she took one breath of his shirt and his warmth flowed into her, and her arms came up and wrapped themselves around his back, almost like she hadn't directed them to do so.

He held her close, without words, and she simply stole his comfort, which he freely gave.

"Things happen," she finally said, stepping back.

Bennett wore a strange look on his face as he said, "Yes, they do," and then he opened the door and stepped through it first, his chivalry apparently spent.

JENNIE LOOKED AT THE HIDEOUS BLACK SNEAKERS ON HER feet—the only pair of shoes even remotely suitable for ripping out walls and tearing down cabinets.

But they did not go with her outfit at all. Her first thought was to change her clothes. After all, she wanted to be sexy and sweaty while working with Bennett today.

Almost immediately, she recalled the thought. She was who she was, and she didn't need to color-coordinate her shoes with her shirt so she could *rip out walls*.

So she turned away from her reflection, feeling powerful and strong in a way she hadn't in years. She'd never realized how much of herself she changed to please someone else, alter how they thought about her, or try to impress them.

But that was the old Jennie. The new Jennie was who she was, and she owned ugly black sneakers that didn't go with anything in her closet.

She blew a kiss to Snowball, her puffy white cat who only showed up to express her displeasure with the dietary options, and skipped out her front door to find Bennett with his head bent over his phone in the cab.

"Someone interesting?" she asked as she opened the

door and climbed in. The ride over to her place had been a bit strained, with unspoken "things" between them. Jennie used to be really good at diffusing tension, but it seemed that skill had fled when Kyle did.

But now, the atmosphere felt lighter. Casual, almost. Bennett looked up from his phone and said, "Just my mom. She's insisting I come for dinner this weekend, but I keep telling her I can't."

"Why can't you?" Jennie reached behind her and pulled the seatbelt down.

"Work," he said, easing out of her driveway and pointing the truck back toward the Mansion.

"How often do you work?"

"Is that a real question?"

Jennie frowned and forced herself not to play with her hair. "Of course it is."

"I'm full-time. We just have to work overnight some-times and on the weekends." He cut her a glance as he looked for traffic at a stop sign. "It's not nine-to-five."

"Neither is my job."

"No, I suppose not." He took another peek at her. "Still a night owl?"

Jennie wanted to fold her arms and deny it. Why, she didn't know. Instead, she said, "Yes," as if she were clip-ping a bullet out from between her teeth.

"No wonder you were trying to burn your place down at midnight last night."

"I wasn't—"

Bennett's laughter silenced her. "I know, Jennie. Jeez. You used to be able to take a joke."

His words stung, and the awkwardness that had lingered between them after the hand-holding and her confession about being stood up at her own wedding returned.

"Look," he said. "I didn't mean anything by it."

"I know."

"All right. Who did you call to come get your outlet fixed?"

Jennie looked away. "Um, Paul, maybe. Enrique."

"Oh, not Enrique."

"He gave me a quote. I might need to save for a few weeks." And by that, Jennie meant she'd have to get a loan or ask her parents for money. Because she didn't exactly have clients beating down her door here in Hawthorne Harbor for a painting.

"You should call Glauco."

"Was he on the list?"

"Yes."

"Why didn't you just tell me to call him?"

"I can't do that," he said. "We have a standard list of tradesmen we send out when necessary. I can't be hooking my buddy up with jobs all the time. I work for the city." He spoke in a somewhat condescending tone she'd heard before. Loads of times. She'd actually told him once in the past how he sounded, and he'd tried to do better.

"I'll call Glauco right now."

"You don't need—" This time she cut off because of his laser glare.

"He's the best," Bennett said as he turned down the drive toward the Mansion. "And you want the best, right?" He searched her face, and Jennie finally let herself look fully at him.

He was the best man she'd ever had in her life, and she'd thrown him away when she'd turned her back on this town, vowing never to return.

She nodded, afraid of so many things in that moment, she couldn't catalog them all.

5

Bennett waited while Glauco's line rang, thinking he'd never be able to get the lemony-citrus scent of Jennie out of his truck now that she'd ridden in it for a while.

"Hey, hombre," Glauco answered.

"Hey." Bennett smiled. "I have an electrical job for you. A kiln that needs a special high-voltage outlet." He looked at Jennie, and for once, she didn't immediately cast her eyes somewhere else.

"And it's got to be cheap, man," he said. "We don't have a lot to pay for it. And not much time."

"Electrical?" Glauco asked. "I can do that."

"I know you can. That's why I called you. When can you come see what she's got and give an estimate for price and timeframe?"

Glauco started muttering to himself and Jennie leaned

toward Bennett. "Tell him I can pay him. It doesn't have to be super cheap."

But Bennett had seen the worry in her eyes. She didn't own a car, and he knew it wasn't because she was a fan of public transportation.

"Tomorrow?" Glauco asked at the same time Jennie whispered something else at him. He held up his hand to get her to be quiet.

"Morning or afternoon?" Bennett asked.

"Seven-thirty, man. I gotta job out in Forks the rest of the day."

"Seven-thirty tomorrow morning." He looked at Jennie, who now wore what could only be described at panic on her face.

Bennett almost started laughing. "That'll be fine, Glauco. Let me give you the address." He looked at her expectantly. Just because he'd been there twice didn't mean he had the numbers memorized.

She recited them and he said them to Glauco, finally hanging up after saying, "Thanks, man. You're the best."

He faced Jennie and smiled. "He really is the best."

"I can pay him."

"I didn't say you couldn't." Bennett twisted to get out of the truck.

"It would be nice if it were cheap," she said. "I mean, I don't want to spend more than I have to, right?"

"Right." He got out of the truck, his mind turning over what kind of secrets she might have. Uno came running toward him, his tongue lagging out the side of his mouth. He looked so happy and carefree, and Bennett laughed as he scrubbed the dog's head and ears.

Jennie, of course, stood at the front of the truck with a horrified look on her face.

"What?" Bennett asked.

"Is that your dog?"

"Nope. He's the fire house mascot. Aren't you, buddy?" He scratched down the dog's back and looked back at Jennie. "I just take him home once a week. Get him out of the fire house. Socialize with other dogs. Train him. That kind of stuff."

"Oh, so you're a dog trainer too?" She practically marched toward the front door of the Mansion like he'd done something wrong.

"Yes, ma'am."

She whirled on him. "Don't call me ma'am."

A lesser man would've fallen back and held up his hands in surrender. Bennett just started laughing. "What? You think you're too old to be called ma'am? You're younger than I am, Jennie." Bennett hadn't minded the gray that had shown up in his beard over the past year or so. He wasn't trying to impress anyone.

Until now....

The thought crept through his mind like a snake in the grass, and it wouldn't go away even when he tried to replace it with something else.

Jennie's sudden fury faded, and she sighed as she

turned around and started toward the Mansion again, slower this time.

Bennett had so many questions for her. Why was she so mad? What had this guy done to her? Why was she back in town? How long would she be staying?

But he valued his life—and he wanted to try holding her hand again in the future—so he simply followed her inside silently. When they reached the stairs, he said, "Nice shoes," in the nicest voice he could muster.

She glared at him, and he wondered if he'd ever be able to do something right when it came to Jennie Zimmerman.

HOURS LATER, MABEL HAD INSISTED THEY ALL STOP TO EAT a late lunch. Bennett wasn't complaining. He hadn't seen free meals in his contract, but he wasn't going to turn down Magleby raspberry punch or the ham sandwich Mabel brought out from the kitchen. He'd attended several events at the Magleby Mansion and the food was always delicious.

Jennie had worked hard throughout the morning, and Bennett liked her drive and determination. He always had. She did seem different, though, but he couldn't put his finger on what it was.

In high school, they'd gotten along great, though their banter sometimes went back and forth as it had today. She'd never been so cold one moment and then boiling hot the next, though. Maybe that was what was different.

He texted her twin brother, a lieutenant at the police department with, *How long has your sister been back in town?*

Jason knew of Bennett and Jennie's teen relationship. Heck, the whole town knew. Bell Hill too. After all, Bennett was set to be a baseball star, and that kept people's tongues wagging for what felt like forever.

Not sure. Three or four months?

You didn't tell me. Bennett didn't put a question mark at the end of the sentence.

She needed to do things her own way, Jason said, as if that explained everything. Maybe for him, but not for Bennett, who frowned at the message and then at the woman sitting down the stone wall from him.

They'd talked a little while they worked, but nothing like the trip down memory lane Bennett wanted. He had learned she'd come from San Francisco, from a ritzy art studio there, as she told Lauren a bit about herself and her art. Bennett had been in the same room, in plain sight, so it wasn't like he was eavesdropping.

Mabel appeared on the front steps of the Mansion, and she waved one weathered arm at him. She yelled something, but Bennett couldn't hear what. So he shoved the last of his delicious ham sandwich in his mouth and got up, crumpling the paper in his fist.

He approached Jennie and saw she'd finished her lunch too.

"Want me to take this trash?" He bent to retrieve it before she could answer.

"Oh, sure," she said, the pleasantries back in her voice. Bennett didn't allow himself to get his hopes up. After all, she'd probably quip at him before the day finished.

He walked toward Mabel, who pointed out in the fields. Bennett followed her finger to find Uno and Gemma in a face-off with a herd of horses.

Fear curdled his blood, and he dropped the trash he'd been carrying. Hawthrone Harbor didn't have many problems with the wild herd, but they were spotted a few times a year.

Rumored to be very territorial and extremely wild, the public had been told never to approach the horses.

Bennett didn't care. He wasn't going to let his dog and his mascot get trampled. He marched down the graveled road and toward the fields on the south side of the Mansion, calling for Uno and Gemma to "Come! Come on, guys! Let's go!"

Gemma, the bigger of the two dogs, and clearly the wimpier, tucked her tail and ran toward him.

"I've got her," Jennie said from Bennett's side, and he almost tripped over his own feet to find her there.

"You don't even like dogs."

"Doesn't mean I want to watch one get stampeded."

Bennett received Gemma with a pat and a quick

stroke, before latching onto her collar and passing her to Jennie. "Thank you," he said, deep appreciation welling in him.

He focused on Uno again, the dalmatian steadfastly refusing to budge though the big, black-coated leader of the pack pawed the ground with his hoof. Didn't he know that hoof could cause some real damage?

"Uno!" he called again, but the dog didn't even flinch. If only he hadn't finished his sandwich before knowing the canines were in trouble.

Bennett slowed his walk almost to a crawl, some of the horses making minute shifts in their position too. His phone chimed, but he didn't move to check it.

"Whoa, now," he said as his boot touched the longer grass of the field beyond the borders of the Mansion's estate.

Guilt pumped through him that he hadn't been paying more attention to where the dogs were, what they were doing. He'd been so caught up in Jennie. The sight of her back in town. The smell of her in the air around him. The hope that maybe, just maybe, they might be able to have a second chance at something meaningful.

Bennett almost scoffed. He didn't even *want* something meaningful with another person...did he?

He held up both hands to show the horses he meant no harm. That was universal language, wasn't it?

I come in peace.

Both hands up.

From somewhere in the herd, a horse whinnied, and that made Uno flatten to the ground. He could probably run circles around these horses, but Bennett didn't want to take any chances. He couldn't even imagine showing up at Fire House Two in a couple of hours with an injured mascot.

"Uno," he said when he was within fifteen feet of the dog. "Come on, boy. Let's go."

He turned toward Bennett just as an ear-splitting whistle rent the air.

Instinctively, Bennett turned toward it, back behind him, taking his eyes off the wild horses.

Jennie stood at the top of a little hill, just west of the Mansion. Even as he watched, she lifted her fingers to her mouth again and let loose with another whistle. What she was trying to accomplish, Bennett didn't know. Maybe she *wanted* him and the fire house dog to get trampled.

The horses launched into motion, the thundering of their hooves shaking the ground beneath Bennett's feet and forcing his attention back to them.

He barely had time to comprehend the situation in front of him when Uno streaked past him.

He took off after the dog, pumping his arms and legs as fast as he could, not daring to look back to see if the leader of the wild horses was bearing down on him.

Jennie waved her arms over her head, almost like *you're good, you can stop.* And while Bennett thought he understood what that meant, he kept running anyway.

The noise of the herd faded and he chanced a glance over his shoulder to find them racing in the opposite direction from him, obviously not interested in a fight today.

He slowed, his chest burning and his muscles screaming that they hadn't warmed up properly and these were the wrong shoes to be wearing while running.

Uno's wet nose touched his hand, and he stroked the dog absently, trying to regain his composure and his temper before he faced Jennie.

Too bad she arrived at his side only seconds later. She pushed out her breath and watched the horses fade from sight.

"What the devil was that?" Bennett barked.

6

"*That* was called helping." Jennie glared at him, her blood on fire and not just because she'd almost witnessed someone get hurt.

Not just someone, her mind whispered though she didn't have time to entertain ridiculous fantasies right now. *Bennett.*

"I don't think you know the definition of helping." He stomped away from her, the Dalmatian he obviously cared so much about going with him, sticking right to his side.

"It broke them up, didn't it?"

"I almost got trampled."

"Please." She scoffed. "I knew they wouldn't follow you."

"You did?" He spun back to her, his beautiful face not wearing any kind of mask now. Oh, no. His anger and frustration were plain to see. "How on *Earth* would you know that?" He didn't wait for her to answer, but turned and marched away again.

She followed much slower, because she didn't have a proper answer. So while annoyance filled her that he hadn't even said *thank you*, she supposed he did have a point.

"Fine," she said when they reached the Mansion again. "I *assumed*."

He tossed a broom in the back of his truck. "Next time, assume with someone else's life." He glared at her and moved around the truck to open the passenger door. "Load up, Uno."

The dog obediently jumped into the cab, and Jennie catalogued the tenderness in Bennett's voice despite the storm still raging on his face. "Where's Gemma?"

"I put her inside."

"The Mansion?" Panic paraded through those dark eyes now, and he started toward the doors at a jog.

"Mabel said it was fine," she called after him, wondering if she could ever do anything right when it came to Bennett. He hadn't been wrong when he'd said she didn't like dogs. Especially big ones, and Gemma was a giant.

But she was gentle, and she'd done exactly what Jennie had commanded her. So maybe she wasn't all bad.

A moment later, Bennett came out again, his apologies to Mabel loud enough for Jennie to hear. A twinge of regret stole through her as she watched him soften, lower his voice, smile, and embrace the older woman.

She caught a snippet of his conversation when he said, "...tomorrow afternoon," and turned to get in his truck.

He glanced at her, and she suddenly knew what it was like to have someone look at her but not really *look* at her. Not *see* her. And she didn't like it. She didn't like it one little bit.

Bennett put Gemma in the truck and climbed in behind her before starting the ignition and driving away in a scattering of gravel.

Jennie watched him, a frown pulling through her whole body. Her muscles ached, and her head hurt, but she hadn't complained once. She did whatever he or Lauren said, and she answered the other woman's questions even with Bennett's listening ears within range.

"Are you coming back in, dear?" Mabel asked, and Jennie startled away from the road where she couldn't even see Bennett's truck anymore.

"Yes, ma'am," she said. "If there's work to be done."

"Oh, there's plenty of work to do." Mabel looked down the lane too, and added, "He'll be back tomorrow afternoon to finish up. He just had to go to work."

Like Jennie had asked. Like she cared where Bennett would be or what he was doing. But as she followed Mabel back inside to resume working, Jennie realized she *did* care. Very much.

"Can I work tomorrow too?" she asked before they could climb the stairs and be joined by Lauren.

"Of course," Mabel said like Jennie had just asked the stupidest question on the planet. "Then I expect your kiln will be fixed and you'll be busy with the new pieces."

"Yes," Jennie said, the weight of seven-thirty in the morning to meet with Glauco descending on her. "Then I'll be busy with the art pieces."

JENNIE ROLLED OUT OF BED AT SEVEN-TWENTY, PULLED HER hair back into a long ponytail and had just put a kettle of water on to boil when her doorbell rang.

She groaned and snagged a hoodie off the back of a kitchen chair on her way to the front door. She'd just stuffed her arms inside when someone knocked.

"Okay," she said grumpily. It had been maybe ten seconds since they'd rung the doorbell. She opened the door to find Bennett standing there, glorious and radiant as the morning sun started to cast it's golden glow over him.

"Morning," he said like it was a good thing people were up this early. "I hope you have coffee going, because I got off late last night."

"Don't like coffee," she said, her voice a bit froggy still.

"Oh, that's right." His shoulders fell as he stepped past

her and into her house, uninvited. "I suppose you'll have tea, then."

As if the kettle had heard him, it started to sing. Jennie liked the way he filled out the gray T-shirt he wore, liked the jeans that hung on his hips, the way he seemed at ease in her space, that he'd come to help her with Glauco.

Without saying anything, she squeezed past him and busied herself in the kitchen, making tea.

She handed him a cup a few minutes later and watched as he lifted it to his lips. He took the smallest of sips, grimacing and putting the cup on the counter. "He should be here in a minute. He just texted me when I got here."

"Great." Jennie didn't know what else to say. And she hated that. Sure, she and Bennett maybe hadn't had the perfect relationship before, but she'd always had something to tell him about, something to say.

"I'll be working out at the Mansion again today," he said, taking a seat at her bar. "Maybe after we're done here, we can go to lunch or something. Then head out there together."

Jennie's eyes flew to his, and he didn't look away. She found strength and determination in his gaze, and she actually liked it.

"I know you just had something bad happen," he said. "We don't have to pick up where we left off twenty years ago." He swallowed, the first sign of nerves from the burly firefighter. "I'd actually like to go a little slow. I, uh, I've been divorced for about seven years now." He left so much left unsaid, but Jennie heard it all.

He'd been hurt too. Maybe they wouldn't like each other now as much as they had then. But he wanted to try.

And as Jennie thought about it, she wanted to try too. So she nodded and said, "Okay."

"Okay." Bennett picked up his cup of tea as if he'd take another drink. He seemed to remember last minute what was in the cup, because his eyebrows pinched together and he set down the cup.

The doorbell rang again, propelling him off the barstool and toward the front door like he owned the place. Jennie let him answer, because Glauco was his friend and she honestly just wanted to get this kiln and outlet problem over with.

Bennett's presence at her side brought her comfort as Glauco examined the kiln, the outlets, the other things she needed to power. He sketched and talked in a heavy accent, and Jennie liked that she could look to Bennett for an explanation when she didn't know what "re-route the lines" meant or "splice the power" would mean in terms of cost.

She'd look at Bennett, and he'd launch into an explanation that a five-year-old could understand. So that, after about twenty minutes, when Glauco stopped talking, Jennie knew about what he was going to do and how much it would cost.

"Well, I have to do it," she said with a sigh. "How long will it take?"

"This?" Glauco waved at the singed outlet like it was nothing. "A day or two. Tops."

"When can you start?" Bennett asked, and it almost felt like Jennie could lean back into his strong body and he'd support her.

She stood as still and straight as possible, surprised by her feelings, especially after she'd sworn off all humans with a Y-chromosome after she'd pulled herself together and addressed the crowd who'd come to see her walk down the aisle.

It had been a different sort of walk, that was for sure.

Maybe you've been living in the anger stage of grief for long enough, she thought as Glauco said, "I come tomorrow. Yes?" He looked from Bennett to Jennie, who nodded.

"Yes, tomorrow would be great." She shook his hand and he left her alone with Bennett again.

"So it's nowhere near lunchtime," he said once the door had clicked shut. "Breakfast?"

"I don't eat breakfast, remember?"

Bennett tilted his head at her as if trying to see inside her mind. "I don't remember that."

"Yes, well." She folded her arms. "I'm not a fan of eggs."

He blinked, his face going blank for a moment. "I'm not even sure what to do with that. Who doesn't like eggs?"

"Lots of people," she said, feeling her defenses shoot right up. She tried to tamp down her impatience and her attitude. "But I could be convinced to go to brunch. I like the coffee cakes and stuff at Riverwalk Pastries." She gave him the sweetest smile she could.

He chuckled, and she knew she had him. He'd always gone where she wanted to, done what she'd asked. He'd been a very, very good boyfriend once, and Jennie's mind wandered down that road again.

"So how long have you had Gemma?" she asked.

"Seven years."

So since the divorce. Maybe she should've gotten a little dog instead of the white furball who hid under the bed whenever anyone came over.

"Tell me about your wife."

His gaze flew to hers, and she tried to make her expression soft and compassionate. But since she couldn't see herself, she had no idea if she succeeded or not.

"It was Cynthia Gray," he said, swallowing afterward. "You remember her, right?"

Jennie did remember Cynthia Gray, right down to the fake Madonna mole she glued to her face every morning before school. "Wow," she said, managing to keep all emotion out of her voice. "I don't see you with her."

"Yeah, well, she didn't either."

Jennie tilted her head, hearing more in those words than he'd said. "What does that mean?"

"I don't want to talk it to death," he said, a flash of frustration filling his eyes. He blinked, and it was gone. Thankfully, so was the mask he usually hid behind.

"She only liked me when she thought I'd be a rich and famous baseball player. Once that dream died, so did our marriage. She's with a football player—or maybe hockey. Something—now." His jaw clenched, and Jennie heard the hurt in his voice though he was very, very good at hiding it.

"I'm sorry, Bennett," she said, meaning every syllable and letting the emotion come out in them. She wanted to ask him why he wasn't a professional baseball player. It *had* always been his dream, and he had to be bored at the fire station, despite the dog he clearly loved.

She didn't ask him, though. She'd already pushed him to reveal emotional things, so she said, "I need to shower and go to the bank. Can I meet you at Riverwalk around ten-ish?

"Ten's fine," he said. "I'll take Gemma down to the beach. She needs to get out." He ran his fingers through his hair and sighed. "She's been cowering under the kitchen table since yesterday's run-in with the horses."

"Horses can be terrifying."

That brought a smile to Bennett's face. "You don't like the look in their eyes."

"They're too smart," she said. "And big. I don't trust them at all."

"I'll take you out again, if you want." A playful glint entered his eye, and Jennie had the distinct feeling that they were reliving the same memory—the one where he kissed her under a star-filled sky after they'd ridden his family's horses to the coast.

She cleared her throat—wishing her mind could be as easily purged—and looked away.

He clapped his hands. "Okay, so ten at Riverwalk." He practically lunged for the door, and Jennie stood back as he strode out.

"You're being insane," she muttered to herself as she cleaned up his undrunk tea and headed for the shower. "There's no way he really wants to get back together with you. You haven't even been nice to him."

As she stepped into the warm spray, her only thought was, *Then start being nicer.*

7

There were literally never emergencies in Hawthorne Harbor. *Never.*

But when Bennett's phone rang as he stepped out of the shower, Charles said, "We've got an emergency."

"I'm ten minutes out." And that was if he was already dressed, which he wasn't. "What's going on?"

"Massive fire in Forks. They're calling in everyone."

"Wow. Must be bad." Bennett's heart pounded like he'd just sprinted the last four hundred yards of a marathon. Forks was an hour away without traffic, and if they needed the Hawthorne Harbor Fire Department on the scene....

He said, "Be there in five," and hung up, focusing on getting dressed and getting out of the house as quickly as possible.

Uno and Charles were already on the truck when he

pulled in, and he swung into the passenger seat to find all his gear there.

"Ready?" Charles asked, his face grim.

Bennett nodded, wishing he had more in his stomach than a couple of swallows of disgusting tea.

He pulled on his fire clothes and checked to make sure he had his helmet and other equipment before he put his thumbs to work.

Bennett texted the Yardleys first. Had a fire emergency. Can you run over and check on Gemma in a few hours?

Nelly will be thrilled! came back their reply. Bennett made a mental note to get something for them and their five-year-old. They were such great neighbors, and he relied on them a lot.

He drew in a deep breath and prepared to text Jennie. Their brunch date was still an hour away, so hopefully she hadn't gone to too much trouble yet.

Just thinking the word *date* got his pulse skipping and he felt hotter than normal. That could've been from the fire suit though.

It was in that moment that he realized he didn't have Jennie's number. His mind rotated, trying to find a solution. He couldn't just stand her up—what kind of trauma would that inflict on her?

He'd have to text Jason, but that caused a wave of frustration to roll over Bennett's shoulders.

Nothing to be done about it, he told himself. So he sent a message to Jason, hoping there wasn't a police emergency too.

Why do you need her number? Jason asked instead of just going with the easy route and giving him the number.

I need to talk to her. Every minute and every mile that went by got him closer to ten o'clock—and losing his temper.

I don't know if I can give it to you.

Bennett growled under his breath. *Fine. I asked her to brunch, but there's a huge emergency in Forks, and I can't make it. I need to text her and let her know.* He ground his teeth together as he waited for Jason to answer.

The number came through, along with a thumbs up emoticon, which Bennett ignored. He put Jennie's number in his phone and got his thumbs moving again.

Hey, it's Bennett. I got your number from Jason, because I can't make brunch. I'm so sorry. Got called down to Forks with a big fire emergency.

He read over the words again and again and then sent them.

Oh, okay, Jennie messaged back. *Stay safe.*

That was all. No call me later, or let's reschedule.

Bennett wasn't sure why he wasn't happy with her response. He dropped his phone on the seat beside him and settled his sunglasses over his eyes for the long drive ahead.

The smoke came into view long before Forks did, and

Bennett leaned forward to see further out the windshield, fear entering his body.

"Wow."

"Chemical plant," Charles said, his fingers flexing on the steering wheel. "Technically not in Forks, but yeah." He watched the sky for a moment before focusing on the road again. "Not going to be pretty."

Bennett hoped there weren't human casualties, but he braced himself for the worst. Charles employed the lights and the siren and they skirted the city to get to the fire.

No less than a dozen other trucks were already there, but as soon as Charles and Bennett stepped out of their rig, a boxy man shouted orders at them. He wore the helmet of a fire chief, and Bennett didn't question him.

They left their hose attached, as the items burning couldn't be put out with water.

"Stay here, Uno," Bennett said, leaving the dog in the running truck. No way the animal could come in and potentially step in something that would injure him. He wasn't even sure Uno should be breathing this air, what with the multi-colored smoke coming from multiple openings in the building.

They joined the line for the chemical retardants, and Bennett strapped his oxygen mask into place.

He'd never been inside a chemical facility before, and he never wanted to be again. All the halls felt too dark and too long, and he got hopelessly lost in only a few minutes.

He entered a room where something bubbled and

fizzed no matter how much powder the firefighters in front of him poured onto it. Discussions broke out, and Bennett stepped forward to listen.

It didn't make sense that they had to bring their own substances to extinguish whatever was foaming and causing steam to rise from the container. Surely the scientists who worked here would have systems in place to contain the chemicals.

He spotted a cabinet that hadn't been opened and stepped over to it. The doors were locked. "What about this?" he asked, his voice robotic through the oxygen mask.

Only one person turned toward him, but he looked strong enough to pry doors open if the situation required it.

"There's got to be something in here," Bennett said, quickly explaining why he thought so.

The man took a small hatchet from his tool belt and wedged it between the doors, twisting it and bending the doors. Bennett used his good arm and wrenched the door back to find containers labeled with large letters.

"This one," the other man said, selecting one that said EXTINGUISH in huge red letters. He stepped over to the foaming tray and poured it on. The smoke stopped—and so did the conversation.

"They have solutions here," he said, pointing to the cabinet. "What else is still active?"

Bennett accepted the nod from the other firefighter,

and the crew moved through the chemical plant, checking every room, every corner, every cabinet until everything was contained and under control.

Bennett would not want to be the one responsible for cleanup, but as he stepped back outside, he realized he wouldn't just be able to head on home.

A huge tent had been set up, and every firefighter who had been inside had to go through an intense decontamination procedure.

Bennett waited, his oxygen mask in place and sweat running down his back, for his turn, watching the sky settle toward dusk.

His shoulder ached, and Bennett adjusted the ice pack to settle over the joint again. He yawned, wishing he could go to sleep. But his insomnia seemed particularly troubling tonight.

He thought about calling Jennie before realizing she hadn't messaged or called him either. Did she know about the huge mess at the chemical plant?

He changed the channel, only to see the blue smoke lifting into the sky and over the ocean. It seemed everyone knew about it, and it would be a miracle if she didn't.

Mabel had called earlier and left a message that she'd bring food by his place. He took another bite of the macaroni salad, reminding himself that he needed to write the woman a thank you card.

His mom had been frantic until he'd called in. She said she'd let his brother and sister know, and Bennett had felt loved for a few moments.

He *was* loved, he knew that. Somehow, he always put how Cynthia felt about him above everyone else.

And she hadn't loved him enough to make it to *till death do us part.*

But it was okay. He scrubbed Gemma's ears, grateful for the dog's presence in his life. She'd been enough, and she always loved him.

But as a few more minutes passed and his eyes drifted closed, Bennett wondered if the love of a black lab was really what he wanted.

And why did he feel so lonely with his trusty companion right beside him?

8

J ennie couldn't tear herself from the images on the TV. So much smoke. So many emergency vehicles going in and out. She felt like she was watching the news coverage of a horrible event, similar to the tragedy of September eleventh.

And Bennett was on the scene. Her fingers went round and round each other, but she couldn't look away.

She'd initially been disappointed when he'd cancelled their brunch. At least she'd had advanced warning, even if she had to endure several very annoying texts from her "older" brother.

She'd reminded Jason that he was four minutes older than her, and had been pushy even inside the womb. She gave him no answers, only that Bennett had helped her with her kiln that morning and they were supposed to meet up to eat.

It doesn't mean anything. That had been the last text she'd sent to him before silencing the notifications for his texts.

What a lie.

Of course brunch with Bennett meant something. Probably a lot of something. Jennie had been trying to figure out how she felt all day, and it was impossible.

It was Bennett Patterson. The boy she'd grown up with. Her first crush. First kiss. She hadn't known as an eighteen-year-old if she loved him or not.

She knew she didn't love Hawthorne Harbor, didn't love that she had no opportunities to pursue art in the town, and knew she wouldn't be able to live with herself if she didn't give herself a chance to go to college and become the artist she hoped she could be.

And so she'd left. Left Bennett here just as his baseball career was blooming. Left everything so she could find out if she was worth something.

The images on the TV didn't stop, just like her thoughts continued to circle. The vehicles didn't either. Then a tent went up and the smoke thinned. Interview after interview flashed on the screen, but Jennie had muted the sound.

She'd just finished dinner—a bowl of cereal—when the first crews started leaving the site. So Bennett would call soon. At least text to say he was all right, and ask her how her day had been.

But the evening wore on, turning to night, and her phone didn't so much as vibrate. Her annoyance turned to anger, and she finally switched off the television and went down the hall to her bedroom, bypassing her art studio, where she and Bennett had shared a few tender moments that morning.

At least she thought they had.

Maybe she'd imagined it all. "Maybe you could call him," she said to her empty room, wondering if the simple sound of his voice would fill it.

She yawned, her mind sluggish and soft since she'd gotten up so early to meet Glauco. It seemed hard to believe that the meeting had happened this morning. It felt like this day had been a week long, and she felt disconnected from real life,

She crawled into bed, checking her phone one last time to make sure the sound was on and it had battery power. It was and it did, but she just hadn't gotten any messages.

She thumbed out a few things to Bennett. Hey, I watched a bunch of news coverage on the chemical spill

She erased that. He didn't need to know that she'd spent her whole day in front of the TV, that she had nothing better to do, that her creative energy she relied on to make art had taken a vacation when the outlet had sparked.

She'd been afraid to admit it to herself, but she'd

wandered into the studio a couple of times today during commercial breaks, only to stare at the pile of canvases and wonder when her muse would strike again, dictate what she should paint for the huge wall at Magleby Mansion.

She didn't need power to paint, but she did need passion, and she didn't have it.

So she'd returned to the living room and the news, drifting into the kitchen to eat or stare out the window into the backyard. She didn't go demo at the Mansion, because she couldn't do much without Bennett, and well, Bennett was miles away, literally and figuratively.

In the end, she didn't type anything to him, but cradled her phone on its standing charger and pulled the comforter up to her chin.

The moonlight fell through the window in silver rays, and as Jennie contemplated it, she whispered, "It's okay to like Bennett Patterson."

She needed to give herself permission, and while she didn't quite believe it yet, at least her heart wasn't totally closed to the idea.

Jennie woke the next morning to the sound of power tools. She sat straight up in bed, her heart hammering like a type of power tool itself.

She clutched the comforter to her chest, wondering

what in the world was going on. After grabbing her phone, she saw that it was past nine o'clock.

A man sang in Spanish and a drill went *whir, whir, whiiiiir!*

All at once, she realized what was going on. "Glauco." She jumped out of bed and padded in bare feet out of her bedroom and down the hall to the studio.

Sure enough, Glauco bent over the outlet on the far wall, a portable radio balanced on a nearby table blaring Spanish music.

"Glauco," she said, and he turned toward her. "I'm sorry. I didn't realize what time it was."

"I just came in," he said. "I hope that was okay. I didn't see a car."

"I don't own—it's fine," she said. "Do you want some tea?"

He shook his head and turned back to his work, the conversation apparently over.

Jennie went into the kitchen, where Snowball sat on the counter, a grumpy look on her feline face. Or maybe that was how she looked all the time. Jennie wasn't sure.

"Hungry, girl?"

The cat meowed, and Jennie fed her, put out fresh water, and set a kettle on the stove. A strange tune met her ears, and it took several seconds for her to realize that it was her phone ringing from down the hall in her bedroom.

She ran to get it, but it silenced when she was only

halfway there. "It's not him," she told herself, feeling ridiculous and put together wrong for hoping that it would be Bennett calling.

She collected her phone from where she'd left it unceremoniously on the bed and took a deep breath.

Why did she feel like she was back in junior high again, hoping the football star would call her? Only in this case, Bennett had been the baseball superstar.

And he'd called her. A smile erupted across her face, and she was in the middle of deciding if she should call him back or send a text when her phone rang again. Bennett. Again.

"Hey," she said, maybe a bit breathlessly.

"Morning," he said. "So listen, I have about sixty seconds before a staff meeting. We had to cancel brunch and I'm working all day today, but what about dinner?"

"Dinner?" Jennie squeaked. That was a step up from brunch. Brunch she could brush off as something friends did. But dinner? Dinner was definitely a date.

"Tonight?" he asked. "About seven-ish?" He didn't sound injured, only rushed.

"I guess so."

"Great. I'll swing by and get you." And then he was gone, leaving Jennie to wonder what had just happened.

"He asked you out," she said to herself as she went back into the kitchen to silence the shrieking kettle.

He'd asked her out plenty of times before, but somehow, this time was different. He was forty-three-years-old, and she'd be forty-two in a couple of months. This wasn't pretend, not that their high school relationship had been.

But this felt more real. A slower smile skated across her lips as she steeped her tea, and she finally allowed herself to be excited to see Bennett that night, about seven-ish.

Jennie didn't have her complete mojo back, especially since the metallic scent of the overheated drill bit Glauco had used still hung in the air. But she looked at the sculpture she'd started earlier that day. It was *something* that had come from her imagination, and right now, after the drought her muse and creativity had been experiencing, she'd take it.

She didn't know what it was, but the pillar had beautiful lines and curves, and she imagined texturing the whole thing and glazing it with light pinks, blues, and golds.

"Maybe a vase," she said aloud, the clay on her hands starting to dry. Glauco had nearly finished the job that day, but he'd be back in the morning. She'd told him to come in like he had today, because she probably wouldn't be up.

No, after a date with Bennett, she'd need hours to detox and examine things from every angle.

"The date." She glanced around for her phone, but

couldn't see it. The clock on the wall read six-thirty, and she cursed herself and her lack of time management as she rushed out of the studio and into the master bathroom.

She had time to get ready, but she rushed through her shower and didn't wash her hair. It fell almost to her waist, and there was no way she could get it dry in time for a seven-ish date.

Seven o'clock came and went without a text or phone call from Bennett. Jennie coached herself into going out onto the front steps to wait.

He'd been at work. He hadn't known the exact time he'd be done. She couldn't expect him to drop everything and show up at her house.

Still, a nagging sense of worry tugged against her patience and her resolve, whispering things like, Maybe a relationship with him is too hard. Maybe you should find someone who had a regular, nine-to-five job.

Jennie hadn't thought she wanted to "find someone" at all. Even the idea of rekindling this old flame with Bennett had her heart tripping in fear.

Trying to tamp down that fear and not let it rule her life, she pulled out her phone and sent him a message.

All ready. What's your ETA?

She hoped it wasn't too pushy. Maybe he'd lost track of the time too. Maybe he'd gotten off work later. Maybe, maybe, maybe. She was really getting sick of the maybe game. She'd played it so much while waiting for Kyle to show up at their wedding, and every day since.

Not anymore, she thought as her phone buzzed.

Running late, sorry. The chief would not stop talking. Leaving my place now. Probably 10 min.

Relief rushed through Jennie, and she realized she had a long way to go before she could truly trust a man. But if there was anyone she wanted to start with, it was Bennett.

To distract herself—and keep from sending him more thank an okay in response—she started texting her best friend she'd left behind in San Francisco.

Hey Lisa! Just thinking about you. How's the bay?

Lisa Nichols and Jennie had been next-door neighbors on the top floor of an apartment building that faced the bay. Their balconies were separated by only a thin railing, and Jennie had loved sitting there and watching the ships, the people, the ocean.

No wonder her muse was on vacation here. Though the beach and another bay, albeit a different one, sat about ten minutes away, Jennie had not taken the opportunity to go see it.

"I will," she vowed to herself as Lisa responded.

Soooo good! I miss you so much. This new guy moved in next door and the whole place smells like onions and beef stock now.

Jennie laughed, maybe for the first time since her

forced exodus out of San Francisco. A pang of lonliness hit her, which made no sense. She had a date with a handsome man only minutes away.

But she knew there were no replacements for her girlfriends. Growing up with only Jason, Jennie had always been close with someone. But she craved her female relationships, and the decade-long friendship with Lisa had filled something in her that Jennie desperately missed.

We should get together for lunch, Jennie typed. Even as she hit send, she knew she couldn't. San Francisco sat almost a thousand miles down the coast, and Jennie had gotten a loan just to pay for the electrical work she needed done.

Lisa wasn't rolling in the dough either, and she said, I wish! I am coming to Vancouver in a few months for a family reunion. How close is that to you?

Vancouver was only a few hours away, and Jennie's heart took flight. *It's about four hours, she said. Totally doable!*

Yay!

A truck pulled up just as Lisa's last text came in, and Jennie stood, her whole body vibrating with nerves.

I have to go, she thumbed out quickly. *I have a date. I'll catch you up later.* She silenced the notifications on Lisa's text stream, knowing her friend would go nuts over the words *I have a date.*

Heck, Jennie was going slightly nuts, especially when

Bennett came around the front of the truck wearing a pair of dark wash jeans and a polo the color of summer grass.

It should be illegal to look as good as he did, and Jennie wondered what in the world she was getting herself into.

9

Bennett couldn't look away from Jennie. Thankfully, she likewise seemed frozen in place, staring at him the way he gawked at her.

He simply didn't remember all those curves, and she hadn't really been into dresses in high school. But she wore a navy blue number with pink polka dots all over it. The fabric hugged her body to her waist, where it flared out and down to her knees. She wore a splashy pair of pink heels with it, and Bennett couldn't breathe, blink, or swallow.

She stepped toward him, breaking whatever spell she'd put him under, a smile curving her mouth.

And wow, Bennett wanted to kiss her so badly. He licked his lips as if he might get the chance later, and walked down the sidewalk to come up her driveway and greet her.

"Hey, there," he said, his voice miraculously smooth. "You look great."

She twirled in the dress, the pink from the polka dots traveling to her cheeks. "Thank you. You too." She wobbled a bit on the heels, and pure panic paraded across her face.

Bennett lunged for her, latching onto her elbow and steadying her. A current as strong as anything he'd ever felt ricocheted through him, zinging his heart, his lungs, and settling in his stomach.

She had to feel that too, right?

Bennett locked his eyes on hers, and sure enough, he saw the electricity in her gaze too. *Thank goodness.*

"So." He cleared his throat and dropped his hand. "I was thinking of going over to Bell Hill for dinner. There's a new place you probably haven't tried." He watched her for a moment to gauge her reaction. Jennie had never been particularly keen on trying new things, but tonight, she grinned and said, "As long as I can get something besides seafood."

"Totally," he said. "This is more of an, oh, I don't know, Upscale place. They'll have seafood too, of course." He opened her door for her and steadied her again while she climbed into the cab of his truck and smoothed down her skirt.

He hurried around the front of the vehicle, mentally coaching himself not to be a fool. *Play it cool.*

He felt so much like he was back in high school, going

on his first date with Jennie Zimmerman and hoping not to screw it up.

A powerful sense of déjà vu hit him as he got behind the wheel and started the truck. A nervous laugh leaked out of his mouth. "This feels like high school, right?"

"A little." She giggled. "But I'm way too old to play games."

He jerked his attention to her. "Yeah, me too."

And with that, she slid across the bench seat and slowly, carefully, so slowly and carefully Bennett could feel and enjoy every sensation, she curled her fingers in between his.

"No games." She looked up at him, an edge of desire in her eyes that really sparked fire in Bennett's blood.

He squeezed her hand, all the response he could come up with. He managed to drive over to Bell Hill without disobeying any traffic laws or going right off the road as the lemony scent of her skin started to infuse the cab.

"Beachcomber," Jennie read off the sign when Bennett pulled in. "Doesn't look busy."

"It's Tuesday," he said. "And it's not in the busiest tourist area." Which he was actually glad about. Sometimes the beaches and pier were overrun with tourists when he just wanted a hot dog from the best stand Hawthorne Harbor had to offer.

They got a table quickly, and he ordered the steak skewers as an appetizer while she got the baked tomato soup.

"That has bleu cheese in it," he said while the waiter still stood at their table.

"I can read." Jennie flicked him a look and nodded at the waiter, who moved away.

Foolishness raced through Bennett, but he wanted to stick to the no-games rule that had clearly been established. "I thought you didn't like bleu cheese."

"I don't."

He frowned at her, which made her giggle again. The sound wormed it's way through Bennett's veins to his heart, and he smiled too.

"It won't be prevalent," she said. "You just have to watch out for bleu cheese when it comes in crumble form or dressings."

"Crumbles and dressings. Got it." He lifted his soda to his lips. "Do you still dislike mushrooms?"

"Ew. Yes." She made a face and consulted her menu again. "And all these fancy places have mushrooms in their dishes. *Fancy* mushrooms."

"Well, if there's anything worse than a mushroom, it's a *fancy* mushroom." He chuckled, and Jennie shook her head at him though she wore a smile.

The waiter returned and they ordered—Bennet got the braised short ribs and Jennie got the roasted chicken, which totally came with fancy mushrooms—and he said, "So it's been twenty years. Fill me in."

Jennie looked like she'd swallowed insects and needed to let them out of her mouth. It hung open, and a few moments passed until she recovered.

"I went to art school. Graduation. Worked in a few studios. Now I'm back in town."

It was Bennett's turn to gape. "Oh, come on," he finally said. "You can't sum up twenty years in three sentences."

"Sure you can. You try it." She looked at him with a small smirk, and Bennett accepted the challenge.

"Three sentences?" He inhaled. "All right. I got married a few years after you left. Hurt my shoulder so I couldn't pitch anymore. Got divorced, finished my master carpentry accretidation, and got a dog."

"See?" She sipped her soda and looked at him with more sincerity in her eyes. "I'm sorry about your shoulder. Does it still give you problems?"

"After a hard day like yesterday tearing stuff out, yeah. But not usually." Bennett wasn't used to talking about himself. The people he spent time with knew everything about him, and it was actually refreshing to release some of the past to Jennie.

The conversation became easy after that, and while Bennett didn't reveal any other major things in his life, he felt comfortable with Jennie.

She laughed as easily as she ever had, and he could see the echo of her former self though he acknowledged that she'd changed too.

And he liked the changes in her. The maturity. The wisdom. The talent.

They walked out hand-in-hand, and he said, "You

want to go visit the bell tower?" Bell Hill had been named for the famous tower on the tallest of the rolling hills sweeping east from the beach.

"Depends," she said.

"On what?"

"We used to kiss behind the bell tower."

Bennett suddenly felt twice as hot, and he cleared his throat. "Yeah, we used to."

"I...don't think I'm quite ready to do that yet."

Bennett was, but only so he could validate this giant spark between him and Jennie. He could wait too. In fact, in that moment, he'd give her all the time she needed, because he wanted to see if she could make it down the aisle *to him* this time.

But he kept that to himself, vowing never to say it out loud. He felt several paces ahead of her, and he'd rather they were on the same page. Because the last time he was this far ahead of her, she'd left town.

"That's fine," he said. "I like this fine." He lifted their joined hands a couple of inches and let them drop.

"You said fine twice in the same sentence." She bumped him with her hip.

"Yeah, but when I say it, I mean it." He grinned at her. "I'm not you."

She rolled her eyes but didn't deny it. "Then let's go visit the bell tower."

Happiness soared through Bennett, and he hardly recognized it. Where he thought he'd been happy before, he realized now walking up the forty-seven steps to the bell tower that he hadn't really tasted true happiness all that often.

BENNETT WHISTLED TO GET GEMMA OUT OF THE SURF. SHE liked to play with the waves as they stroked the shore, and she sometimes fell behind on their morning runs. She barked and one of Trent's German shepherds yipped in response.

Bennett normally ran alone, but today, he had a pack of people and canines with him. Jason ran beside him, matching him stride for stride. And Trent, the K9 specialist on the police force, had joined them too.

He'd brought all four of his K9 dogs, and they ran beside him like a little army. Two on each side even, and Bennett really liked the way they looked trotting along the sand, never getting too far ahead or too far behind Trent.

Which, of course, made Gemma seem like a wayward toddler. Thankfully, Uno had come too, and he wasn't as disciplined as the shepherds either.

With twice as many dogs as men in the line, anyone on the beach this early gave them a strange look and a wide berth.

Bennett kept waiting for Jason to say something about Jennie, but he didn't.

It was Trent who said, "I heard you were going out

with someone, Bennett," that almost caused Bennett to fall down on the smooth sand.

"What?" he asked, his breath puffing out at having to talk.

"My sister said she saw you and someone at that new restaurant in Bell Hill the other night."

Bennett had forgotten that Trent's family was from Bell Hill too. "Yeah," he said, hoping that would be it.

But Trent only let a few strides go by before saying, "Who was it?"

"My sister," Jason said before Bennett could decide if he was going to answer.

"We're not dating," Bennett said quickly. "It was dinner."

"Oh, okay. So Jennie." Trent turned around and started jogging backward. "I'm looking to try dating again."

"Oh, yeah?" Jason slowed to a walk, and all three men did too. "Even after the Terra incident?"

"It's been what? Almost two years," Trent said. "I don't know. Porter is only five. He needs...." He pushed his breath out. "More than I can give him."

"And you think he needs a new mom?" Bennett asked, not accusing, just wondering.

"Maybe, yeah." Trent turned around and ran his fingers down the back of the dog closest to him. "I don't know. My sister helps out a lot, but she's been sick lately." He shrugged, like maybe he'd find a new wife and new mother for his son by next week. Knowing him, he might.

Bennett had no advice for him. He'd been married before, but he hadn't lost his wife in a car accident. Didn't have a kid to raise. Couldn't even get back together with an old flame very quickly.

"Who are you thinking about?" Jason asked. "Kaitlyn probably has a dozen names she could come up with."

Trent looked like he might throw up and he kept stroking that German shepherd like the dog was his sole source of comfort. "Ask her."

"Yeah?" Jason exchanged a glance with Bennett, looking dubious.

"Yeah," Trent said. "I like brunettes."

"Oh, so Jennie's out." Jason's look changed to more of a smirk, and he didn't look away. "She's a blonde."

Bennett remembered the happiness from the other night, and he'd enjoyed the texting sessions with Jennie when they hadn't been able to see each other in person. So he looked steadily back and said, "Yeah, and I like blondes."

10

Jennie's phone chimed but she ignored it. She'd finally seized onto an idea for an entire series of sculptures that included a bowl, a vase, and three other pieces that would flow and drift together to make a stunning collection.

She'd need the kiln to get the collection done, but the outlet was fixed and Glauco paid, and everything seemed right with the world again.

Well, as right as Jennie's world could get in Hawthorne Harbor. Her mind moved immediately to Bennett, and she twitched thinking maybe the message that had just come in had been from him.

And she'd really liked messaging him. They hadn't done much texting in their previous relationship, and it was a whole new way of conversing that Jennie thrived in.

She found it easier to ask him questions, give him answers, and flirt when she wasn't face-to-face with him.

Her phone rang next, and she knew that wasn't him. In fact, there was only one person who called her, and that was Mabel Magleby. Jennie refused to rush the clay, though, and if she stopped now, she'd have to start the piece over.

So she kept the wheel going, and kept carving and pressing and moving the clay in the shape her mind could see.

About twenty minutes later, she had the effect she wanted, and she slowed the wheel and leaned back to stretch the tightness in her muscles.

After washing up, she checked her phone and confirmed that the call had come from Mabel, and the text was from Pepper.

She groaned at the reminder that she and Pepper were going to the dress shop tomorrow on Wedding Row. Jennie had said yes to help shop for a wedding dress, because Pepper was her best friend and Jennie wanted to be supportive. But now that the actual event was upon her, she wanted to cancel. Maybe she'd get sick before tomorrow afternoon.

She ignored her friend for now and called Mabel. "Hey," she said. "Sorry, I was at the wheel and couldn't get to the phone."

"Oh, it's fine. Fine. You said you needed to meet with me and show me something."

"Yes." Jennie exhaled and pushed her hair out of her face. "When's a good time?"

"I've got a big breakfast tomorrow," Mabel said. "And there will be lots of leftovers. You should come eat some, and we can talk."

"What time?"

"Eleven?"

So not the afternoon, and she couldn't cancel with Pepper. "Can I bring a friend?"

"Is it Bennett?"

"No," Jennie said quickly. "Pepper Howard. She's getting married—"

"I know Pepper. She's booked her event here. Of course, bring her."

"Great. See you tomorrow." Jennie hung up and caught sight of her snow white cat loitering in the doorway. Her stomach grumbled, and she realized Snowball had come out of hiding because she was also hungry.

So Jennie wandered down the hall and into the kitchen to make sure neither her nor Snowball would starve to death.

PEPPER PUT THE CAR IN PARK OUTSIDE THE MANSION, AND Jennie said, "Thanks for driving." The thought of having to ride her bike up the hill to this beautiful venue in this heat wasn't something Jennie wanted to do very often.

She got out and took a deep breath of the heated, salty air of the ocean, a flash of gratitude for this beautiful place where she'd grown up. She had the distinct thought that she should go visit her parents soon, as she hadn't been by in a few weeks. Jason and his wife Kaitlyn had dinner with them every week, but Jennie hadn't been able to bring herself to attend yet.

She and Pepper met Mabel near a long breakfast bar, the smell of bacon and maple syrup in the air. Jennie's mouth started to water, and she reached for a plate—a real plate, no paper here—and started loading up with fruit, French toast, and as much salted, cured meat as she could fit.

"I'll have Jaime box this stuff up." Mabel waved to someone Jennie couldn't see and didn't even try to argue. Mabel would send her home with enough food to feed her for a week, and why should she argue with that?

A couple of assistants moved around her and Pepper as they ate, cleaning up and taking down from the event.

Mabel disappeared for a few minutes, and then she sat down at the table with Jennie and Pepper. Jennie hoped she'd have the energy and drive Mabel did in forty or fifty more years, but she sort of doubted it. She could barely get out of bed before nine a.m. She reasoned that Mabel probably went to bed by eight o'clock, and that was when Jennie started her best work.

"So tell me about this piece. You said it's actually five pieces?"

"It's a collection, yes," Jennie said, reaching for her napkin. "It's got five pieces, and they're inspired by the beach. So we'll have some of those blues and seafoam greens from the water. The lighter peach and tan from the sand. And just a hint of white or gold for the sun. They'll be spectacular."

Jennie was actually really excited about the pieces, and she could see them all in her mind's eye.

"One is a vase," she said. "Since you have all those flowers in the gardens. And one is a bowl. The others might just be pillars or driftwood type of pieces. Maybe another vase." She couldn't really decide.

"Bennett is building a big buffet," Mabel said. "So five pieces should be okay. Do you have a drawing?"

Jennie did, and she pulled the sketches out of the satchel she'd brought with her. She showed Mabel the flow of the pieces, pointed out where the colored glazes might go, and couldn't curb her enthusiasm about the project.

When Pepper cleared her throat and tapped her naked wrist as if she wore a watch, Jennie startled.

"Mabel, I've kept you for hours," she said. "I'm so sorry." She stood, surprised Pepper had lasted so long.

"Oh, it's nothing." Mabel looked around the empty hall. "I don't have another event for a couple more days. You've saved me from wandering outside in the sun." The old woman smiled, and Jennie leaned down to embrace her.

After thanking Mabel for breakfast, Jennie followed Pepper out to the car. "You sounded happy about the project," her friend said.

"I am." Jennie leaned her elbow against the door and cradled her face. "It took forever to get an idea, so it feels nice to just have that."

"You've had a rough few months. A big move." What Pepper didn't say was *a broken heart*. But Jennie heard the words anyway.

"Yeah," she said.

"So what's with you and Bennett Patterson?"

Jennie immediately regretted leaving her house. Working from the home-based studio had been so nice. No one to run into. No gossip to deflect.

"We're...friends," she said carefully, though they didn't agree all that often.

"You went out with him."

"How do you know?"

"A-ha!" Pepper practically punched the steering wheel. "So it's true. And I had to hear about it from Mary at the groomers?" Pepper turned toward her, a look of hurt on her face combined with absolute glee.

"Mary at the groomers?" Jennie didn't even know a Mary.

"Mary Stinner. She's friends with Cheryl, who is like, BFFs with Kaitlyn."

"Jason," Jennie muttered. But she hadn't told him

anything either. Perhaps Bennett had. She knew he'd asked Jason for her cell phone number.

"So?" Pepper asked as she navigated the windy road back down the bluffs toward town. "Is it true? You're dating again?"

"I mean, sort of," Jennie said, thinking of the hand-holding and the promise not to play any games. He hadn't tried to kiss her at the bell tower, and she hadn't seen him in the flesh since. Her muse had struck, and he had a job with odd hours.

"Oh, I've heard this before." Pepper laughed, played with her Mohawk, and pulled into an empty space on Wedding Row that sat right in front of Bows and Ties, a parking miracle if there ever was one.

"It's strange," Jennie said as she went into the dress shop with Pepper. "After Kyle stood me up, I didn't think I'd ever want to be with a man again."

"Oh, you're not with a man," Pepper said, fingering a dress on display near the door. "This is Bennett Patterson we're talking about."

Jennie snorted. "He's not a god."

"No?" Pepper made a beeline toward the sales associate who'd just waved at her. "Whatever you say, Jennie." In the next breath, she squealed, hugged the woman in the expensive skirt suit, and disappeared with her down a hall hidden by at least a hundred wedding dresses.

"You can wait over here," another associate said, this

one just as polished and poised. "She'll come out and show you all the ones Leann's picked for her."

"Great, thanks." Jennie flashed a fake smile and sat on the poufy, pink couch, wishing she were anywhere but here.

Had Lisa felt nauseous when she'd gone gown shopping with Jennie? Of course not. Her best friend in San Francisco had *loved* everything wedding-related, and she'd spent more time looking at magazines for the perfect dress than Jennie had.

She lifted her phone and snapped a photo, quickly sharing it with Lisa. *Guess where I am?*

Why are you looking at wedding dresses?

Shopping with Pepper. She got engaged. Or she's going to. Jennie wasn't even sure if Hunter had even proposed yet.

Pepper had always been one to over-prepare, and when she came out a few minutes later wearing an all-lace ensemble, Jennie couldn't help standing and ah-ing over the dress.

She didn't necessarily want to be in Pepper's shoes, and not just because they were literally the ugliest wedding slippers she'd ever seen.

She tried to see herself putting on another white dress. Ordering more flowers. Renting a facility. Getting pictures taken. The whole wedding affair exhausted her, and she'd already done it once with no payoff.

Could she do it again?

The quick thought in her mind said *No way, Jose.*

But a slower, quieter, more burning thought whispered, *What if it were Bennett at the altar?*

Jennie couldn't answer that question, and she distracted herself by fiddling with the buttons on the second gown, and helping to secure the veil with the third.

After all, if there was one thing Jennie had gotten good at since Kyle's sudden departure from her life, it was avoiding unpleasant things she didn't want to think about or deal with.

Long after the dress fitting finished and she returned to her studio to work, Jennie still fretted over which category Bennett belonged in.

Boyfriend or bother?

Bennett answered his phone when he saw Jennie's name on the screen. She didn't call very often, and he thought maybe she was hurt.

"Hey," he said.

"I'm thinking boyfriend," she said, making Bennett lower the dumbbell in his left hand.

"What?"

"No games, right?"

"Right." He glanced around the gym located in the fire house. Alex Benson and Ray Alpin worked with each other at the bench press.

"So I've been having some weird thoughts," she said. "If you should be my boyfriend or if it's all too much of a bother, and I've decided boyfriend."

Bennett wondered what it would be like to live inside

her mind, even for an hour. "You do a lot of thinking," he said.

"So maybe bother, then."

He laughed, glad when she joined in. "No," he said. "Boyfriend's fine. Are we going public with that?"

"People think it anyway."

"What people?"

"Kaityln apparently told Cheryl, who told Mary *at the groomers*, and Pepper found out."

"Ah, I see." All thoughts of weightlifting had left Bennett's mind. "So, lunch today? I'm done here at the station at eleven-thirty."

"I want a hot dog from Ruby's."

"Perfect. I'll come pick you up."

She didn't argue with him, and they hung up. So a very public lunch date on the pier, where everyone in town could see. And a lot of people would be there, as this was the last weekend before school started for kids. So families would be squeezing in one last beach trip.

From the other room, the radio blipped, and Alex practically sprinted for the doorway. Bennett chuckled, glad he wasn't the only one fighting off the boredom at the station.

"It's probably a cat," Ray said, setting the weight back on the supports. "But he'll take anything."

"I'm next," Bennett said. "I hope nothing else comes in. I need to get off on time today."

Ray, a big, tall man who'd worked for the department for about a decade, looked at him. "Oh yeah? Was that your girlfriend?"

"As a matter of fact." Bennett shrugged, though he expected the ribbing that came from Ray.

"I thought you were *happy*," the dark-haired man said. "Content with Gemma and all that."

"I was."

"So you'll do our calendar this year? The bachelor auction?"

Bennett had forgotten about that. Kind of. He'd refused to put on only the lower half of his fire suit and stand there with his shirt off for the photographer. The woman had brought six assistants with her—six! As if it took seven twittering women to snap a picture of someone holding a fire helmet and wearing a look like he'd just tamed the wildest flames in the known universe.

And letting someone spend money to go out with him? No, thank you. He wouldn't be good company anyway, he'd told Ray last year. And this year...this year, maybe he'd be with Jennie once the New Year rolled around. She definitely wouldn't like him splashing himself all over a calendar.

At least he didn't think she would.

"Put me down for a maybe," he said. He liked Ray, and the man worked hard on the calendar and the auction. They both brought in a lot of money to the fire house for new equipment and supplies. Bennett had just never been able to make quite the big deal out of it as other people.

He wasn't finished working out, but he didn't care to get back to it. So he put his dumbbells away, wiped down the bench he'd been using and waved to Ray on the way out.

His step felt lighter than it had all week, because he was going to get to see Jennie in the flesh in just a few hours.

BENNETT HURRIED UP THE FRONT STEPS AT JENNIE'S HOUSE and practically smashed his fist against the doorbell. He was running late—again—and he loathed being late.

She opened the door, and he blurted, "I'm so sorry. Chief Harvey grabbed me right as I was leaving, I swear."

Her smile came slowly, but it came, and Bennett took the few seconds it took to spread across her face to bask in the warmth of it. Watch her emotion change from guarded and closed off to accepting.

"You're only forty-five minutes late," she said. "And you texted." She plucked her purse from a side table by the door and stepped out onto the porch with him. "I am about to eat my own arm, so I hope you know how to drive fast."

He slung his arm around her, glad he was able to do

such an action without getting slugged. "Oh, I can drive fast, sweetheart."

She nudged him with her hip, and he drew in a deep breath of her citrusy scent and admired the plum-colored blouse and simple jean shorts she wore. She somehow managed to look sophisticated and artsy with classic gold jewelry around her neck and on her ears, and Bennett found himself wanting to touch those parts of her with his lips.

His heart racing and with him trying to tame his fantasies, he opened her door for her and helped her climb into the truck.

Go slow, he told himself, even muttering it out loud as he rounded the front of the truck.

"So your studio is back up," he said as he put the vehicle in gear and got going.

"Yep. Back up."

"What are you working on?"

She gushed about the sculptures she'd envisioned, and he really liked listening to her talk. She carried the conversation for the quick ten-minute drive to the beach, and fell silent as Bennett crawled through the lot, looking for a parking spot.

He cursed himself for being late, because the lunch crowd had obviously already arrived at the beach.

"Over there," Jennie pointed to the right, and Bennett saw the spot. He took it, ignoring the fact that they had a long walk in front of them, and laced his fingers through hers once they'd both gotten out of the truck.

"How's work?" she asked.

"It's boring," he said, not even trying to play up his job. "We just sit around and wait for a call to come in. Today, Alex practically wet himself when he got to go rescue a cat that had fallen into a window well." Bennett squeezed her hand as she giggled. "And I use the term 'rescue' lightly."

The cat hadn't been in any danger. It just couldn't get out, and the owner was too elderly to get down and help. Alex had been gone for a total of thirty-five minutes, but he'd had this unearthly glow about him when he returned.

They joined the line for hot dogs, and Bennett turned his face into the sun. "I love summer," he said. "It's almost over."

"Just for the kids," she said. "Well, and their parents. And the teachers." She edged forward. "But you realize you can still come here, right?"

"Ha ha." Bennett watched a couple walking the other way, both of them with hot dogs and fries, and his stomach growled too.

"Mabel wants to meet with us about the buffet," Jennie said.

"Oh?" A stitch of guilt pulled through Bennett. He still hadn't gone up and finished the demo in the west wing. At this point, Lauren Michaels had probably done it. "What's a buffet?"

Jennie laughed then, a full laugh that shook her shoulders and sent her joy cascading into the sky.

Bennett watched her with wonder, the need to make her laugh like that every day of her life strong and powerful. When she quieted, he said, "What? It's a legitimate question. When you say 'buffet' I think all-you-can eat."

"It's a piece of furniture," Jennie said, still chuckling. "Mabel said you were going to build it, but my sculpture is now a collection of five pieces, and she wants to go over the design with you to make sure the *buffet* goes with my collection."

"Oh, a fancy collection," he teased. Since he hadn't even given a second thought to the pieces he'd be building for Mabel, he said. "I'm sure it will be fine."

"Do you have a design in mind?"

"Nope." It was almost their turn to order. The number of people standing around with receipts didn't comfort him, but Jennie wanted a hot dog, and so a hot dog she would get.

"What do you do all day?" she asked, a note of incredulity in her voice.

"Work out," he said. "Run. Lift weights. Clean. Cook."

"*You* cook?" Her eyebrows went up like it was the most ridiculous thing she'd ever heard.

"Well, I watch Charles cook. Or Ray. He's actually really good on the grill."

Jennie pressed her lips together, her opinion probably

smashed behind them. But she didn't say anything. Just curved those lips into a smile and nodded.

"Remember when your dad almost burnt down the house when he tried to fry a turkey?"

The memory surged forward, and his own laughter spilled from his mouth. "We had Thanksgiving at the pie shop that year. Everything tasted like pumpkin."

"And you hate pumpkin." Jennie tucked herself closer to his side as the teenagers in front of them completed their orders and turned around.

Bennett wanted to keep her there—right there against his ribs—for a lot longer than he got to last time. He leaned down and swept his lips across her temple, squeezing her waist for a quick moment before stepping up to the counter and ordering for them.

He catalogued this moment too, right here on the pier with her, hoping they'd be able to talk about these memories together over the next twenty years.

As he realized the permanence of his thoughts, he pulled back on the reins. Just because Jennie had uttered the word "boyfriend" didn't mean she was ready to get married.

"How was the dress shop?" he asked as they stepped away with their receipt. "You never said."

"It was...." She let her voice hang there, and Bennett waited too. She wouldn't look at him but wandered down the pier a bit more, her eyes focused out on the horizon.

"I don't know." She leaned against the wooden railing, and Bennett stepped next to her.

"I bet it was hard. Being in a gown shop and all that." He tried to make his voice nonassuming, compassionate.

"It was hard."

"But you did it."

"Yeah." Several seconds passed with just the sound of the gulls and the waves, the dull roar of chatter from the people around them. "I don't know if I'll ever have the courage to go through that again."

Bennett's insides squeezed, tightening to the point of pain. "I know what you mean."

She twisted toward him slightly. "Do you see yourself getting married again?"

"I hadn't really thought about it."

Jennie gave him a soft smile. "You're not a great liar."

He smiled and shook his head, deciding to be real with her. No games. "I got Gemma when Cynthia left. I decided then and there that I didn't need a wife, or a girl-friend, or anything like that. I had a dog, and she's always happy to see me. Always wants to lay by me. Always wants to play."

"I got a cat."

"Oh, cats are terrible." He scoffed and threw her a playful look. "No companionship there. They just want you to feed them."

Jennie laughed again, but she didn't disagree. "I prob-ably should've gotten a dog."

"You can get small dogs, you know."

Jennie tucked herself back into Bennett's side. "So I guess I just have one question."

"Only one?"

"Very funny."

"Go on then," he said.

"If neither of us wants to get married, are we just playing pretend?"

12

Jennie's heart danced around in her chest as the seconds passed. Why wasn't he saying anything? Why had *she* said anything?

Because she liked him too much already, and if the possibility of her having to lace herself into another wedding dress was in her future, she needed to know now.

"I'm not playing pretend," Bennett finally said, his voice thick and low. Husky. Beautiful. Sincere. "I'm not playing anything here."

He hadn't come right out and said he liked her, but she could feel it in his touch. See it in the way he looked at her. Taste it in the very sea air they both loved.

"Are you?" he asked, direct and to the point, as he'd always been.

"No," she said, hearing his name called behind her. "That's our food."

"I'm not saying we have to get married next week," he said.

"Good," Jennie said. "Because even next summer would be a stretch." She paused and looked at him. Right at him. "I don't think either of us are ready for that."

She continued walking to get her hot dog, her stomach practically eating itself. The first bite of French fry was salty and delicious, and Jennie moaned.

"No," Bennett said as he loaded onions, ketchup, and mustard on his hot dog. "I'm not ready for that."

"Right." Jennie squirted ketchup and mustard on her dog too, bypassing everything else. "Because you thought you could be happy with a dog for the rest of your life."

"Hey, plenty of people have dogs as companions."

Jennie giggled and bit into her hot dog, another moan seeping through her throat. She chewed and swallowed and said, "I know, Bennett. But it speaks to your state of mind."

And his wife had left seven years ago. Kyle had been out of the picture for seven *months*. Jennie felt slightly crazy even contemplating another relationship, but as Pepper had told her as they'd left the dress shop, *He's not Kyle. Don't make him Kyle.*

Jennie had been thinking about that a lot lately, and while she didn't know everything, she did know she was happier when she saw Bennett and after she texted Bennett than before he'd re-entered her life.

"I'm in a fine state of mind," he said.

"I didn't say you weren't."

"Hm." He found a bench and sat, scooting down to the end to make room for her. They ate with the glorious sunshine spilling over them, the sound of the waves hitting the shore, and the squeals of children playing in the ocean.

Jennie had always loved coming to the pier, and now she had this new experience with Bennett in the place she loved.

Of course, she had other memories with him here too, but she wanted grown-up ones. Not romanticized, teenage remembrances that felt like they'd happened in another lifetime, to a different person.

"You still doing puzzles?" she asked before taking another bite of her hot dog.

"You know what? I'm in between puzzles right now." He cast her a sly look. "We can go look for one at the toy shop if you want."

Warmth curled through her. "Only if you let me pick it."

He laughed and shook his head. "Oh, no. I've done that before. That puzzle was a *monster*. It took me six months to finish."

Jennie gave him a blank stare. "I don't know what you mean."

"Yes, you do." He didn't even go on to explain.

"Don't you have hours and hours to fill at the fire house?"

"Sure, I guess."

"I've seen those memes, you know." Jennie really liked this conversation, this easy flirting and back and forth. It felt like she could be herself with him in a way that didn't take hardly any effort.

"What memes?"

"You know, how the firemen are all lying around compared to the cops."

Bennett made an exploding noise with his mouth. "Those aren't true, you know. We work just as hard as they do."

"Really?" she challenged. "Working out, running, and cleaning. I don't think the police department is doing that."

"They give tickets for dumb things like having the taillight out in your car." He twisted fully toward her. "You're telling me a fix-it ticket is better than what I do?"

Jennie loved the semi-angry glint in his eye. "I honestly don't know what you do. I asked you and you told me working out, running—"

"I know what I told you." He stuffed the last of his hog dog in his mouth, and Jennie wondered if he was really angry.

She started laughing, only stopping to choke a little when a glob of ketchup slipped off the end of her bun and landed on her shirt.

"Smooth move," Bennett said, a smirk on his face.

"Serves you right for saying cops do more than firefighters."

"I'm just saying."

"Yeah, yeah. I know what you're saying." He handed her a napkin, but there was no way she could make this shirt presentable.

"How about you take me home so I can change, and then we'll go to the game store over by Wedding Row?" Saying the words didn't scorch her throat as hotly as she thought they would.

"You can barely see it."

"I'm not wearing ketchup for the rest of the night." She glanced around as if a ketchup patrol would slap cuffs on her and lead her away in shame. "Plus, you can see my collection." She shrugged like it was no big deal, but her gaze caught on Bennett's, and they both knew it was.

After all, Jennie didn't normally let anyone into her studio. Or see her art until it was finished and set just so. Bennett knew this, and he stood and extended his hand toward her.

She slid her fingers along his as easily as she breathed, and she felt a layer of tension melt from her shoulders. So maybe she could envision herself with another man, wearing another white dress, in the far, far distant future.

Several minutes later, he pulled into her driveway and killed the engine. Jennie got out without waiting for him to come open her door, and she went up the steps first, her heartbeat rippling a little strangely.

A streak of white zipped down the hall when she stepped inside to the blessedly cool house. Behind her, Bennett sighed, and Jennie made a beeline for the hall. "I'll be right back."

"Okay," he said and she went in her bedroom and locked the door behind her. Pulling off the stained shirt, she exchanged it for a green one with a cartoon version of the Washington Hawthorn trees the town was named after.

"Snowball?" she said, but of course the cat didn't make an appearance. "I'm going to close you in here." Jennie wasn't sure why she was speaking to the feline like it could understand her, but she didn't want to just trap the cat in the bedroom without warning.

But Snowball didn't come out, and Jennie did close the door behind her. Bennett was not waiting in the living room where she'd left him, nor the kitchen.

Jennie wiped her palms down her jean-clad thighs and stepped toward the art studio. Sure enough, Bennett's tall, broad frame stood right in front of her collection, which now had four complete pieces waiting to be glazed.

"So the fifth will be twice as tall as this one," she said, joining him in front of the table and indicating a tall, twisted pillar. "It won't be as curved, as it'll actually hold water and flowers."

"They're nice," he said. "Tell me about them." Bennett delicately traced one fingertip down the handmade ridges in the pillar, and Jennie imagined what his hands would feel like doing that down her shoulders, across her face, along her cheekbone.

The temperature in the studio increased by ten degrees, and Jennie took an extra moment to center herself before she launched into the explanation of the collection, the color scheme she'd been planning, and how it had came to her mind.

Bennett seemed to be interested in her ramblings and didn't say a word until she finished.

"They're great." He beamed at her, and the moment between them strengthened and lengthened.

Jennie's pulse went wild and things that should've been warm turned cold.

He cleared his throat, the spark in his eyes not dulling even when he took a step away from her. "I'm not sure how you create in this mess, though."

Instant heat shot through Jennie, anger as hot as anything she'd felt before. "Out," she said, her guts quaking.

"It was a joke, Jennie."

"This is why I don't like people in my studio." She turned and headed for the door, wishing she could unclench her fists and take back her outburst.

"Jennie, come on." Bennett's footsteps sounded behind her, but Jennie didn't turn back. "It was—"

She silenced him by spinning back to him, and she felt dangerously close to losing it. She felt certain her eyes blazed pure lasers, because Bennett pressed his lips together, almost like he needed to physically keep himself from speaking.

"I am who I am," she said.

"I know that. I like who you are."

"I'm not going to change." Jennie felt a measure of insanity enter her mind, and she took a deep, deep breath to push it out.

"I'm not asking you to change." Bennett reached out and slid his hand down the side of her face, cradling her cheek in his palm. "Jennie, I'm sorry. I didn't mean anything by it."

Jennie's anger faded moment by moment until everything didn't seem held behind a screen of red.

Bennett watched her, and she knew the moment she'd defused because he knew it too and she saw the recognition of it in his eyes.

"Kyle was constantly nagging me to keep my studio clean," she said, the words a bit hollow even to her own ears.

"And Kyle was the ex-fiancé?" Bennett asked.

"Yes." Jennie turned, feeling completely in control, and moved into the kitchen. She didn't know why, only that she didn't want to have this conversation with him standing at the mouth of the hallway.

"And?" Bennett asked.

"I thought we were going to go get a puzzle," she said.

"I want to know more about Kyle," Bennett said, advancing toward her.

"Can we drive while I talk?"

"Sure." Bennett gestured for her to go first, and Jennie walked on shaking legs outside to the truck. She took extra seconds to situate herself, buckle her seatbelt, and watch the beautiful countryside roll by as Bennett drove toward the center of town.

Wedding Row was off Main Street, but it created a second downtown area that thrived with shoppers, boutiques, and eateries that never seemed to have a single empty table.

"Kyle was the office manager at the art gallery where I was commissioned," Jennie said, glad to have some life back in her voice. "That's how we met. We dated for a couple of years. Were engaged for a couple more. And then he didn't show up to the wedding."

Jennie sighed, wishing she were back on the Memory Lane where she got to kiss Bennett at the bell tower or beneath the pier or on his back porch.

"Is that why you left San Francisco?"

"Well, I couldn't just show up on Monday morning like nothing had happened."

"What did you do?"

She could feel the weight of Bennett's eyes on her, and she didn't entirely hate it. So, progress. "I took my honeymoon."

"By yourself?" The level of surprise in his voice caused her to turn from the landscape rolling by.

"Yes," she said. "By myself. I mailed his engagement

ring back from Cancun, and I asked my neighbor and best friend, Lisa, to go clean out my studio." Jennie cocked her head to the side. "Now that I think about it, Lisa said I was messy too."

Bennett did the lip-pressing again, and Jennie found it adorable and annoying at the same time. A sigh leaked past her lips and she said, "I know I'm messy. It's just how I work."

"It's fine," Bennett said. "It honestly was a joke, Jennie. Remember how I'd sneak into your bedroom and say the same thing?"

"One time," she said quickly, her face heating. "You snuck in one time and nothing happened."

Bennett gave her a long look. So long, she thought he'd drive them right off the road. "I kissed you while I dangled from your window. That was *something*."

It definitely had been, but Jennie lifted one shoulder in a shrug as if she could barely remember it. But now that he'd said it, she remembered the way her whole body had lit up, as if someone had made her swallow a star.

She remembered how he'd held her close as they talked about his forthcoming graduation and then hers. She remembered the emotion in his voice as he explained how he was going to try out for the major league baseball team in Seattle, the Spears.

And she wanted those intimate moments with him again. Her eyes dropped to his mouth, and thankfully, he was focused on driving again and didn't see her.

"Kyle wanted to change a lot about me," Jennie finally said, breaking the silence between them. "I didn't even realize who I'd become until he left, and I vowed I wouldn't change like that again. Not for anyone."

"Again, I'm not asking you to change." Bennett pulled into the parking lot down on the north end of Wedding Row. They could walk anywhere from here and have an enjoyable time. He found a spot and swung the truck in, turning toward her once he'd put it in park.

"In fact, I like you just the way you are."

13

Bennett stared at Jennie, refusing to blink or look away. He didn't have to use a lot of words to say a lot, and he didn't know what else to add anyway.

"I like you, too," she finally said. "I just sort of lost my temper back there."

Bennett nodded, glad the freaky, fiery version of Jennie had cooled pretty quickly. He'd seen her go ballistic like that before—once—when Jason had stolen her prized pink pony and used it for target practice.

She was nine-years-old, but had tiny fists of fury. At least this time it hadn't come to blows.

"So no changing," he said.

"Obviously, I'm going to change." She got out of the truck, and Bennett killed the engine and joined her on the sidewalk, carefully drawing her hand into his. "It's just...*I* want to decide when and what to change. I don't want someone else to tell me how I should be or what I should do different."

"Too old for that," Bennett agreed. He glanced left to find all the glittery, shiny wedding shops. Rings, tuxes, flowers, photography, and party rentals. He steered Jennie away from Wedding Row, with all it's glam and painful reminders, using his body to block her view of them, and over into the other side of the block.

This side had restaurants, bike rentals, beachwear, shops and stores, and snack stands. He went into a hat shop just to look, something he'd done with Jennie probably a half a dozen times before.

"You want another fedora?" she asked, trailing her fingers along the brim of a cowboy hat.

He shook his head. "What about this one?" He picked up a golf cap and set it on his head. Jennie laughed and shook her head, and Bennett relaxed all the way.

They browsed and looked, not buying anything, until they got to the game store. As a kid, Mitch's Magic Emporium had truly been magical. There were board games, card games, and magic sets. Toys, and dolls, and things Bennett couldn't get in any other store. Candy, jelly beans in every flavor, and sodas from other countries.

His parents had never allowed him to buy more than the cheapest of things here, but as he'd grown up and gotten his own jobs and earned his own money, he came and bought all those exotic treats and sweets he'd always wanted.

None of them were as good as he'd hoped—except the candy apple chewing gum. He swiped a package of that off the shelf by the check-out before moving further into the store to the jigsaw puzzle aisle.

"I get to pick," Jennie reminded him.

"Fine," he said, giving up the fight. He looked too, because there was no rule saying he couldn't buy more than one puzzle. She'd cajole him, and tell him he had to do hers first, but she didn't live with him and would never know. He could take one to the fire house and do one at home, just in case she ever came over.

The simple thought of having her in his house left his mouth dry and his fantasies running rampant.

"What about this one?" she asked, pointing to a color puzzle. "It's fifteen hundred shades," she read off the box. "Every piece is a slightly different color."

"Fifteen hundred pieces," he said, dreading the idea of how long it would take to complete. No pictures. Literally a color wheel, with all the shades and tints in the known universe. Fifteen hundred of them, anyway.

"If you want." He tried to make his voice nonchalant and moved further down the aisle to another selection of puzzles. Strange as it may seem, Bennett liked the puzzles called Fairy Garden or The Enchanted Library.

They also had extremely difficult sections with brickwork that took concentration to piece together, but they were fun at the same time.

He selected A Waterfront Party, looking at the sky and

the ocean that were almost identical in color. Tea lights had been strung over the wooden trellis, and people and animals alike were having a quaint picnic in the sand.

"I want this one," he said, returning to Jennie.

She looked at the front of the box. "There's a raccoon eating a cucumber sandwich."

"Are you going to make me do that color one?" He gave her a stern glare, but she didn't put the puzzle back on the shelf.

"I think so." She scanned the very top shelf and apparently didn't find anything worse.

She met his eye with absolute glee in hers. "Yep. This is the one."

Bennett rolled his eyes, not really upset, and walked away. "All right. Let's get this stuff and get over to Mabel's."

He paid for the puzzles and the gum—and a deck of spam cards Jennie threw on the counter at the very last moment.

"Recipes," she said by way of explanation.

"Do you even eat spam?"

"Sure."

"You don't cook."

"I do sometimes."

Bennett didn't argue further, because he didn't really cook either. A grilled cheese sandwich, maybe. Spaghetti sometimes. Easy things he didn't have to use a recipe for.

At Magleby Mansion, evidence of construction sat out

front in the form of a big dumpster, a flatbed truck, and Lauren's company truck.

"Oh, boy." Bennett exhaled. "Guess we better go see what's going on." Immediately inside the foyer, nothing was different. But upstairs, a piece of plastic drifted in the air currents, blocking what was through the door that led into the west wing.

Bennett and Jennie climbed the staircase and went to investigate. The scent of lumber met Bennett's nose, and his whole body sighed.

"I love working with wood," he said, suddenly yearning to get out into his shop. He hadn't had a project for a while, and he missed the sound of the saw screeching through the wood, the precise measurements, the satisfaction when everything lined up and looked beautiful.

The west wing had been completely gutted. The wall that had separated this receiving room from the rest of the wing was gone, and Lauren stood near the window, speaking with another man.

They both turned toward Bennett and Jennie when they entered. "Hey," Lauren acknowledged them, finished her conversation, and came over.

"This is Gene," she said, indicating the other man. "He's my foreman. We were just talking about you two." She flashed them a friendly smile.

"Just here to see the progress," Bennett said. "I guess I

better get into the shop. You'll be done with this in no time."

Lauren chuckled. "Oh, it'll be weeks still. We're on schedule." She glanced around too, her eyes coming back to them. "Not that it matters, but it kind of does. Mabel wants wood accents in each room. We—" She exchanged a glance with Gene—"Thought it would be nice if they matched your furniture."

"Oh." Bennett should've read his contract. He wasn't even really sure how many pieces he was making. Nor out of what. Or what color the stain would be. All questions Lauren would ask.

"That would be great," he said. "I'm in the planning stages right now." He refused to look at Jennie. "Can I get back to you?"

Lauren shrugged like she didn't care, but Bennett knew she had a tight construction schedule. If something or someone didn't come through when they said they would, she'd be behind.

"I'll text you tonight," he added.

"That would be great," Lauren said. "Then Gene can get the same materials and colors. Let me give you his number."

She recited a number while Bennett typed it into his phone, and she and Gene moved further into the wing, already talking about something else.

"I'm glad I didn't go into construction," Bennett said.

"You like working with wood," Jennie said. "You literally just said so."

"Building furniture," Bennett said. "Not walls, or dealing with flooring, lighting, all of it."

Jennie wandered over to the window where Lauren had been standing. "You haven't even thought about your pieces, have you?"

Bennett thought about denying it for about two seconds. Then he said, "No," with a big sigh. "Want to come over to my shop with me and brainstorm?"

She turned from the window, a mixture of surprise, apprehension, and need on her face. She'd never been good at hiding how she felt, and Bennett had never appreciated it more.

"You can call me a slob, if you want." He grinned at her, glad when she shook her head and laughed before crossing the room to him and taking his hand in hers.

"I already know your shop will be spotless," she said. "So let's go brainstorm some furniture, but we need to talk to Mabel first."

Bennett made it through the conversation with Mabel about the buffet without having to know a whole lot, thankfully. He felt like he was walking on clouds as he descended the steps and helped Jennie into his truck. He simply could not believe she'd come back to town, back to him. He hoped it was a permanent thing, and then he decided to ask her.

"Jennie, are you planning to stay in Hawthorne

Harbor?" He cut a quick glance at her as he turned onto the road that led back down the bluff and into town.

As a second passed, and then a couple of blocks, and then a mile and she hadn't spoken, Bennett's heart fell like he'd pushed it out of an airplane.

14

Jennie's mind wouldn't settle. Bennett didn't ask his question again, and he didn't turn on the radio. The silence between them felt suffocating, and Jennie hated it.

But she also hated that she couldn't answer his question easily.

"I don't know," she finally said. "I'm here for now, and the money from Mabel's job will be enough for a few more months." She looked at him, mentally begging him to understand. "But there's not much use for me here. I'm an artist, and a high-end one at that."

"Open a gallery," he said.

"Here?"

"Sure. There's that posh place on Wedding Row."

"They do photography," she said. "And sure, it's expensive, but brides will pay for pictures. They don't pay for wedding day pottery." She looked out the window, wishing her attitude about staying in town wasn't so fatalistic.

"Seattle has a big art scene," he said.

She swung her gaze toward him, trying to figure out what he meant, but he didn't elaborate.

He reached over and turned on the radio, pushing buttons until he found a station that wasn't playing a commercial. Jennie let him retreat, because it was easier than having a difficult conversation.

He lived basically in a diagonal line from her place on the north end of town, down the street from the most popular building in Hawthorne Harbor—Duality.

No wonder he didn't cook. Jennie smiled to herself as he pulled into the driveway of a cute little white house with one of those big, wide porches.

"I've always wanted a porch like that," she said, admiring it.

"I remember that." He gave her a tight grin and got out of the truck.

Sure enough, his lawn had been trimmed to exactly two inches high. She wondered if he knelt down and used a ruler to keep it so even. He obviously watered regularly, and did the weed and feed, probably aerated, all of it, because the grass almost looked like turf in its perfection.

The carport where he'd parked was clean, of course, and Jennie felt a twinge of disappointment that he bypassed entering the house in favor of walking into the back yard. She had the insane desire to know if the man had left his breakfast dishes in the sink or not.

His back yard was as immaculate as the front, and a large shed waited in the back corner. Easily half as big as the house, the shed had a white P painted in bright white paint on the side.

"Patterson?" she asked.

"This was my grandmother's house," he said. "I don't think I ever brought you here when we dated in high school."

Jennie suddenly remembered that he'd come here almost every weekend for Sunday meals, but no, he'd never brought her. Not even when they'd been talking about babies and diamonds.

"When did she pass away?" Jennie asked.

"Oh, at least ten years ago." Bennett didn't carry any pain in his voice, but Jennie knew it had to be there. Time dulled things, but Jennie knew death had a special way of stinging for a long, long while.

"And you moved here?" she asked.

"She left it to me."

"So you have no mortgage?"

He paused at the door to the shed and looked at her. "That's right." He unlocked the door and went inside. "Let me get the cooler going and I can hear Gemma barking, so let me go let her out."

Jennie startled as he entered her personal space,

partly because of the quick way her heart suddenly started beating and partly because of the dog.

"She's coming out here?"

Bennett gazed down at her, the heat between them intensifying exponentially within a single breath. "She'll run around in the yard for about five minutes. Then she'll come lay right under the fan."

He didn't move, and Jennie was very glad for the solid wall behind her to keep her standing.

She stared at his mouth before finally nodding, and that broke the spell between them, allowing him to walk away from her. Jennie watched him go, thinking it would probably be easier to kiss him and get it over with.

Her lips tingled at the very thought.

She turned away from the sight of his broad shoulders and entered the shop. It was a big space, but thankfully heat rose, and the cooler was pumping hard into the shed.

It looked very manly, with a table saw running down the middle of the space, loads of lumber, wood scraps, and sawhorses on one side, with the other wall holding a full-length counter. Various tools hung on the wall above that, not a single thing out of place.

A rush of affection for Bennett hit her with the force of a tidal wave. He was nothing if not predictable, and she ran her fingertips along the edge of the counter, trying to feel closer to him.

The woodshop emanated his spirit, his goodness, his perfectionism, and Jennie liked it all. Her heart slowed and filled with love for him, and with that, came a heavy dose of fear.

Was she ready to love someone again? *Could* she even love someone again?

Maybe Bennett, she thought as barking filled the sky.

She pressed into the counter as a black streak flew past the entrance to the shed. Barking, barking, barking.

Bennett's laugher joined in with the joy of the dog, and Jennie edged to the doorway so she could see him. He interacted with Gemma like he really loved her, and Jennie thought it was entirely unfair of him to bring her here.

Because she felt herself falling, and it was the good kind of falling in love.

Gemma spotted her, and she trotted over, her big tongue hanging out of her mouth already.

"Gemma, stop." Bennett's voice was commanding yet kind, and the dog paused. "Sit." The dog sat. Bennett came up beside her, positively beaming. "Good girl." He scrubbed her head, and Gemma's eyes closed halfway as she leaned her head back, clearly in bliss.

Jennie was suddenly jealous of a dog.

A *dog.*

"See?" he said, drawing her attention back to him. "She's nice."

"She's probably just hot." The dog was black all over except for some white hairs growing in around her mouth. Still, Jennie felt a pull to the canine she didn't understand,

and she reached out and patted her. Gemma didn't snap or growl, but put that blissful look on her face.

Jennie giggled, and Bennett stepped past her. "Told you. C'mon, Gemmy."

Gemmy. Such a cute nickname from the tough firefighter. Jennie had a hard time making all the different sides of him match up.

He spread several papers across the counter and pushed his breath out. "Okay, let's see what I agreed to build."

Jennie laughed, unable to help herself. She joined Bennett at the workbench and peered over his bicep. "I know there's a buffet."

He pointed to a spot on the paper. "Yeah, that's here. Looks like several end tables, a huge armoire...and the buffet." He glanced down at her. "What do you think?"

Jennie met his eye. "What do you mean, what do I think?"

"What would you like the buffet to be made of? Maple? Oak? Redwood is kind of nice."

"I only know one of those."

"Cherry would be pretty too." He focused back on the paper. "I should probably ask Mabel if that would go with her interior design. It's a redder wood."

"My parents had a solid redwood table from a fallen tree from California. It's beautiful."

"Had?" He fell back a step and looked at her.

Jennie's nerves bounced around in her body, almost

like they had decided to have a dance party and forgotten to tell her. He was so handsome, and that falling sensation happened again, and why couldn't she look away from his lips?

"They still have it," she said, realizing she'd misspoke.

"Do you see your folks often?" he asked.

"Here and there," she said. "They're thinking of buying an RV and traveling all over."

Bennett smiled, a soft, beautiful smile that drove Jennie's thoughts irrationally toward kissing. "I think that would be awesome."

She returned his smile. "I know. You've already got plans, don't you?"

"Not really, no." He stepped back over to the workbench and looked needlessly at the papers.

Jennie trilled out another laugh. "You really can't lie to me, Bennett."

He cut her a glance full of heat and playfulness. "One day."

She shook her head and leaned into him, threading her arm around his. "I don't think so."

"You're not great at hiding things either, you know."

"Better than you."

"If you say so."

Jennie leaned away without removing her touch from him. "What do you mean?"

"It means I can see you staring at my mouth all the

time." He settled his weight on his far leg and smirked at her. "You're dying to kiss me."

Jennie wanted to deny it outright, but the words stuck in her throat. "So what?" she finally challenged. "You wouldn't let me?"

Bennett's dark eyes devoured her, making her simultaneously cold and hot. Oh, so hot. He leaned toward her again, the glint in his expression saying he wanted to kiss her too. "I'd let you," he said, his voice somewhat croaky.

"All right, then." But Jennie couldn't seem to make her body close the eight-inch distance between them and get the deed done. Her head swam with the nearness of him, what it would be like to kiss him as a grown woman, not a teenager, and it seemed like her brain had frozen.

The air filled with the scent of wood shavings and cologne, and only she and Bennett existed—even though Gemma's panting was loud enough to wake the dead.

"So?" he asked. "Are you going to kiss me?"

Jennie wanted to, but she didn't want to be the instigator. She wanted him to sweep his arm around her waist and draw her close, whisper something romantic, and claim her mouth. Why, she wasn't sure. Bennett just had that power over her, she supposed.

She tipped up on her toes, putting more pressure on his forearm to steady herself, and pecked him on the cheek. "There. You big baby."

He growled, clearly not satisfied with the kiss, and said, "That wasn't a kiss."

"I never do anything right when it comes to you," she said with a smirk.

He searched her face for a few moments, then leaned down, bypassing the romantic whisper, and touched his lips to hers. Feather-light, almost seeking for permission she'd basically already given, the touch lasted long enough to send Jennie into a tailspin but not nearly long enough to be labeled a kiss.

Her eyes had drifted closed, the world around her marshmallow soft. "Bennett," she said, the one doing the throaty whispering.

"Hmm?" His breath washed across her cheek, so he couldn't have pulled back too far.

"That wasn't a kiss either."

One hand slipped around her waist while the other trailed down the side of her face, causing her to open her eyes. He hovered only inches from her, wearing a look of complete adoration in his expression.

"I really like you, Jennie Zimmerman."

Before she could tell him she really liked him too, Bennett matched his mouth to hers and kissed her. Now, *this* was a kiss, and since Jennie hadn't been able to tell him how she felt, she poured her emotion into the action, hoping he'd get the message loud and clear.

15

Bennett had kissed other women, and none of them compared to Jennie. It was as if she'd been made for him to kiss, and no one else would do. She leaned into him and kissed him back with as much passion as he felt coursing through his body. He couldn't get her close enough, couldn't kiss her long enough.

When he finally pulled away, the temperature in the woodshop could never be cooled by the weak air pumping out of the swamp cooler. He opened his eyes and looked into Jennie's light ones to find happiness there.

"Wow," she said.

"That good, huh?" He grinned down at her.

She playfully slapped his chest as she giggled. "It's just...better than I remember."

"We were seventeen before," he said, skating his lips across her cheek to her earlobe. She pressed into his touch, and Bennett's ideas about spending the afternoon measuring and cutting wood flew right out the window.

He wanted to lead Jennie over to the hammock in the corner of his yard and hold her while they talked the rest of the afternoon away. Fine, he wanted to kiss her in between every word, but he certainly didn't want to build a buffet when he could be kissing Jennie.

"So I think redwood," she said, stepped out of his arms. Bennett let her go, because Jennie probably needed some time to process what had just happened. Bennett himself felt buzzed, and he forced his focus back to the contract.

"Let me text Lauren."

"What for?"

"Measurements." He glanced at her. "Oh, wait. You have them, don't you?"

"Yes...somewhere in my studio." Her eyes sparkled, and she burst out laughing a moment later. Bennett joined her and swiped open his phone anyway.

"I'll ask her about the interior design." Twenty minutes later, he'd decided on the redwood and had the dimensions for the end tables and the armoire. He sketched ideas on a notepad while Jennie took his truck back to her place to get the dimensions for the buffet. When she returned, she had a plastic bag hanging from one arm and two sodas, one in each hand, from Duality.

"You're an angel," he said, taking the drink she handed him. "It's hot in here, right?"

"It's not as bad as outside." She put the bag on the workbench. "I got some of those cheddar bacon tots you like." She met his eye. "At least, you used to like them."

"I still love 'em," he said. "And there better be a Kit Kat in there."

She produced a king size candy bar and grinned. "Right here."

Bennett smiled and took the chocolate bar. "And what did you get? Wait. Let me guess." He cocked his head like he was really thinking about it, but he'd been to Duality a zillion times with her. "Some of that crusty mac-and-cheese...with a ranch packet to squeeze on top."

She reached into the bag and left her hands in there as if preparing for a big reveal. "Ta-da!" Sure enough, she had a container of mac-and-cheese—which looked entirely too orange to be real—in one hand and a packet of ranch dressing in the other.

"I guess we're both predictable," he said, opening his box of tots. "Did you find the measurements?"

"Yep, right here." She pulled a folded piece of paper out of her back pocket and handed it to Bennett.

The sound of clicking claws came over, and Bennett turned toward Gemma as the dog sat, an expectant look on her face. Her eyes were earnest, like *I sat, Dad. Aren't I so good? I have some of those tots?*

Bennett gave her one, along with a quick scrub behind the ears, and looked at the numbers Jennie had scrawled on the paper. He quickly started a new drawing, adding the numbers she'd provided and turned it toward her.

"What do you think?"

She studied the sketch, taking a few bites of her afternoon snack as she did. "No ornamental stuff on the doors or anything?"

"I thought your pieces would be the ornamental stuff."

"It would be kind of cool if the same swoops from the pottery went down into the wood."

"But what if Mabel wants to put something else on the buffet?"

"Then it would have character."

Bennett took the paper back and started to add a few swooshes down the front of the doors. "Like this?"

Jennie nodded and said, "Yeah, like that. How hard is that?"

"I can do it with a carving gouge," he said. "I've got three of them." He indicated the shelf where his carving tools were. "Big, medium, and small." He collected the tools and handed them to her. "I'm thinking medium."

"Show me," she said, looking at the gouges like they'd attack her at any moment.

Bennett turned from the workbench to get a piece of scrap wood. "So it would be sanded and ready to assemble already," he said as he sifted through the pile for a good sample. He found a decent sized piece of oak and moved back over to her. "So imagine it was a finished piece."

"Yeah, sure I can imagine that."

Bennett looked up at her dry tone. "Oh, you think you're so funny." He chuckled and had the desire to kiss her again.

She grinned at him like she was indeed funny and shrugged. "I don't expect you to know what my art is going to look like."

"But I can imagine the difference between a finished piece of pottery and one that's raw." He held up the wood. "So this would be better than this. You just gouge in the pattern you want. This is a pretty hard piece of wood—it's oak—so each gouge might need multiple passes." After picking up the carving gouge, he positioned it against the wood and pressed it away from him, creating a riverbed in the wood.

He repeated the action several more times, leaving some high areas of wood and making some deeper. "See? It's kind of like the swooshes on your pots."

She picked up the wood and studied it, lovingly stroking her fingers along the ridges and valleys. "It's beautiful. Exactly like my pottery." She gazed at him with wonder, and Bennett couldn't fathom why.

"What?" he finally asked when her gaze got a little too heavy.

"You're an artist."

He shook his head. "No, not like you."

She looked back at the wood and set it on the workbench. "I think that would look beautiful on the front door panels."

Bennett did too, and he turned to sort through the redwood stock he had. When he turned back to the bench, several lengths of lumber in his arms, he found Jennie perched on his stool, Gemma at her side. She patted the dog and said, "Don't say anything."

So Bennett laughed and shook his head, glad his dog had won Jennie over so quickly.

BENNETT GOT USED TO A NEW SCHEDULE OVER THE COURSE of the next couple of weeks. He worked his shifts at the fire house, trying to keep Jennie's voice out of his head about the memes. There were no more emergencies—not even a badger had fallen into a window well and scared a homeowner. Nothing.

In his off-hours, he worked in the shop, putting together tables and the armoire. He'd been saving the buffet for last, hoping to work on it while Jennie was too busy to come watch. He knew she'd completed her collection, because she'd texted him to say how great the kiln had worked.

And no flames!

She'd been so proud, and Bennett liked the long text conversations they had too. He saw her a lot too, as he'd taken to texting her when he was leaving the station to see if she'd like to eat breakfast, lunch, or dinner with him, depending on what kind of shift he'd just finished.

She always said yes, and then she'd come linger in the shop while he worked. A couple of times, he'd hardly gotten anything done because she'd spent so long kissing him.

Not that he minded. But if she thought she'd need to wait until next summer to marry him, Bennett sometimes wondered what she was doing. Because he felt himself already knee deep in love with her, and he'd started imagining what it would be like to have her waiting at home for him when he got done with his monotonous shifts at the fire house.

One day, she didn't answer his query about lunch, so he headed past Duality and toward his house. As soon as he turned into his driveway, he spotted her bicycle. *This is new*, he thought as a smile carved its way across his face. She'd never come over to his place without him before, and he wondered if something was wrong.

He went in the house with a "Jennie?" but was only greeted by silence. That was when he knew something serious was going on, because even Gemma wasn't there to slobber all over him and wind between his legs like a cat.

"Gemma?" he called. The dog barked—from outside.

Bennett stepped over to the door that led onto the back deck and went outside. Gemma barked again, but she didn't come running over. Instead, she sat next to the hammock, near Jennie's head.

"Come on, girl," he said, but the dog didn't move.

Bennett's heart twisted in his chest as he went down the few steps to the grass. Something was seriously wrong. "Jennie?" he asked as he drew closer.

Sniffling came from behind Gemma's huge head, and the dog turned and licked Jennie's arm. Bennett half expected her to yelp and shove the big dog away. But she didn't. In fact, she turned onto her side in the hammock and wrapped both arms around Gemma's neck.

"What's wrong?" Bennett could clearly see tears now. He reached out and patted Gemma's head, glad the canine could give Jennie some sort of comfort. He pushed Jennie's hair off her forehead and she opened her tear-filled eyes and looked at him.

"It's my mom," she said. She started to say more, but her voice broke and a fresh wave of tears spilled down her face.

"Oh, honey." Bennett nudged Gemma out of the way so he could climb into the hammock with his girlfriend. She let him take her into his arms, and she cried into his chest for a few seconds. Bennett had several questions, but in that moment he just let Jennie take all the comfort she needed, his heart breaking for her.

Finally Jennie regained some control, but she didn't relinquish the grip she had on his body. "She's been diagnosed with breast cancer."

"I'm so sorry," Bennett made his voice say. "She just found out?"

"This morning."

"Did you call me? I didn't get a message."

"I didn't call." She snuggled deeper into his side. "I just came over. Gemma kept me company."

"What are the doctors saying?"

"They're still doing a bunch of tests, but it's already in her lymph nodes." Jennie sniffed. "She's only sixty-four, you know?"

"I know, sweetheart," Bennett said though he wouldn't have been able to pinpoint Jennie's mother's age. "Have you seen her?"

"Yes, just for a few minutes. They had another appointment this afternoon up in Seattle."

"I'm sorry," Bennett said again, wishing words could be adequate enough to erase heartache. But he knew they weren't. Cynthia had apologized when she'd left, and it hadn't even come close to helping Bennett understand or accept her decision to leave him.

He pushed his ex-wife from his mind, determined to be with Jennie, be present, while she needed him.

16

Jennie lay with Bennett for a long time. Until the sun started going down and she realized that his stomach was complaining loudly that he hadn't eaten in a while. He hadn't said much, and Jennie hadn't either.

She couldn't explain why she'd come straight to his house after learning about her mother's health problems. Only that she knew this quaint home would provide her with the comfort she needed. She'd gone inside only to let Gemma out, and the dog had sensed her distress instantly, staying beside her and giving her an occasional lick when the tears got a little too thick.

She'd almost cried herself out by the time Bennett got home, but she'd had one good sobfest into his chest before exhaustion had finally stemmed the flow of tears.

"Let's go to dinner," she said.

"I can order in," he said. "Or go pick something up."

"I'm okay." She pushed herself up enough to look at him. She'd kissed him so many times over the past couple of weeks, but somehow doing it now would feel brand new to her. She leaned over and touched her mouth to his. He let her set the pace, didn't move his hands to cradle her face and twine his fingers through her hair, as he'd done previously.

She kissed him tenderly, almost with gratitude for simply being there with her. Holding her. Letting her take as much from him as she wanted. She felt tender, soft things for him that seemed like love.

Pulling back, she let her emotions roll through her without censoring them. Fear for the future. Love for her parents—and for Bennett? Worry. Doubt. Hope. Joy.

"You're right," she whispered. "I don't want to go out."

He stroked her hair now. "What do you want? I'm not great in the kitchen, but I can make toast and eggs. Or Dutch pancakes."

Surprisingly, a giggle escaped Jennie's lips. "You've tried those Dutch pancakes once, Bennett. They spilled over into the oven and then filled the house with smoke."

"I've gotten better at them," he said, adding a chuckle to the end of his sentence. "Plus, I know how to get rid of smoke now that I'm a firefighter."

"Everyone knows how to do that." She gave his torso a playful nudge. "It's called opening a few windows and blowing a fan."

"So no to the Dutch pancakes. Grilled cheese sand-wiches? Or I can put some hamburgers on the grill. Or I can order pizza." He stroked his fingers up and down her arm and shifted to look at her. "Tell me what you want, and I'll make it happen." He spoke with such adoration and reverence that Jennie's heart expanded with love for him.

At the same time, her first instinct was to push him away. Keep him at arm's length. Put up a wall between them, even if it wasn't very high. So she swung her legs over the side of the hammock away from him, her back to him now. "Whatever you want," she said, though she wanted a big plate of Chinese noodles and vegetables from Nod to Noodles down the road a ways.

She wouldn't send him on an hour-long round trip just for her. Because she knew he'd go, and she didn't want to face that fact right now. Didn't want to face her own growing feelings for Bennett, didn't want to be beholden to him for more than a few hours of comfort in his back yard.

"You like the vegetable Alfredo pizza from Jovani's, right?"

"Yes," she said, in the mood for anything but pizza. But she let him order it, let him lead her into his spotless house and park her on his couch. She ate a few bites of the piece of pizza he gave her, she leaned into him when he turned on a romantic comedy, and she let him take her home when the hour grew late.

She missed Gemma, especially when her companion became a surly, white cat who hadn't been fed since that morning. She managed to fill Snowball's bowl without getting scratched to death. On her way down the dark hallway to her bedroom, the glow from the light on the neighbor's back patio caught her attention as she passed her art studio.

Pausing in the doorway, she let the astringent smell of the cleaners and paints and glazes she used to create beauty seep through her. What was she going to do when she finished Mabel's pieces? How could she stay in town? She honestly didn't think she could. She'd leased this house because of this utility room she'd converted into an art studio, but she'd need more than one job a year to make her life here permanent.

How could she leave Bennett for a second time? She knew she couldn't do that again, but he'd never left Hawthorne Harbor, even after his divorce. Which meant he didn't *want* to live somewhere else, and she couldn't ask him to follow her until she happened to land somewhere.

Turning away from the studio, she turned off her thoughts too. Her phone rang, and she nearly jumped out of her skin. Her heart pounded, and then started drumming like crazy when she saw her father's picture on the screen.

"Hey, Dad," she said, making her voice strong. "How did the tests go? How's Mom?"

"She's doing okay." His voice sounded far away and

utterly spent. "We decided to stay in Seattle. Rather, the doctors wanted to see her again in the morning."

That didn't sound good, and Jennie said as much. "They want to do another test for a new experimental medicine." He exhaled. "She's going to be fine. They can remove the lymph nodes and the mass in her breast. They just want to make sure the cancer isn't growing anywhere else. It was stage four."

Jennie didn't know much about cancer, but she knew stage four was bad. Spreading to other parts of the body was too. "Okay, Dad. I'll go by the house for Patches in the morning."

"Thanks, Jennie." He wore a slight smile in the way he said her name. "We'll be home by mid-afternoon."

"I'll be there," she vowed. Just like Bennett had set aside all his plans for that day and had just been with her, Jennie could be there for her mom and dad. They'd never said anything, but she knew now she'd probably hurt them with her sudden disappearance from Hawthorne Harbor all those years ago. All the missed holidays. The selfish way she'd pursued her dreams until they'd come true. Suddenly, being an artist didn't mean quite as much as being a good daughter, and regret laced itself through Jennie's bloodstream.

"I'm glad you're home," her dad said. "I talked to Jason today, and he's going to take the next couple of days off work."

"Okay, I'll coordinate with Kaitlyn for dinner tomorrow." And by that, Jennie meant she'd offer Jason's wife some money, as Jennie couldn't actually cook much more than boiled eggs.

She hung up with her father and continued into her bedroom. Pure exhaustion filled her, but she managed to get things set with Jason and Kaitlyn for the following day before she allowed herself to drift into unconsciousness.

THE NEXT DAY, SHE PACED IN HER PARENTS' LIVING ROOM while Kaitlyn worked into the kitchen. Since their home was on the older side, walls separated everything, but Jennie could still hear the hissing of a pot and smell the delicious scent of roasting meat. How Kaitlyn did half of what she did in the kitchen, Jennie wasn't sure. But it didn't matter. She could peel potatoes and chop carrots, so she felt like she'd contributed at least a little bit to the meal.

The front door opened, and Jennie spun toward it though it didn't make sense for her parents to enter that way when they'd park in the garage and come in that door. Sure enough, Jason entered the house, looking as anxious and tired as Jennie felt.

"Hey," he said, drawing her into a brotherly hug. "No word?"

"Not since Dad texted to say they'd left."

"That was almost three hours ago." Jason frowned.

"They should be here by now. I was worried I'd be late." His blue eyes held the worry, but all Jennie could do was shrug. Jason's mouth tightened and he moved into the kitchen to kiss his wife.

Jennie's fingers wound together and pulled apart, her nerves sure to make her explode. Her niece and nephew played in the back bedroom that used to be hers, their chatter just loud enough for Jennie to catch on the fringes of her attention.

"The stew is ready," Kaitlyn announced, and Jennie left the living room in favor of the kitchen. Not only did Kaitlyn have a steaming pot of beef stew waiting on the counter, but a big bowl of salad and a dozen gloriously browned rolls. Jennie knew those had come out of the freezer, but they were still impressive.

"Should we feed the kids?" Jason asked. "Then if Mom and Dad are tired, we can send them back to the playroom." He and Kaitlyn could have whole conversations without saying a word, and Jennie had never felt anything but annoyed about it. But now, as she watched them shrug and then as Kaitlyn moved to the mouth of the hall and called her kids to come eat, Jennie wondered what it would be like to have someone who knew her so well that she didn't even have to speak to have her voice heard.

And like lightning had struck her, she realized she had never had that with Kyle. Never. She busied herself with helping her niece get her roll buttered as she thought through the four-year relationship and why she'd never achieved that level of closeness with Kyle.

Because she'd never truly been herself.

The answer was always there, but Jennie had never known it—at least until she'd endured some of the hardest hours and days of her life.

She sat at the bar with the kids so Jason and Kaitlyn could huddle in the living room and talk. Jennie had never felt so complete as she did in that moment, with her family gathered around. A rush of gratitude that Kyle had not shown up for their wedding hit her. She couldn't imagine being married to him now, living with him, starting a family with him.

No, when she thought of those things, it was now Bennett's dark eyes looking back at her from across the altar.

The sound of the garage door lifting drew her away from her thoughts, and she hurried over to the door leading outside. She stood in it as her father pulled into the garage. She couldn't quite see her mother's face in the dim light, and Jennie pressed her emotions back, back, back. The last thing her mom would want was a blubbering daughter.

"We made it." Her dad went around the back of the car and opened the passenger door for his wife. "Something smells good."

"Kaitlyn cooked," Jennie said as she got her first look at her mom. She looked great. Not too tired. Maybe just emotional and trying to hide it, the way Jennie was. She came up the steps first and Jennie let her into the house before seizing onto her and saying, "I love you, Mom."

Jason and Kaitlyn joined them, and everyone took a turn hugging Jennie's parents. Finally her mom said, "I'm starving, and that stew looks delicious." She smiled at everyone, and they sat down to dinner.

"Tell us everything," Jason said. So their dad launched into technical medical things Jennie would have to look up later. The main point was what he'd told her last night —the doctors thought they could get her cancer-free through radiation, chemotherapy, and surgery.

"We'll do the removals first," her dad said. "Two weeks, we'll be back in Seattle."

"Two weeks," Jason said. "Wow."

"We'll be in Seattle a lot," her dad said. "We're thinking of getting an apartment up there, at least for the next several months while Mom goes through her treatments and recovers from her surgery."

A twinge of panic blipped through Jennie. She wouldn't be able to help much if they went to Seattle. At the same time, something Bennett had said slithered through her mind like a snake in the grass.

Seattle has a big art scene.

Maybe she could check into that. See if there was a studio or gallery that would take her pieces.

Jason asked a question, but Jennie missed it. She did catch, "So you've already found one. Wow." He looked at

Kaitlyn and then Jennie. "I'm sure between Jennie and I, we can take care of the house and Patches."

"I can take Patches," Jennie said.

Her mom looked at her, only surprise on her face. "He's a *dog*, Jennie. You realize that, right?" She grinned, the first smile Jennie had seen on her mom's face since she'd returned.

"He sheds all over the place," her dad added. So Jason taking him wasn't really an option. Kaitlyn was allergic, and while she could come around the house for a few hours, she'd be sneezy and wheezy before they left that night.

The adults all looked around the table while Jennie prepared herself to say what was on her mind. "Bennett will take him." She shrugged like Bennett was just a casual acquaintance—one she knew well enough to take her parent's golden retriever at a moment's notice.

Jason snorted and covered his mouth with a napkin while her parents stared at her. "I'm, um, sort of dating him again."

"Sort of?" Jason said with much incredulity. "They've been dating—full-on—for weeks."

"Not that long," she said.

"How long?" her twin challenged, and Jennie remembered all the things about him that annoyed her.

"I'd say maybe three and a half weeks?" Another shrug. "Something like that."

"And it's not 'sort of.'"

Kaitlyn reached over and touched her husband's hand, shaking her head at him in a silent way of saying *Shut up, Jason.*

"Well," her mom said. "I've always liked Bennett Patterson. If he'll take Patches, that would be nice."

Jennie nodded and put more stew in her mouth so she'd have a few seconds to think before she had to answer her mother's questions. Because she could see them building up. She'd always liked Bennett Patterson too, but she didn't have an answer for her mom when she asked, "How fast is this relationship going?"

But she could answer "Are you thinking of staying in town then?" with a "Yeah, Mom. I'm thinking about it."

17

Bennett eyed the friendly golden retriever as it circled Gemma and Uno, sniffing like it had never sniffed before. "Do you think I'm a dog hotel?" he asked, though he'd gladly take Patches—and any other dogs Jennie brought to him.

Jennie just kept watching the dogs as they started chasing each other in his back yard. She'd been distant and busy since her mother's diagnosis, and Bennett had done his best to simply be there whenever she needed him. Admittedly, it wasn't as often as he'd like, but she'd always responded to his texts, so he hadn't pushed the issue. Everyone dealt with grief in their own way. Bennett knew that better than most.

Jennie had shown up that morning with the golden retriever and the words, "My parents are staying in Seattle for a few months, and Patches needs somewhere to stay."

Bennett sat on the back steps, waiting for Jennie to join him. Sit by him. Say something. When she finally did, she slipped her hand into his and laid her head against his shoulder.

"You okay?" he asked, squeezing her fingers.

"Just worried."

"Everything you've told me sounds like they're going to be able to beat the cancer."

She exhaled and snuggled closer. "Yeah, I know."

Bennett let a minute go by before he said, "So tell me about what you're working on now." She'd finished her five-piece collection, but she hadn't invited him back to her studio, nor had she expounded much on what she was working on next.

"It won't come together in my mind."

"The unveiling is next month."

"I'm aware."

Bennett watched the dogs as the sun continued to lift into the sky. "I have to go to work soon," he finally said. "Want to come into the shop for a few minutes?"

"Sure."

He stood and led the way over to the wood shop. He'd started cutting the pieces for the buffet last night, late after everyone else in town was probably asleep. They were stacked against one wall, but Jennie went straight over to the finished pieces.

"These are so beautiful."

"I could build you something," he suggested with a

shrug, not wanting to add more to her life when she needed simple.

"Yeah?" Her face brightened. "So you'll take my parents' dog and build me something."

"What can I say? I'm a good boyfriend." Bennett gave her a playful smile, hoping her mood would improve before he went to work. He'd seen Jennie in his melancholy state before, when she thought she couldn't afford to go to art school. In the end, she hadn't been able to let go of the dream—though she'd let go of plenty of other things.

Jennie grinned at him and walked over to him, snaking her arms around his back. "You are a really good boyfriend." She sobered and looked right into his eyes. "You always were. You know that, right, Bennett? I didn't leave because I was unhappy with you."

"I know," he said, though it hadn't erased the ache in his chest to know that all those years ago. And she'd never come back, at least not for more than a few days around Christmastime.

"I was lost," she said. "And it took a long time to find myself."

Bennett nodded, because he felt like he'd been wandering for a while now—since Cynthia's departure from his life. Really, since his injury and the long recovery road. Giving up on his dream of playing baseball had been hard, and Bennett didn't really fault Jennie for leaving town and pursuing her dream to become the artist she was.

"I think I'm going to stay in town," she said, causing Bennett to flinch with her in his arms.

"Yeah?" Hope lifted through him like helium. "That's great news, Jennie."

"I might have to travel a bit," she said. "I'm going to check out the studios and galleries in Seattle. See if they'll display my pieces if I'm not local or the artist-in-residence."

"That's a good idea." Just the fact that she had plans, or ideas, or solutions to her future income problems was a good sign to Bennett. Maybe he could keep her in his life this time. "Let me know how I can help."

She stepped away from him, wiping one hand through her hair and tightening her ponytail. "For now, I need you to take Patches." She admired the armoire and the tables he'd completed. "And bring me some of those cheddar poppers when you get off work tonight." She gave him a sly look, and Bennett laughed.

"I can do all of that."

"Great." She drew in a big breath and turned to survey his shop. "You haven't even started the buffet?"

"I cut some of the pieces last night."

"You know the unveiling is next month, right?" She threw him a devilish look over her shoulder.

"Ha ha." Bennett swept his arms around her and pulled her against his chest. "I'm aware." He kissed her neck, glad when she twisted in his arms and pressed her lips to his. And he knew he'd never survive if she didn't stay in town, didn't find a way to make her life here...with him.

"CHILI," BENNETT REPEATED, LOOKING AT THE HUGE CAST iron pot on the stove. Charles wore an apron and finished tossing the salad. "It smells so good, Charles."

"Thanks." The other man flashed him a smile and reached for a bowl. "With cheese, or without?"

"Cheese me." Bennett grinned at his friend, took his bowl of chili, and joined the other firemen at the table a few feet away. Chief Harvey was in today, and he was in the middle of a story about one of his granddaughters.

Bennett was content to eat and listen, so that was what he did. As the group burst into laughter, he did too, and a sense of contentment filled him. Right here, in this fire house, he'd found a sanctuary when he'd needed one the most.

"So," Alex said from across the table. "I hear you're dating Jennie Zimmerman."

"It's not a secret," Bennett said, putting another spoonful of chili in his mouth.

"Alex is looking for a date," Ray said with a laugh. "He's been striking out."

"I have not." Alex glared at Ray but when he looked

back at Bennett, he wore a ridiculous amount of hope in his eyes. "You used to date Jennie in high school, right?"

"Yeah," Bennett said slowly, not sure where this conversation was going. "So?"

"So, his high school girlfriend just broke up with her long-time boyfriend, and he still thinks he has a chance with her."

"Who is it?" Bennett asked.

"Hilary Steele."

"Hilary?" Ray asked. "I thought it was Tahlia."

"Tahlia's the one with the cat who keeps getting stuck." He rolled his eyes. "I'm so sick of that cat."

"You went out with her too, I'm sure of it," Ray said.

"Once," Alex said, his neck turning a shade of red Bennett hadn't seen in a while.

"Oh, I sense a story here," he said, digging in for another bite of chili.

"No. No story," Alex said, ducking his head. But he had nothing to hide behind, and Ray started laughing. The rest of the men at the table turned to look at them, interest in their eyes.

"Alex has a story," Bennett said, leaning back in his chair with a huge grin on his face. "And he won't share."

"It's nothing," he said, casting a nervous glance down the table. He was one of the newest firefighters in the house, and he'd been talking about taking some wildfire classes just to add more to his resume. Get more experience. Have something to do at work.

Bennett didn't blame him, but he didn't want the life of a wildfire fighter. It was completely different out there, no fire house, blistering conditions, and unpredictable winds that could steal a life as quick as a blink.

"Oh, come on," Ray said. "Maybe we can help." He turned down the table. "He's looking for a girlfriend."

That riveted everyone to Alex, who looked at Bennett for help. "I don't know the story," Bennett said. "Just because I have a girlfriend doesn't mean I know how to get one for you."

A few men laughed, and Bennett finished his chili while Alex started the story about going out with Tahlia just to make her sister, Hilary, mad. "Or jealous. Or something. It didn't work."

Alex took a huge bite of cornbread and glared at Ray.

"Maybe she'd go out with you again," Ray suggested.

"Tahlia? No." Alex shook his head with finality.

"Why not?" Bennett asked.

"We don't have anything in common."

The conversation moved on to something else, but Bennett fixated on what he had in common with Jennie. Their love of the pier. Ruby's hotdogs. Teasing each other. Duality. And the fact that they both liked to make things from ordinary materials. Her, with the art. Him, with his carpentry.

But she disliked dogs, and she was messier than anyone he knew. His fingers twitched just thinking about her studio. And they got along okay, he thought.

More than okay, he amended as he remembered the way she'd kissed him before he'd come into work. But she wasn't ready to put on another engagement ring, and Bennett recommitted himself to letting her set the pace in their relationship.

His shift ended—he'd gone out on one call to help a dog who'd gotten tangled in his leash when the owner had tied him to a fire hydrant—and he stopped by Duality for the cheddar poppers Jennie had requested.

"Evening, Bennett."

He turned to find Mabel standing behind him in line, her own assortment of hot foods in her hands. He grinned at her. "I love those cheddar burger pockets."

Mabel looked at what she carried. "They're my favorite too. How's the furniture coming?"

"Just fine, ma'am."

"And Jennie?"

Bennett wasn't sure what the older woman was asking. He apparently wore the confusion on his face, because Mabel nodded him forward in line and said, "How are you and Jennie?"

"Uh, just fine, ma'am." He didn't normally discuss his relationships with anyone, especially someone like Mabel. Sure, everyone in town knew her, but Bennett didn't *know* her.

"She's a spitfire, that one." Mabel chuckled. "Reminds me of myself when I was younger." Something sharp entered her eyes, and Bennett edged forward again, only one more person in line before it would be his turn to pay.

"You don't let her drive you away, okay?"

"Ma'am?" Bennett desperately wanted to understand what in the heck Mabel was talking about.

"I did that once to a nice man like you, and he let me. Don't you let her do that." She nodded that it was his turn, and Bennett turned to put his purchases on the counter. Mabel's words hung in his mind as he paid, drove to her house, and sat with her on the front steps while they ate their late-night snack.

"Heard from your parents?" he asked.

"Yep." She nodded, in a much better place tonight than she'd been that morning. "They're settled in, with somewhere to sleep and eat. Mom's got an appointment in the morning for her surgery."

Bennett enjoyed this moonlit time with Jennie and felt himself slipping a little more in love with her. "That's great. Any headway on the art?"

"You know, I think I got a new idea today that will be great in the west wing."

"Your contract doesn't specify what you have to make?"

"Not really. I have to do some sculpture, some painting, and a couple of other undefined pieces. I'm going to talk to Mabel tomorrow about them."

"Sounds great." He didn't ask her if she could finish them on time. Jennie was a professional artist who wanted to work, and she wouldn't risk her reputation, even to satisfy her muse.

Bennett finished eating and stood. "Well, I better go. I've got two dogs waiting at home, and they've probably eaten each other by now."

Jennie laughed as she joined him. "Thank you, Bennett." She tipped up on her toes and kissed him, and he knew her gratitude was about more than the cheddar poppers. He kissed her back, hopeful yet hesitant that they could make a future together work this time.

18

"I was thinking of something like a mirror," Jennie said, watching Mabel for her reaction first. The old woman didn't even blink.

Lauren cocked her head and said, "I could see that here."

"A huge frame." Jennie put her hand on the sheetrocked wall. Lauren had just told her that this room would be robin-egg blue. "Probably wood, but I'll put leafing on it to make it look like metal," she continued, the concept of the mirror coming together in her mind. "It'll look old and rustic. Regal. But also new and modern."

"I've never thought of a mirror as art," Mabel said.

Jennie repressed her sigh. Maybe her ideas were too forward-thinking for somewhere like Hawthorne Harbor. She hadn't put out any calls to Seattle yet, unable to deal with one more thing at the moment.

She had her mom constantly weighing down her mind, the three more pieces she needed to finish in the next twenty-four days before the unveiling, and Bennett. And talking to the landlord about buying the house she was currently leasing.

"It is art," Jennie said. "It'll be a focal point of this room, and every bride will look at themselves here." She glanced at Lauren for help, but the woman said nothing.

"I'll still have the pottery in the reception room," Jennie said. "And a painting for the bridesmaids room." She'd been thinking about that painting for a few days too, but since her mother's diagnosis, she saw browns, dark reds, and mustard yellows. And this west wing in the Mansion wasn't doom and gloom, autumnal colors of death and decay. So she needed to give herself some space to get into a new place before she could paint.

"And I've been thinking...." She gestured for Mabel and Lauren to follow her into the room Mabel had called the family gathering room. It was the room right off the landing, the first spot everyone would see when they came to the Mansion for any type of event and had access to the west wing.

"Your family has such great history for this town," Jennie said, choosing her words carefully. "I know you didn't want anything too huge, but I was thinking of a sculpture for this room that would depict some of that family and town heritage." She stood in the corner of the room, directly down from the doorway. "Here. And it would be three-dimensional, as if coming out of these two walls and welcoming everyone to Magleby Mansion."

"Sounds brilliant," Lauren said.

"I'm thinking hawthorn trees," Jennie said. "Maybe the family crest, a large monogram, something." She'd sketched out a couple of things late last night after Bennett had gone, but the piece hadn't quite come together yet.

"I'd need your help to install it," she said to Lauren. "And the mirror too, most likely. If you want the mirror." She looked at Mabel hopefully. "I really think it'll be a showstopper."

"I just can't see it," Mabel said. "Can you show me a picture?"

Jennie pulled her phone from her pocket and started searching. "It's like this," she said, tapping a picture to make it fill the screen.

"Oh, it's huge." Mabel took the device and Jennie started to feel excited about the project.

"Yes," she said. "It'll be like a piece of art. Sculpture, almost, but not quite. But functional, adding beauty to the room, but not take up the room you need for a mirror. Because it *is* the mirror."

"It's awesome," Lauren said, peering over Mabel's shoulder. "You can do that?"

"It'll be a darker piece," Jennie said. "Which will stand out against the lighter walls and accents. It'll look like a really expensive piece of metal. And yes, I can do that. I'll carve the wood for the frame, and leaf it with nickel and aluminum."

"It sounds like it'll take a lot of time." Mabel handed the phone back.

"Yes," Jennie said, her determination rising within her. "But I've never missed a deadline, Mabel. I won't let you down."

"Am I paying you enough for a piece like that?"

"Be honest," Lauren said.

"Well, what were you going to spend on the mirror?"

Mabel looked at Lauren. "I believe that was part of your build."

"Just get a plain mirror," Jennie said. "I'll give you the dimensions. We'll mount the frame around it." She smiled at the other two women. "Okay? This is okay?"

"This is great," Lauren said. "This place is going to be amazing." She smiled at Jennie again before she left the room.

Mabel said, "Yes, Jennie. It's going to be great. Work with Lauren to get everything installed. Let me know if you need anything."

Jennie nodded, a sense of pride filling her that she hadn't felt in a while. The collection of pottery had been great, a real wave she'd ridden for a week or so. But to have additional inspiration felt spectacular—made her feel like she could be a working artist again after she'd failed to get married.

She hugged herself, her thoughts immediately flying

to Bennett. Could she see herself with him? Living in that immaculate, white house? He'd probably build her an art studio in the back yard, beside his wood shop. The more Jennie thought about it, the more she wanted that future. The little white house, with the little picket fence. The big back yard, with the big black dog. The wood shop, where Bennett worked and wiled away his free time, and her art studio, which she could keep as messy as she wanted.

She couldn't believe this train of thought, but she definitely tasted the fear it brought with it. She'd have to open herself up again, and she'd vowed never to do that again while she stood in front of a mirror in Cancun.

Even for Bennett? she thought, and as she admired the height of the ceilings in the west wing, she realized that she'd already let him in. At least part of the way. And she wasn't horribly afraid of widening the door and allowing him a place in her heart.

I'LL JUST COME OVER AND WATCH THEN.

Jennie ignored Bennett's last text. With only two weeks left until the unveiling, Jennie didn't have time to do much more than work on her art. She was even getting into the studio before noon, which was a real feat for her.

And Bennett was feeling a little neglected. Her busy schedule had been fine while he built the buffet, but he'd finished a day or two ago, and now he wanted to take her to dinner, hold her in the hammock, or as his latest string of texts had promised, go grab something at Duality and watch the sun set into the ocean.

Jennie wanted to do all of those things too, but she also wanted to get paid. *Needed* to get paid. And that meant she had to buckle down and get these pieces created.

The mirror frame turned out to be a real bear of a project, with carving, construction, and covering, and Jennie had rapidly fallen behind schedule on it. Luckily, Lauren didn't need it to finish the rooms, and it could literally be hung an hour before the unveiling if necessary.

"But that is not going to be necessary," Jennie said as she concentrated on picking up another piece of nickel leafing so it wouldn't rip. It had taken a learning curve to figure out how to get the metals on the wood the way she wanted, around all the intricately carved things she'd done without ripping, and adding just the right amount of tarnish to make the piece look old. Now that she had the system down, she was moving along at a good clip, and she could *not* break for dinner.

Even if she was hungry.

She kept on, determined to finish the whole side of the frame, all the way to the corner, before she allowed herself to rest. And she'd have to get back in the studio in the morning to finish the painting, which sat drying in the corner by the kiln.

"Knock, knock."

She startled at the sound of Bennett's voice in her house. Annoyance sang through her. She'd never responded to his text, but he'd obviously shown up anyway. The scent of hamburgers came with him, but thankfully, no dogs did.

"I brought dinner," he said, pausing in the doorway. "You have to be hungry."

"I am, yes." She finished with the piece of nickel leafing, dabbing to get it tight against all the crevices and divots on the frame. She sighed and leaned back, her bicep and her back aching a bit.

"Are you mad?" He stayed in the doorway, not entering.

"I want to be." Jennie stood and smiled at him. "But that food smells amazing." She walked toward him, thinking *he* was the amazing one. "And you look great, too."

He dropped the bags of food onto a nearby table and received her into his arms. "I missed you," he murmured right before he kissed her, a slow, sensual kiss that awakened every cell in her body. "Sorry. I just couldn't sit home by myself for another evening." He matched his mouth to hers again, and Jennie melted into him, kissing him like she missed him too, because she did.

When she finally came to her senses—with the help of her stomach, which growled at her to *stop kissing and get to the food!*—she stepped back and tucked her hair behind her ears. "So, come in. Which one of these is for me?"

He picked up the bags and dug around inside for a moment, moving a box of French fries from one bag to the other before handing it to her. "I got you a crispy chicken sandwich," he said. "I thought I remembered you liking them."

"Harvey's has nothing better." Her stomach roared at her and she plucked a few fries from her bag.

"Actually." Bennett made quite the ruckus reaching into his bag and pulling out a massive foil-wrapped burger. "That would be the bacon brutus."

Jennie laughed as he unwrapped his burger. "Nothing we eat should be named brutus."

"I disagree." He bit into his burger, and Jennie pulled out her chicken sandwich, glad to see that he'd also got the special sauce for her to dip in. Anxiety pulled through her that Bennett was sitting in her studio. But he didn't say anything, didn't even glance around. She'd told him plenty about the projects she was working on, but she wasn't used to having someone see her art before it was finished.

She pushed away her walls, wanting Bennett to be here with her. She bit into her sandwich, and everything got better with food. She asked about Patches, and Bennett said he was doing really great with Gemma.

"I find them curled up together on the couch when I

get home," he said. "Gemma doesn't even come greet me anymore."

"I don't believe that." Jennie took a long pull of her soda.

"Fine." Bennett grinned at her and picking up one last French fry. "She does, but it's delayed."

Jennie giggled and shook her head at him. "So." She stood. "Do you want to see what I'm doing?"

"Absolutely." Bennett wiped his hands like he'd be touching something in her studio, but Jennie thought she might actually swat his fingers away if he did.

"So I'm making a huge mirror frame as a piece of art. Lauren will be getting the actual mirror, but this beast is taking forever." Jennie thought about kicking the unfinished wood for a moment, but she didn't.

Bennett stood back and took several moments to take in the frame. "This is gorgeous." He reached out like he might touch it but drew back quickly. "Did you carve this?"

"Yes."

He gazed at her with wonder then, and it made Jennie's stomach squirm. With everything she'd eaten, it was not a comfortable feeling, and she turned away from him. "I'm doing silver leaf, nickel leaf, and aluminum leaf. Then I tarnish it all. I'll probably need some help getting it out of here and over to the Mansion."

"I can help with that."

"I'm counting on it, Mister Muscles."

He came up beside her and slipped his arm around her waist. "You're very talented, Jennie."

"Thank you." She exhaled and turned toward the kiln. "I'll be done with this painting tomorrow." She led him across the room, through the mess, to the painting in the corner. It was bright and sunshiny, with a huge grove of hawthorn trees. Just in front of them, far and on the horizon, stood a bride and groom.

"I need to do the finishing blacks," she said. "I'll do them in the morning, and then I'm starting the huge showpiece." She blew out her breath, the panic of not finishing hitting her square in the chest. "I'm going to have to work constantly until the unveiling."

"What can I help you with?" Bennett kept his eyes on the painting as if he liked it so much he couldn't look away.

"Keep bringing me food?"

He laughed and tugged her tight against his body. "I can do that."

"Okay." She faced the frame again, wondering what she'd been thinking. "I don't work super great under pressure."

"Well, let's get back to it." Bennett sat in the same chair he'd been in while eating and pulled out his phone.

Jennie sat beside the stack of metal leafing and ignored the pull of exhaustion on her muscles and mind. She worked until her fingers hurt and she simply couldn't lift another piece of metal leafing from the pile.

Bennett still sat in that chair, and he'd hardly moved in the time he'd been there. She turned toward him, her heart expanding for his thoughtfulness and his kindness and his company.

"Thank you, Bennett," she said, drawing his attention.

"Done for the night?"

"I think so." She twisted to look at what she'd done. She had made it to the corner she wanted to, but she hadn't done any of the tarnishing. She flinched toward the bottle but didn't pick it up.

"What's your last piece?"

It still hadn't quite come together in her mind, so she shrugged and said, "I have a vague idea, but I'm not sure yet." *Thirteen days* echoed in her head, and again the panic hit her.

"All right, I'll bring you lunch tomorrow. I'm not going in until four, so the dogs will be with my neighbor."

"They'll take Patches too?"

"And they just got a puppy for their daughter." He chuckled. "The Yardleys are great. You'll have to meet them next time you come over."

Jennie leaned into him and closed her eyes, wondering what time it was. When she checked her phone, she startled to see it was almost midnight. "Bennett, you've got to be dead on your feet. Go on home."

He yawned. "You're worth it." He kissed her quick and headed out the front door. Jennie fed her cat and went to bed, but sleep took a long time to claim her, Bennett's words revolving around in her head and keeping her awake.

You're worth it.

Was she? If that was true, why wasn't Kyle waiting for her at the altar?

Bennett rode in the passenger seat as Jaime drove the moving van that he'd brought over from Magleby Mansion. Together, the two of them had gotten all of the furniture Bennett had completed loaded up and they were on their way to the Mansion now.

Lauren's truck sat out front, but on this Thursday morning, hers was the only vehicle. The unveiling celebration sat only a few days away, and he felt the anticipation in the very air at the Mansion. Lauren, her foreman Gene, Jaime, and Bennett got all the pieces upstairs and put where they belonged.

"These are beautiful," Lauren said, standing back to admire the armoire. "Go stand over there by that and let me take your picture."

"Where's that going to go?" he asked as he walked over to the piece.

"Oh, I don't know. Aunt Mabel will have a photographer here on Saturday. Wear your best suit." She grinned at him and he smiled for her phone camera.

"Send me that, would you?" He took several pictures too, thinking he could at least add them to his blog, which was woefully outdated and neglected. But he really did enjoy his carpentry hobby, and maybe he should try to get more work than that that happened to fall into his lap.

He'd been spending a lot of time with Jennie in her studio, and he'd gone to every take-out eatery in Hawthorne Harbor over the past couple of weeks. She'd finished the painting and the pottery, and the frame, and when he and Jaime had finished with his furniture, he directed the man over to Jennie's.

She stood elbow deep in plaster, and Bennett just stared for a moment. The unveiling was in two days. There was no way whatever she was doing was going to be done by then. Was there?

"Hey," he said, refusing to say anything about her pieces. "We'll get everything loaded up and over to the mansion. Lauren is ready to attach the frame."

Jennie looked like she'd be better off if an earthquake happened and swallowed her whole, but she nodded. Redness sat in each cheek, as if she'd been working really hard without a break, and Bennett added, "I'll bring you a chicken salad from Amie's, okay?"

"Yes, please."

Bennett threw her another worried look, but she'd

already gone back to work on some sort of pillar, where she kept forming and shaping the plaster. He couldn't imagine what kind of eye it took to do what she did, though he supposed it was a lot like how he took wood and made it into a table or a rocking chair.

He'd been stewing about something to make for Jennie, and as he followed Jaime back out to the moving van, he stalled in her living room. He hadn't asked her again if she'd be staying here in this house or if she'd buy a place of her own, maybe with a studio in the back yard instead of the home. She had everything she needed, and he came up blank with an idea of what he could make for her from his shop.

He went out to the van and worked with everyone at the Mansion to get everything in place.

"Lauren," Mabel said as she entered the west wing. "Tell me where we're at."

Lauren started leading her through everything from light fixtures to baseboards, and she pointed to the large corner in the first room with, "Jennie's last piece goes there."

"Do we know where she is on it?" Mabel looked at Lauren and then Bennett, and his heart started pounding, hard. He knew Mabel didn't have any kids—had never been married—but somehow he suspected she could see right through a lie.

"I haven't heard," Lauren said.

"She'll have it ready," Bennett said. "I've seen it, and she'll have it ready."

"She'll still need help with the install, right?" Lauren asked.

"For sure. And the use of that van to get it over here."

"It better be done tomorrow then," Mabel said, and they moved through the doorway and into the next room. Bennett didn't need to go with them, but he did, because he enjoyed this tour from the other side of the veil. He knew by Saturday night that this place would be completely transformed, even though it already was.

He grabbed the salad for Jennie on his way back into town and hurried into her studio to find it empty. "Jennie?" he called, moving back into the hallway. Her bedroom sat down a bit and across the hall, but he wasn't going to check in there.

She wasn't in the living room or kitchen, but he caught a swatch of pink fabric through the window and found her sitting on her back steps.

"Hey," he said, sitting down next to her.

"I can't finish it," she said. "There's no way. Not enough time for it to dry." She sniffed and wiped her nose.

Bennett handed her the plastic bowl with the fork balanced on top. "What can we do?"

"It has to be completely dry for me to paint it," she said. "I waited too long." She shook her head and popped the lid off her salad. She squeezed dressing onto it and stirred and stirred and stirred.

"I have an industrial dryer," he said. "It's for wood, but we could try that."

"I have the heat up," she said. "I can't get it to dry."

"What about a blow dryer? I could hold it right where you need it." Bennet's mind started sifting through the appliances he had at his house. "I've got two pretty big fans too. I'll go get them. We can get it dry."

Jennie put her first forkful of lettuce in her mouth, chewed, and swallowed. "I don't know."

"Well, we have to try," he said. "I'll call in tomorrow. I'll help you get it done." He hadn't seen the piece inside, but he'd only checked for her and left after a moment. She took ten minutes to eat, remaining silent.

Then she stood, exhaled, and said, "All right. If you really will help, let's go see what we can get done." She led the way back inside, and Bennett followed her, his thumbs moving over his phone quickly to send a message to Chief Harvey about getting tomorrow off.

That's fine, his boss said. But you'll have to take the next weekend shift.

No problem, Bennett texted back. He'd work every weekend if it meant he could help Jennie with this project.

The heat inside Jennie's studio was intense, but Bennett stood next to her, listening as she outlined how she had to mold the plaster while wet. It was going around a hawthorn trunk about ten feet tall. At the top, she'd sculpted trees around the front two-thirds already, and she indicated where the roots would drip down, where crest would go, and then finally where the name MAGLEBY would land.

Bennett felt overwhelmed, and all he had to do was get things dry. "Okay," he said when she finished. "And you need the plaster dry enough to paint by tomorrow morning."

"Yes."

"I'll go get everything I have at my house, and I'll dry as soon as you finish sculpting."

Jennie pressed her lips together and nodded. "I'll get back to sculpting." She didn't waste another moment, but started mixing up more plaster. Bennett hurried back to his house, made sure the dogs had food and water, and loaded up his fans and the dryer. He wasn't sure what the wood dryer could possibly do, but he'd have it just in case.

Back at Jennie's, he got the fans plugged in and running, which added a bit of relief to the dry heat from her furnace. He ran an extension cord from the wall over to the structure and plugged in a blow dryer. If he stood on a chair, he could aim the steady stream of air at the top portion Jennie had already sculpted.

"Not too hot," she said. "I don't want it to weep or start to melt the plaster."

"Not too hot." Bennett looked at the blow dryer, trying to figure out how to make it not hot.

Jennie said, "Switch that top button to one."

He did, and the air cooled. He moved it back and forth in sweeping arcs, thinking his arm was going to get tired really fast. With the three fans blowing and the hair dryer, the noise level seemed like standing in an airplane hangar with jet engines about to rev up.

Talking was impossible, but every once in a while Jennie would look up and say, "That section is done. See how chalky it is? See how white?"

Bennett learned what to look for, and he eventually could move down the sculpture without Jennie telling him. His arms ached, and this boredom was akin to what he experienced at the fire house. But there was no camaraderie, no good food, and no dog to keep him company.

But he wanted to be there. Wanted to help Jennie.

"No, Bennett." Disappointment and frustration filled his name.

He looked up from his phone and jerked the hair dryer away from the piece. "What?"

"That section isn't done yet." Jennie exhaled like he'd just shattered the whole thing and wiped the back of her hand over her scalp. Her hair wisped everywhere, and she looked exhausted.

Bennett was exhausted too. And hungry again, as he stomach growled, reminding him of how many hours he'd been standing in this studio, waving a blow dryer back and forth. He felt sure he'd never get the sound of these fans out of his ears, and he wondered if police officers used this type of noise as a way to break criminals.

Because Bennett felt dangerously close to breaking. "Sorry," he said. "I thought it was finished." She'd done the roots and the crest, and he'd simply followed her progression toward the bottom of the piece as she got everything pinched and smoothed.

"I needed to do the details."

"Well, you didn't say anything."

"I didn't think I needed to." Her eyes flashed, and exasperation filled Bennett.

"Obviously, you did."

"Obviously." She put her hands on her hips, not backing down.

"I'll go get us some dinner." He would've never left a project this huge for the last three days before it needed to be seen. Never.

"I'm not hungry." She picked up the plastic container of water and started running her fingers over the part of the crest he'd just dried. He couldn't stand there and watch her undo his hard work.

"Fine." He started for the door.

"I don't need you to come back," she said. "I'll finish up tonight."

No thank you, Bennett. No you've saved me, Bennett.

He'd already taken tomorrow off of work—just to be beside her and make sure she finished this piece on time. And she didn't need him now, because he didn't know every knob and line in the Magleby family crest?

He didn't need a lot of praise, honestly. But he didn't need to be blamed for drying something when he'd dried eight feet of plaster singlehandedly.

"I'll get you a salad anyway." He left the studio before she could protest or say anything else. Out in the front yard, without the constant sound of the fans and the dryer. He breathed in deep, deeper, enjoying the silence.

His head pounded, and he hadn't even realized it. He kept the radio off in the truck as he drove into town, realizing that it was quite late by the lack of people and traffic. Or maybe it just seemed that way because the sun was going down sooner and sooner, and there was no moon.

No matter what, he felt a sense of foreboding hanging in the air, and it made him cranky.

Duality was always a bright spot, and he went inside to get as much food as he could carry. And a salad. Instead of going right back over to Jennie's, he sat in the parking lot and ate his way through a pizza pocket and two containers of tater tots.

He went home and checked on the dogs, telling them to come with him and load up in the back of the truck. Driving was one of Gemma's favorite things to do, and Bennett took the long way around town to get back to Jennie's.

Even being gone for an hour, he sat in the truck, trying to convince himself to go back inside. Gemma and Patches wouldn't be able to come in, but they'd stay in the back. Finally, after sitting out front for five minutes, Bennett gathered his courage and went inside.

He knocked on the front door as he opened it and called, "Jennie?"

The low sound of the fans hit him square in the face, but he walked toward it anyway. The light in the studio was still on, the fans still going, but Jennie wasn't there.

Bennett gripped the plastic container of her salad and examined the structure in the middle of the room. In the time he'd been gone, she'd fixed the crest—not that he could tell—and finished the name at the bottom. She'd moved the fans closer and apparently left everything to dry.

So maybe she'd get the piece finished after all, though he had no idea what she had in mind as far as the painting went.

He turned away from the studio and went back into the kitchen. Jennie wasn't sitting on the back steps either, and Bennett pulled out his phone to text her. *I brought your salad. Where are you?*

She didn't answer right away, and he felt uncomfortable being in her house and yard without her there. Worry needled him, and he checked her car port for her bicycle. It was there, leaning up against the house, so she hadn't gone anywhere.

He entered the front yard, wondering where he should go and what he should do. His phone buzzed in his pocket and he found Jennie's name on the screen.

I went to bed.

That was all. No explanation. *No thank you for the food. What time should I come in the morning? You don't need to come.*

"Jennie," Bennett rolled his eyes and the ridiculousness of her statement. He suddenly heard Mabel telling him not to let Jennie push him away. But what was he supposed to do? Bang down her front door and demand she eat the salad he'd bought?

In the end, he took the salad and himself and the dogs and went home, wondering if he'd go to Jennie's the next day or not.

Jennie knew she needed to apologize, but she didn't know how. The pressure around her chest and radiating down into her legs was indescribable. She shouldn't have left this project to the end, even if she didn't have every piece in place. She could've sculpted the tree and the roots two weeks ago, and she hadn't.

And Bennett had given up his entire day to stand in her overheated studio and sweep a blow dryer in a near circle.

Jennie honestly didn't know how to sort through her feelings, nor how to juggle everything going on in her life. She hadn't been able to get up to Seattle and see her mother the way she would've liked, and while the surgery had gone well and her mother was recovering, Jennie would've liked to have been there.

But she barely had her head above water in Hawthorne Harbor.

She sighed and gave up trying to fall asleep. She sat up in bed and picked up her phone, staring at Bennett's name in her texting app. "Can't text him," she said to herself and she pushed the button to call him.

The line rang and rang and eventually went to voice-mail. Frustrated in an instant, Jennie jammed her finger on the redial button and put the call on speaker.

"Hello?" Bennett answered on the fifth ring, as if he didn't know who was calling. He didn't sound like she'd woken him either. Wasn't out of breath.

"Hey," she said just as he said, "Hello?" again.

"Hey." Jennie stared into the darkness draping her bedroom. "Look, I wanted to say thank you for coming to help today."

"Sure."

Jennie's emotions stormed through her. "I didn't mean to snap at you. I just...I'm still worried this piece won't get done."

"Right."

"Are you going to use single-word sentences for the whole conversation?" Jennie regretted her words immediately and ran her fingers across her eyes.

"Probably."

"Why?"

"Because I get in trouble when I say something you don't like."

Jennie's heart pinched, and she felt like a complete jerk. "You should be able to say what you want."

"Okay."

But he said nothing.

"Bennett."

"What, Jennie? What do you want me to say? That you should've started this *huge project* weeks ago? What would that accomplish?"

"I know I should've started it earlier," burst out of her mouth.

"Exactly. So why should I say it? So you can snap at me?"

"I'm sorry," she said, the words finally there. "I'm sorry, Bennett. Please come tomorrow and keep me company while I paint. I might—" She clamped her mouth shut so she wouldn't say she needed him.

But she did need him.

And not just to get her a salad or keep her company or dry a section of paint so she could go back and add details. She *needed* him in a way she hadn't needed anyone for a while, and she had no idea what to do with those feelings.

Bennett sighed. "What time tomorrow?"

"Nine?" Her voice sounded like she was seconds away from crying, and that was how she felt too.

"I'll bring bagels."

Jennie nodded, though he couldn't see her. "I'm sorry, Bennett."

"I know, love. I heard you." His voice held a soft edge too, and the endearment he used made her blood bounce around in her veins. "Talk to you tomorrow." He hung up, and Jennie watched her phone screen darken when the call ended.

She lay back down in bed, utterly exhausted in every way. She'd get up early and check the sculpt, make sure every line was right. Then she'd call her parents, feed the cat. The mundane things worked through her mind until everything was lined up.

Then, she was finally able to sleep.

THE NEXT MORNING, JENNIE WOKE TO KNOCKING ON HER door. And not the front one. Oh, no. She sat straight up in bed, her heart hammering out of control. The knocking came again, a little heavier this time, along with "Jennie? Are you in there?"

Bennett.

Panic threatened to flatten Jennie, but she breathed. Again. Then she said, "Yes, I'm here."

"Okay."

Through the door, she heard him retreat down the hall, and she made a swipe for her phone. Nine-twenty, and her alarm for seven that morning had been turned off. She had a brief recollection of doing that, vowing to get up in just five more minutes.

"Nine-twenty," she muttered, getting up and hurrying into the bathroom. Her hair looked like a horrible version of rope, but she didn't have time to shower. She could bathe and eat when the piece was installed in the Mansion.

But Bennett....

She took precious minutes to brush her teeth and wrangle her hair into a braid. She had the distinct thought that she should cut it, then it would be easier to deal with. She'd loved her long hair in California, but she wasn't even close to the same person here as she'd been there.

Deal with that another time, she told herself as she changed out of yesterday's sculpting clothes and into today's painting ones.

Ten minutes after she'd been awakened, she stepped into the hall, expecting to see Bennett waiting there. He wasn't.

He was, however, perched on a barstool at her kitchen counter, sipping coffee from one of her mugs, a half-eaten orange scone on the counter next to him.

Her mouth watered, and not only at the sight of pastries. "Morning," she said with as much dignity as she could.

He looked up, his vulnerability there on his face for a fraction of a second before he covered it. "Good morning. I hope I didn't startle you. I couldn't find you, and you weren't answering your phone."

"I silenced my alarm." She tried for a smile, but it

didn't feel quite right on her face. She approached him, her nerves hopping around like rabbits. "We're okay, right? I mean, I know I was a jerk-face, and I'm sorry—"

"We're fine." Bennett nodded toward the stove. "Hot water there for your tea."

Jennie glanced at the kettle but didn't move toward it. She threw her arms around Bennett and buried her face in his neck, taking a deep breath of his skin, cologne, musk, and a hint of dog and wood in there that belonged uniquely to him.

"I'm sorry," she whispered.

"It's fine," he said, bringing his arms around her and holding her tight. "We all get stressed."

She pulled back but didn't step out of the circle of his arms. "You should get to say what you want."

"I'll work on that." He looked at her with soft eyes, lifting his chin so his mouth aligned with hers better. She kissed him, waiting for his eyes to drift closed before she closed hers. And while she wasn't completely convinced that everything was okay between them, she felt his affection for her in the stroke of his mouth against hers.

"So," he said as he pulled away. He cleared his throat. "We should get to work, right? I mean, the clock's ticking."

Jennie stepped away and poured herself a mug of hot water, opening her cupboard as she said, "Yes, let me just make a cup of tea real quick, and we'll get in the studio." She put in her tea bag and turned when he rattled the paper bag he'd brought.

"Cinnamon raisin bagel with strawberry cream cheese," he said. "Gotta keep your strength up."

She obliged by eating the best bagel in town, sipping her tea as Bennett talked about Patches and Gemma. "I don't think you'll get them apart," he said. "How's your mom doing?"

Jennie groaned. "I was going to call them this morning." She glanced at the clock, the minutes slipping by like water down a drain. "I'll do it once the piece is done."

His phone chimed, and he glanced at it. A frown pulled at his eyebrows. "Lauren's texting me?" He picked up his phone as Jennie wondered where she'd put hers. She'd had texts that morning when Bennett had knocked her awake, but she wasn't sure who they were from.

"She says, do you know where Jennie is? I need to know when to be available to install that final piece and I can't get ahold of her." Bennett looked up from his phone, expectation in his eyes.

"I'll go find my phone and let her know." Jennie walked with purpose out of the room, but her knees were shaking. She had no idea what to tell Lauren. The piece might not be done until midnight tonight.

She'd left her phone on the bathroom counter and she called Lauren without looking at the texts.

"Jennie, there you are."

"Sorry," she said, and really meaning it. "I've been busy."

"I'm sure. I'm just wondering when you need me at the

Mansion to install. We have a few minor touch-ups today, and then we're done."

Jennie looked at herself in the mirror and took a deep breath. "What about first thing tomorrow morning? I'm finishing the painting today, and it'll need overnight to dry." Not a lie. She didn't need to disclose that she hadn't even started the painting yet. She'd definitely be finishing it today.

"Ten, maybe? The unveiling isn't until seven that night. We should have plenty of time to install at ten."

"Ten sounds great." Relief rushed through Jennie. She wouldn't sleep through her alarm again.

"Mabel told you about the photographers, right?" Lauren said. "Apparently she's called every paper and magazine from here to Seattle."

Jennie's throat tightened. "She didn't mention that, no."

"Well, I hope you have a nice dress," Lauren said. "Because she'll want some of you with your pieces, and without, and probably everything in between."

"A dress," Jennie said flatly. For weeks, she hadn't even thought about anything but finishing her pieces. And now she had to go shopping too?

"See you at ten tomorrow. Should I send Jaime with the van?"

"Definitely," Jennie said. "This piece is huge."

Lauren said, "Can't wait to see it," and they hung up.

Jennie turned and faced the hallway. She couldn't wait

to see it either. She went into the studio to find Bennett already there, standing back and admiring her unfinished work. A terrible moment descended upon her, where she wanted to jump in front of him and shield her piece, snap at him that he shouldn't have come in here without her permission.

He slid his arm around her waist, breaking the moment, and said, "It's awesome, Jennie. I can't wait to see what you do with the color."

"Well, everyone keeps saying that." She exhaled, not quite ready for the long day of work ahead. "So I better get to it."

"Careful," she said. "Careful." She hovered behind Bennett as he carried most of the weight of the now-finished piece. Jaime was in the front, guiding them down the hall and out the carport door, which she'd propped open with a box.

Bennett grunted, the only sign that he'd heard her. Of course he'd heard her. But Jennie felt two breaths away from a mental breakdown, and the last thing she needed was something getting damaged in transport. Because there was no more time to fix anything.

Every bump on the way over made Jennie cringe, and she was sure when Jaime opened the back of the van, she'd find her sculpture in shambles.

But it was fine. Bennett and Jaime got it upstairs, and Jennie stood back and watched while Lauren drilled and nailed and got it positioned perfectly in the corner. Everyone joined her several feet away and admired the piece, and Jennie couldn't help the massive smile that stretched her mouth.

"It's stunning," Lauren said. "I mean...I don't even know how you do it. I thought the mirror was gorgeous."

"Thank you," Jennie whispered, still admiring her work. Art was always different when put in the environment where it belonged, and the dark piece drew the eye from first entrance into the room. The hawthorn had brilliant red, orange, and brown leaves and flowed downward into more earthy browns, greens, and even some metallic golds in the roots.

The Magleby crest was traditionally red and gold and black, and Jennie had stuck to that color scheme, finally putting all the letters in MAGLEBY at the bottom in black. It had seemed dark and foreboding in her studio, but in this light, airy room, with a few other metal accents in the lamps and light fixtures, and it was perfect.

"I've never done anything with plaster, paint, and wood before," she said. And not just wood, but a natural log from the environment surrounding the Mansion.

"Get over there," Bennett said. "Hand me your phone and I'll take a picture."

"Just use yours," Jennie said.

"You don't know where yours is, do you?" Bennett grinned at her, but Jennie didn't feel the sting of his tease.

She posed next to her piece while Bennett took her picture, and she went around with him as he took pictures of her pottery collection, her next to the mirror and beside the oil painting. Everything in the west wing felt made of magic, and Jennie couldn't wait for that evening.

Lacing her arm through Bennett's as they walked down the huge staircase to the ground floor, she asked, "So lunch?"

"Absolutely."

"Then I need to go dress shopping. Then I'm taking a nap." She laughed, but she wasn't joking.

At the bottom of the steps, Bennett swept her into his arms. "I assumed we were going to the unveiling together." He looked deep into her eyes, and Jennie felt herself falling, falling, falling. "We are, right?"

"There's no one I'd rather go with."

Bennett's face burst into a grin and he kissed her quick. Too quick. "Great. So I'll come by and get you around six-thirty?"

"Sure."

"All right. Let's go get lunch so you can get to your nap."

21

———

Bennett knotted his tie, a deep purple one with silver and bronze paisleys stitched into it. He wore a navy blue suit that almost looked black, and thankfully, it still fit. He hadn't worn it since Miles Montgomery's funeral, four years ago. And before that, at his own wedding.

So it seemed fitting he'd wear it one more time to this unveiling. Then he'd probably need to get a new suit—because he wasn't going to marry Jennie in the same suit he'd worn to marry Cynthia.

"You're thinking too far ahead," he muttered to himself. After all, Jennie had just tried to push him away two days ago.

But she'd apologized, and that was huge for her. He knew what it took for her to say *I'm sorry*, and it meant something for them.

"Okay, guys," he said to the dogs upon walking into the

living room. "There's water and food. I'll be out late."

Gemma didn't even get off the couch like she used to. She looked at him with hooded eyes, as if to reprimand him for waking her during her evening nap with something as trivial as food and water.

Patches's tail started to thump against the couch, and Bennett gave both animals a healthy body rub before heading for the door. For some reason, his nerves seemed to be electrified, and his collar felt too tight as he pulled up to Jennie's house.

All the windows were lit with yellow, and when he knocked on the front door, she called, "Come in, Bennett!" from somewhere inside.

He caught a swish of cream fabric as she dashed down the hall. "I just need to put on jewelry."

Jennie didn't wear much jewelry, but she returned to the living room thirty seconds later with diamonds dripping from her ears. Bennett was struck speechless with her beauty, the radiance she carried in her face, the confidence in her shoulders.

Her dress was indeed cream, but it was laced with gold stitching. It hugged her torso and chest, left her shoulders bare, and flared at the waist. She wore a pair of ivory heels with it, and she was flawless from head to toe.

"How did you do that with your hair?" he asked, gazing at the three knots poking up from the back of her head.

"I didn't," she said. "I paid Charlotte to work her magic

and get my hair off my neck." She smiled and stuffed her phone in a tiny purse with no strap. It too was cream colored with a gold hummingbird sewn into the quilt-like fabric.

"You're gorgeous," he breathed, taking a step toward her. "Stunning. Radiant." He took her effortlessly into his arms and kissed her.

She kissed him back, and Bennett thought he couldn't have asked for a more perfect start to an evening.

"You'll ruin my lipstick," she said against his mouth, but she didn't sound upset about it.

"You can redo it," he murmured, claiming her mouth again. He never wanted to stop kissing her, and he almost dropped to both knees right then, ready to proclaim his love and ask her to marry him.

He didn't, because he knew that would effectively *ruin* the evening. Just because Jennie kissed him like she loved him didn't mean she did. And just because she acted like she was ready to take their relationship to the next level didn't mean she actually was.

So Bennett waited while she went to fix her lipstick, and then he put his hand in hers, determined not to kiss her again until it didn't matter if her lipstick was smeared or not.

"You've got some on your lips," she said with a giggle. "Unless you want to walk in wearing romance in red."

Heat filled Bennett's face, and he ducked into her guest bathroom to make sure he looked presentable. He did want romance in red—or any other color Jennie dictated—but not all over his face.

They finally started toward the Mansion, but the lots were full. So he parked down at the beach and rode the shuttle up with dozens of other people. Jennie clutched his hand tightly as they walked inside, the atmosphere festive and lively. Classical music pumped from the speakers overhead, and fancy yellow lights hung from trellis and archways, along with greenery.

The chatter seemed at an almost intolerable level, but he and Jennie managed to find their seats. Surprisingly, they sat at one of the front tables, with a large RESERVED sign on it. Lauren and her date, Trent Baker, had already arrived, and Bennett felt a rush of gratitude that he was with familiar faces and friends.

He started talking with Trent about the K9 unit, as he had four German shepherds he was training to be police dogs for the force in Hawthorne Harbor. Trent had grown up in Bell Hill too, and though he was several years younger than Bennett, they'd still been friendly.

The minutes ticked closer to seven o'clock, and right on the dot, Mabel stood up from her spot at the head table. Some of her extended family sat up there with her, as did all of her staff right down to the gardener.

Bennett like that. Mabel was a huge personality in town, but she didn't run this place on her own, and she honored those who worked with her to make Magleby Mansion the jewel it was.

"Good evening," she said, her glittery silver dress sending sparkles into the crowd from the string of lights overhead. She wore a bright smile that Bennett had actually never seen before. "Welcome to Magleby Mansion. We'll eat first, do a short program, and then the west wing will be unveiled!" She clapped her weathered hands together, and the audience copied her, applauding for much longer.

"Our local tradesmen and artisans who worked on the wing are seated to my left." She indicated the table Bennett sat at, and when Lauren stood, Bennett scrambled to his feet too. "You'll be able to meet them all in the west wing, where they'll talk about their creations and vision."

Bennett's throat turned to sand. "What did she say?" he asked Lauren, but the audience was clapping once again, and the general contractor didn't answer. They sat, and Bennett looked at Jennie. "Did you know we have to talk about our creations and vision?" He didn't have a vision. Mabel had ordered some end tables and he'd built them.

Jennie looked pale, and she shook her head.

"Great." Bennett looked back at Mabel, but she didn't stand at the podium anymore. Waiters emerged from the stone walls and started serving dinner, and Bennett was quite happy to quell the nerves in his stomach with prime rib and mashed potatoes.

"Maybe it'll help me get another job," Jennie said as

she buttered a roll. "I mean, I don't have anything else lined up." She met Bennett's eye, and he could see the worry in hers.

"Did you ever find out about Seattle?"

She shook her head. "Too busy."

Bennett accepted her answer, but he didn't like it. Something screamed in his head that she wasn't permanent, that she'd leave town as soon as this event was over. He talked himself off the ledge while managing to maintain a polite conversation with a few others at his table. All too soon, Mabel got up again, apparently ready to begin the short program.

She started by calling Lauren up to the front of the room. Flashes bounced around the ballroom while the photographers Mabel had notified of the event took pictures, and Bennett suddenly remembered flashes from when he'd stood at the beginning of the dinner. So they already had his picture. Maybe he could sneak out during dessert.

One look at Jennie, and he knew she wouldn't. Which meant he'd stay too. After all, if he could get her another job that would keep her Hawthorne Harbor.... Well, he'd do almost anything to secure her spot in his life, even smile for the camera while talking about the doors on the buffet and how they were all Jennie's idea.

THE VERY NEXT WEEKEND FOUND BENNETT TAKING A SHIFT he normally wouldn't have worked. But he'd asked for a day off to help Jennie, so he got up on Saturday morning and headed over to the fire house, where the scent of the overnight crew's dinner still hung in the air. And it wasn't great, by the slightly charred scent twisting in his nose.

He'd said good-bye to Jennie the night before, as she'd taken this week to clean up her studio and make arrangements for a trip to Seattle. She'd left that morning, having rented a car to make the two and a half hour journey.

Bennett put his bag beneath his cot, wondering where everyone was. The fire house wasn't usually a hotbed of activity, unless there was a foosball tournament going on, but that generally happened in the spring, around the same time as the Spring Jubilee. A pair of representatives went to the Jubilee as Fire House Two battled for bragging rights in the town's foosball tournament.

Sometimes they put a movie on and everyone disappeared into one of the ground-floor rooms. But Bennett didn't see such an event on the giant calendar hanging beside the fridge. He put his lunch inside and turned to face the empty fire house.

Both engines were in the bay downstairs, and he wasn't sure why the place felt like the zombie apocalypse had rolled through town but left him behind.

It seemed like even the undead would leave him behind in Hawthorne Harbor. His chest felt so tight, so tight, and he couldn't stand to be alone in the fire house for another moment. He went downstairs and strode over to the back door to let himself out. The wind hit him square in the face, but at least it was air.

He stood staring at the park down the hill, his chest heaving for a reason he couldn't name. All he knew was that everything felt different when Jennie was gone.

"You've done this before," he told himself, almost dismissing his insane feelings. She'd just gone to visit her parents. Her mother, who was sick with cancer and had just had surgery. It was unfair of Bennett to miss her so much and assume she wouldn't come back. Her departure this time was nothing like what had happened two decades ago.

But somehow, his heart thumped and wailed as if it were exactly the same, and he didn't know how to soothe himself.

"There you are." Chief Harvey stepped up to him and faced the park with Bennett.

"Where is everyone?" he asked, glad for the fatherly comfort of the fire chief beside him. It was a very good reminder that he needed to get up the road to Bell Hill and visit his parents. Maybe that would fill some of the time he usually spent with Jennie.

Armed with a plan and feeling much less like he was about to implode, he listened as Chief Harvey explained how everyone had gone out shopping for their big weekend stew cookoff.

22

J ennie had not driven in a very long time, but she managed to make it to Seattle without causing or getting into an accident. Her parents had gotten a simple apartment only a couple of blocks from the hospital, and Jennie parked in the underground structure before realizing she couldn't get in the building without a code.

And her father wouldn't answer his phone. He'd always been the hardest to get ahold of, but Jennie didn't dare disturb her mother. She could be napping, as her dad had indicated that her mother did that quite often, especially after her chemotherapy treatments.

She'd just had one on Thursday, and Jennie honestly had no idea what to do, or what to expect.

After waiting about a half an hour, she tried calling

her father again, this time getting him on the line. "Dad," she said. "I got in the parking garage, but the elevator needs a code."

"Oh, of course. Right. Just a second." She heard the rustling of paper coming through the line. "The owner left it here somewhere...."

"Where do you park, Dad?" she asked. He didn't have the elevator code memorized?

"Oh, we're in the lot," he said. "But we walk most places, and the front door has a key, not an electronic keypad."

"Okay, well, just come down and let me in the front door." She started walking up the ramp she'd driven down.

"Here it is. Three-four-seven-one. And our apartment is four-seventy-one."

Jennie changed directions and went back over to the elevator, saying, "Thanks, Dad. Be right up." She hung up without asking how her mother was doing, if today was going okay or not, so she still had no idea what to expect on the other side of the door at apartment four-seventy-one.

She knocked, and several moments later, her father opened the door, a smile on his face. "You made it."

"I made it." She stepped into his embrace and held him tight. He seemed bonier than she remembered, and it had only been a few weeks since they'd left town and she'd shown up at Bennett's with the request to watch a new dog.

"How's Mom?" She stepped back and readjusted her purse on her shoulder, trying to peer past her dad to get an idea of what kind of condition her mother was in.

"She's sleeping right now," he said, stepping back and letting Jennie in before closing the door. "She's had a rough time the last day or so. Can't keep anything down." He gave her a sad smile and moved back into the tiny dining room, where he'd clearly been sitting as two books were spread before the seat he took.

"Coffee? Tea? How was the drive?" He closed one of the wordsearch books and looked at her like he really wanted mile-by-mile details.

"It was fine." Jennie sat without getting herself any tea. "The unveiling was magical." She spent several minutes telling him about the event, absorbing the pride and love in his eyes as he listened.

"Do you have pictures of your pieces?"

She swiped open her phone and showed him the ones Bennett had taken on Saturday morning, explaining her inspiration for each piece all over again. The unveiling had indeed been magical, and she'd enjoyed herself immensely as she presented her hawthorn log sculpture and then the pottery collection.

Even Bennett had done a great job of talking about the buffet and how the carved doors mirrored the patterns on her pots, bowls, and vases. Once the official tour had ended, the guests had been allowed to linger, chatting near their favorite pieces. Jennie had spoken to at least five reporters, posed next to her pots alone, and with Bennett as his buffet and her collection really did flow together seamlessly.

She hadn't seen any of the articles yet, but most of the reporters and photographers that had come were from small towns around northern Washington, and they didn't publish all that often. Mabel said she'd make sure everyone was notified when something came available, but Jennie hadn't heard anything yet.

"Well, I have an appointment with a gallery in a half an hour," Jennie stood, her stomach growling too. "Should I bring back lunch for all of us?" She glanced over her shoulder. "Do you think Mom will be awake?"

"Even if she is, she'll drink one of the shakes in the fridge. It has all the vitamins she needs, and with how little she eats, it's important to get in as much as possible."

Jennie honestly had no idea what her father had been through, or what her mother needed. She'd been so preoccupied with her art and the unveiling. Guilt hit her hard, making swallowing difficult.

"Surely you eat," she said. Maybe she'd only be able to snack in private, away from her mom so she didn't feel bad.

"Sure, bring me back something from wherever you go." Her dad moved to the couch, settled his reading glasses on his nose, and looked at a piece of paper he'd picked up from the sidetable.

Jennie took a few extra moments just to watch him, his undying devotion to his wife and the quite strength he had to be here, in this life in Seattle when all he'd ever known was down the road a few hours.

She ducked outside, because she didn't want to be late for her meeting with Jacque LeRange, the curator of one of Seattle's premier art galleries. She had her pictures, and she had the program from the Magleby Mansion unveiling. Not only that, but she had credentials in another big city, and she hoped her position of artist-in-residence at the San Francisco Gallery of Art would win her some points.

She stepped out of the wind and into the gallery, struck by the sculpture only feet inside the door. Made of soda cans, it stretched impossibly high by tiny aluminum strings. Or so it seemed. Jennie gazed up at it, vaguely aware that someone had approached her.

"It's wonderful, isn't it?"

Tearing her gaze from the structure that looked like it belonged in a Dr. Seuss book, she met the light-colored eyes of another woman. She was exotic and beautiful, and she wore a smile that spoke of kindness.

"I'm Nancy Petitt." She extended her hand.

"Jennie Zimmerman. I have an appointment with Mister LeRange."

"Yes, he told me." Her smile didn't slip, but her eyes took

on a new emotion Jennie couldn't quite name. "I'm afraid he won't be able to make the meeting. He sends his apologies and has asked me to show you 'round the gallery."

But Jennie didn't necessarily need to be shown around. She wanted the time with the curator, and she'd been counting on the personal connection so she could work her charm and show him her work.

So the whole hour was a waste of time, and by the time Jennie had seen the whole gallery, she hadn't shown Nancy one picture. She'd learned that Nancy was the artist behind the soda cans, and as she walked away from the woman and back into the main show room, foolishness raced through her. She'd been smiling and nodding for sixty straight minutes, and she really just wanted a big plate of pasta and a pair of pajama pants.

A phone rang from somewhere to her left, further in the gallery, around the corner and down a hall Nancy had said led to her studio and a few offices.

"Jacques LeRange," she heard in a deep male voice, and Jennie's feet froze to the smooth, unmarred floor.

He was here?

He'd *lied* to her to get out of the meeting?

Not only that, but Nancy had gone along with it.

Jennie's whole face grew hot, and her fingers curled into fists. She wanted to give him a piece of her mind, rage at him that she was worth one hour of his time because she was a talented artist.

At the same time, she absolutely could not let him see her. She spun toward the door, her long hair whipping around and hitting her back as she nearly broke into a run to get out of the gallery as fast as possible.

Tears spilled down her cheeks as she ducked right and pressed her back into the smooth, gray building. She sucked at the air, trying to get the humiliation out of her system. But it wouldn't go.

Her stomach grumbled at her that she still hadn't fed it, and she wiped her eyes. Focusing on her basic needs drove out the irrationality streaming through her. She walked away from the gallery, her heels making entirely too much noise. She went through the line at a local deli and went back to her parents' apartment to find her mother was awake and sitting at the dining room table.

With only two seats, Jennie once again felt like an outsider trying to elbow her way into something which she wasn't quite part of. She leaned over and gave her mother a kiss, noting the gray quality of her skin.

"How are you, Mom?" Jennie peered at her as she handed the Reuben sandwich to her father.

"Feeling a little better this afternoon." She took a sip of her nutrient shake. "It's so good to see you. Tell me about the unveiling."

Jennie didn't want to go through all of it again, but she didn't want to dwell on the events of that afternoon either. She thought of Bennett and what she'd tell him about the visit. She wanted to have good news for him, but she felt like a complete failure.

So she relayed the happenings from last weekend's unveiling, watched a movie with her parents, went and grabbed dinner when it was time, and ignored her phone when Bennett called later that night.

"I'm looking for a big change," Jennie said, looking at herself in the mirror at the salon. "I want it cut. Most of it. All the way off."

The blonde woman who Jennie had looked up online eyed her hair dubiously, and then met Jennie's eye. "You're sure? You have beautiful hair."

But Jennie didn't need beautiful hair if she didn't even recognize herself when she looked in the mirror. She hated this feeling, like she didn't know the woman looking back at herself. She wished she didn't keep coming back to mirrors and wondering who she was. She'd thought that maybe, just maybe, her time in Hawthorne Harbor had solidified what she wanted in her life, but now, sitting in a beauty chair somewhere in Seattle, Jennie thought maybe she didn't belong in her hometown.

Her heart wailed, but she'd stopped making decisions with her heart twenty years ago, the first time she left Hawthorne Harbor.

"I'm sure," she said to her reflection. "Give me something short, sassy, and sexy."

The woman reached for her scissors. "If you say so."

Jennie did say so, and she hoped this would be the first decision of many that would bring her the happiness she couldn't seem to grasp.

She closed her eyes as the first snip of the scissors sounded, and her mind immediately conjured up an image of Bennett. She hadn't had the heart to speak to him at all since she'd arrived in Seattle, and she owed him some sort of explanation for her radio silence for two straight days.

But it sounded stupid to tell him she was still drifting, still searching, still trying to decide who she was and what she wanted with her life. She'd be forty-two by Thanksgiving, after all, and women half her age seemed to have more figured out than she did.

Later that evening, when Bennett's name lit up her phone, she escaped out of the apartment and said, "Hey," hoping the sigh passing through her body didn't come through in her voice.

"Hey," he said, a measure of surprise in his voice. "I thought maybe I'd have to drive up there myself and make sure you were still alive." Of course he wasn't happy about being ignored for almost seventy-two hours.

"I'm still alive."

He sighed, and she imagined him to be releasing his

frustration with her. "Well, tell me all about it. The gallery tour. Your mom. Everything."

Jennie felt so, so tired. "I cut my hair," she said instead. He didn't need all the nitty gritty details of her mom's illness, or the failed studio tour from Saturday, or the lazy Sunday she'd spent strolling around the city and feeling guilty she wasn't back in the apartment with her mom who threw up everything she swallowed.

23

Bennett could hear something off in Jennie's voice though she talked just fine and even laughed a few times. But something was definitely wrong. He wanted to push her, but he felt rather lucky to get her on the phone at all, so he put up with her secrets, which she obviously didn't want to tell him.

Her mom was not doing well, but the surgery had been a success and the side-effects to the chemotherapy were normal and to be expected.

Jennie had said nothing of the gallery tour, which meant it hadn't gone well. She'd spent the time on the phone talking about her new haircut and some of the markets she'd wandered through the day before.

"So what about the gallery?" he asked. One of the major reasons she'd gone to Seattle was to figure things out with her future in art.

"It didn't work out," she said with a heavy dose of nonchalance in her voice.

Bennett didn't know what to say. He sat on the back steps as the dogs ran around the yard, the sun setting quickly now that November was nearly upon them. Finally, he decided to be brave and ask, "What aren't you telling me?"

The silence coming through the line didn't exactly settle Bennett's thrumming pulse, but he forced himself to wait.

"The curator pretended not to be there." Jennie's voice held so much hurt it made Bennett's heart pinch.

"Oh, sweetheart. I'm sorry."

"I honestly don't know what to do."

"You said the art scene was big in Seattle. Surely that isn't the only gallery."

"No, I'm sure it's not." But her voice sounded haunted and so, so far away. Bennett felt impossibly far from her, and he didn't know what to do about it.

"So you'll just stay until you find a home." He wanted her home in Hawthorne Harbor. Wanted to find her lying in his hammock with those two silly dogs when he got home from the fire house. Wanted to tell her that her future was with him, in this old white house that had once belonged to his grandmother.

"Yes," she said. "I'll stay until I figure things out."

Bennett nodded to the near-darkness and said his

good-byes, feeling like they were final though neither of them had said as much.

He sat on the steps for a long time, way past dark and beyond the time when the dogs had stopped playing and flopped at his feet. His thoughts wouldn't line up and make any sense, and he'd felt like this exactly once before, and that was when Jennie had left town the first time.

Even with Cynthia, he'd hated her decision but at least he understood it. At least she'd never hidden who she was and what she wanted from her husband, her marriage, and her life.

But Jennie.... Jennie didn't even know what she wanted, so how could Bennett make sure *he* was who she wanted?

He eventually got up and went inside with the dogs, went through the motions of locking the house and turning off the lights, plugging in his phone, and brushing his teeth. One question wouldn't leave him alone long enough to fall asleep.

Should I go to Seattle and talk to Jennie?

He finally decided that he'd talk to the chief tomorrow and see which days he could get off, because he didn't think he'd get to the bottom of Jennie's feelings without seeing her face-to-face.

So the next afternoon, when he went into the fire house for his shift, his first stop was Chief Harvey's office. "Do you have a few minutes?"

The fire chief looked up from his tablet, which lay flat

on his desk. He ducked his head so he could peer over his glasses and said, "Of course. Come in."

Bennett checked behind him before entering the chief's office, his pulse bobbing around somewhere in the back of his throat. He wasn't sure why he was nervous now. He had plenty of vacation days, and it wasn't a high fire season.

"So I need some time off," Bennett said as he sat down across the desk from Chief Harvey.

"Oh? Things okay?"

"Yes, yes," Bennett said. "It's just...I need to go to Seattle for a few days." The chief didn't need all the details of his personal life. Mabel's words hit him again, and Bennett straightened his back. He was not going to let Jennie run away to Seattle and keep secrets from him. If she didn't want to be with him, okay.

Well, it wasn't really okay, but he could at least deal with cards that were on the table. But she was keeping hers close to the vest, and Bennett needed to get a peek at them.

The chief pulled a calendar book out of the top drawer of his desk. "Let's see what we can shuffle around."

Fifteen minutes later, Bennett had the next ten days off, and he sat at the table in the big fire house kitchen making a packing list.

"What are you so focused on?" Alex stood over him and looked at the notebook. "You goin' out of town?"

"Yes," Bennett said, glancing up. "So you have to take

care of Uno. I won't be able to take him home." In fact, he had no idea what he'd do with Gemma and Patches. He scrawled *Call Yardleys about dogs* on his to-do list and went back to listing things he needed to take with him to Seattle. Honestly, it was a big city. He could probably jump in his truck and go right now, if he didn't have to stay in the fire house tonight.

Plus, he needed to figure out what he was going to say when he found Jennie.

Alex sat at the table with him, a bowl of cereal in front of him. "So you really like this woman."

"Not talking about it." Bennett didn't mean to growl.

"I saw you at the unveiling."

"So what?" he asked. They hadn't done anything inappropriate. Held hands. Danced, along with Lauren and Trent, Gene and his wife, and Mabel and Jaime—and dozens of other people. It wasn't a crime to dance, though Bennett sure had enjoyed holding Jennie right against his chest and whispering about what they might say during the upcoming tour.

"So nothing. It's just now you're going to Seattle to see her."

Bennett looked up, ready for this conversation to be over. "That's what you'd do too, if your girlfriend lived in a different city." Even as he spoke, he realized what Jennie had been hiding.

She'd left Hawthorne Harbor and hadn't said anything.

"It's just a visit." He swallowed and ducked his head back to his list. "It's normal for people to visit each other."

"Yeah, sure." Alex shoved another spoonful of cereal in his mouth, and Bennett took his list into the weight room, ready to leave now and he still had hours to go on his shift.

Finally, the next day, after a somewhat restless night in the fire house with Alex snoring on the cot across the room, Bennett had his bags packed and loaded into his truck. "Come on, guys," he said to the dogs, and he grabbed their leashes, along with a box with their food and a few toys. "We're going next door."

He took the animals out the front door, and they ran down the steps and started frolicking on the front lawn. He let them play for a moment, but his impatience to get driving had him calling them to come with him.

Nelly came flying out of the front door before he'd crossed the driveway, her face filled with joy. "Gemma," she called. "Patches."

Both dogs trotted ahead to the little girl, who let them lick her face while she giggled. Her mother, Montana, came out on the porch and Bennett climbed the steps to give her the box with food and toys.

"Thank you so much," he said.

She smiled at him and looked at her daughter. "She'll do all the work."

"Still, it means a lot."

"Where are you headed?" She watched him with interest, as Bennett never traveled.

He rubbed his palm up the back of his head. "Oh, Jennie's up in Seattle. I'm going to see her." His voice sounded false, even to him.

Montana grinned at him with kindness in her eyes. "You two are so cute together."

Bennett didn't know how to respond, so he just nodded and went back the way he came, stopping to crouch down and talk to Nelly for a moment. He also gave both dogs a good scrub along their ears, and then he got behind the wheel of his truck and set it north.

He arrived in Seattle by lunchtime, his desire to text Jennie and ask her for the best place to eat in the city, and *hey, would you like to join me?*

He honestly couldn't predict how she'd react to him driving to Seattle to see her. *I should get to say what I want too*, he thought, and he picked up his phone and dialed Jennie.

"Hey," she said. "I'm just sitting down to lunch with my parents."

That was code for I can't talk right now.

"Your mom must be doing better," he said, which was nothing he'd thought about the whole drive to Seattle.

"She is, a little bit."

"So...." He cleared his throat. "I'm wondering if you have time to have dinner with me."

"When I get back?"

"No, tonight."

Silence poured through the line, thick and heavy like honey.

"I'm in Seattle," he said. "I wanted to see you."

"Sure," she said brightly—totally falsely. "I'll text you later."

"Sounds good," he said just as falsely. He had serious doubts that she'd text later, but there wasn't much he could do about it. Either she would or she wouldn't.

He drove around a bit, found a great fish and chips shop on the pier, and checked into his hotel before his phone so much as buzzed again.

It was an address, from Jennie, along with a time that said 5:30?

I'll be there.

I'll meet you out front, she sent back.

Bennett felt like he'd swallowed live fireworks by the time he pulled up to an apartment building downtown. A woman stood on the front steps, but she didn't look like Jennie at all. At least not the Jennie who'd left Hawthorne Harbor only four days ago.

This blonde woman had super short hair, with a long piece that hung to her chin on one side while the other side was pretty short. She wore blue jeans with a pink polka dot blouse, flip flops, and a pair of sunglasses.

She came toward his truck when he pulled to a stop, and she walked like Jennie. Bennett could just stare as she opened the door and slid onto the seat. "Hey."

"You cut your hair."

"Really? I hadn't noticed." She gave him a sly smile and buckled her seatbelt.

"It's just so...shocking." It was not the picture of Jennie he held in his head.

"So is you showing up in Seattle." She looked at him full-on then, her eyebrows lifting above her sunglasses.

"We need to talk," he said.

"Oh, boy," she said. "We haven't even had dinner yet."

"Do you want to go to dinner?"

"Of course."

"Tell me where to go."

She directed him a bit further north, to a vibrant restaurant that had loud music playing and an eclectic menu. Bennett felt like he'd entered an alternate universe, and he simply didn't like city life.

But he swallowed his thoughts of what dinner would be like in his backyard instead of in this place which was practically impossible to talk.

"So why are you here?" she asked as she unwrapped a straw and put it in her water glass. She didn't take a drink but simply watched him.

"I heard something in your voice on the phone the other night," he said. "And I guess I thought it would be better to talk face-to-face."

Jennie looked away, obviously uncomfortable with the idea. Of course she was, because he was going to say things to upset her.

Starting with, "I have a feeling you're trying to figure out how to break up with me."

Her gaze flickered to his and danced away again. "That's not true."

"What *are* you trying to figure out?"

The waiter returned and took their orders, and now Jennie did lift her water glass and take a long pull on the straw. He let her stew, and fidget, and watch the TV mounted behind his head.

"Are you coming back to Hawthorne Harbor?" Bennett almost didn't want to know the answer. At the same time, he couldn't stand *not* knowing.

"Honestly?" She sounded like she might cry, but it was hard to tell with the buzz of activity and the music.

"Honestly, Jennie. I'm not getting any younger."

"I don't know."

Bennett didn't like that answer, and he didn't try to hide it. Their food came, and they started eating, this huge elephant between them. Bennett barely tasted anything, and he couldn't wait to get out of this noise. It was almost like being back in her studio with those fans blowing non-stop.

He had a strong desire to take her hand and pull her close and assure her that he'd be waiting in Hawthorne Harbor whenever she decided what she wanted. But he couldn't do it. He tucked his hands in his pockets and strolled down the street, glad she wasn't storming or marching away.

"Tell me what's going on," he finally said.

"I need a job, Bennett." She sounded desperate. "I don't think I'll get one in Hawthorne Harbor."

"So, where does that leave us?"

"I don't know, Bennett." She tucked her hand through his elbow, and he let her because it was comforting. They walked for a while, and then he took her back to the apartment. She didn't get out right away, and Bennett didn't want her to go.

He felt like his world was being ripped in two—again. Because of Jennie's desire to be a fantastic artist, just like she'd always dreamed.

What he didn't understand was why her success in Hawthorne Harbor, at the Magleby Mansion, wasn't enough for her.

Jennie couldn't get out of Bennett's truck. It felt very much like good-bye, and she knew he'd see it that way.

"Can I call you later?" she asked, turning toward him.

"Of course." Pain flashed across his face, but he leaned toward her and she kissed him, one chaste union that lasted long enough for her to know he thought this was good-bye too.

She pressed her lips together, said, "Okay," and got out of the truck. She hadn't said half of what she should've. Or maybe her kiss had said it all.

Inside the apartment, her mom had retired, and her dad stood from the couch like he'd been waiting up for her. Her, a forty-one-year-old woman.

"How's Bennett?"

"Oh, I don't know." Jennie exhaled and collapsed onto

the couch where her dad had been sitting. "I don't know what to do about him."

"Do about him?"

"He's committed to Hawthorne Harbor. Has a good life there. Dogs. A house he doesn't have to pay for. I can't ask him to move here." She couldn't, because she currently didn't *have* anything here. Not even her own bedroom, and frustration pulled through her as she remembered she'd have to pull out the couch into a bed.

"Why can't you stay in Hawthorne Harbor?" her father asked.

Did no one get it? "I don't have a job, Dad."

"Something will come along." He gave her a reassuring smile, but Jennie didn't return it. The lease on her house was up in a few weeks, and she didn't see the point in renewing it if she didn't have a reason to stay in town.

What was she supposed to do? Go on blind faith, hoping someone would ask her to make them a vase? Her work at the Mansion had been exquisite, sure. But it wasn't the type of art people put in their homes, not in a beach-side town like Hawthorne Harbor.

She got up and took the couch cushions off, setting them aside for the moment. She pulled out the mattress, put the couch cushions back on the bed, and collected the quilt she'd been using from the coat closet.

Curling up, Jennie brought the blanket to her chin and stared into the kitchen. The bright green time on the microwave clicked minute by minute, and still no answers came.

Things didn't seem better in the morning light, and she didn't call Bennett. He didn't try to contact her either, and she supposed he'd gone back to his perfect life in Hawthorne Harbor. He'd always known exactly what he wanted, and how to get it. And he *had* done it.

As she walked down to the pier, thankful for her wind-breaker on this stormy morning, she knew his life hadn't been perfect. He'd wanted to play professional baseball and had only had the opportunity for a limited time. In fact, he'd never been called up from the minors, had lost his marriage because of his injury, and turned to his second choice in life.

Problem was, Jennie wasn't even sure what her second choice was. The wind coming off the water didn't tell her, and when it started to rain, she bought an umbrella from a stand and headed back to her parents' apartment.

A couple of weeks went by, and Jennie visited five more art galleries in Seattle. Only one seemed promising, but the manager there had said they weren't taking on new artists before January. Jennie had rented a small studio space from an artist's conglomerate and begun work on a few pieces to show him.

Her lease was up on her house in Hawthorne Harbor, but she couldn't bear the thought of returning to the town where Bennett lived. So the week before Thanksgiving, she called Jason.

"Hey, sis," he said, panting into the phone.

"Is this a bad time?"

"Just getting off the treadmill." A loud clank came through the line, and he added, "What's up?"

"I'm just wondering if you and Kaitlyn and the kids are coming for Thanksgiving." Not entirely true, though she was wondering that.

"I think so, yes. But we can only come for the day. The Festival of Trees starts the next day, and I'm on the schedule."

"That's fine. Mom said she can make a turkey." Jennie sat on a couch in the posh lobby of the building where her parents lived. The apartment was too small almost all of the time, and she surfed her social media at coffee houses, threw pots in her rented studio, or spent time walking the city.

"Hey, I'm wondering how busy you are, and if you might be able to go clean out my house." Even as she spoke, Jennie cringed.

"So you're moving up to Seattle?"

"There's a gallery here that's promising," she said.

"I am not touching anything in that studio," Jason said. "If I put something in the wrong box, you'll freak out."

"I will not." She didn't tell him that her best friend had cleaned out her studio in San Francisco. This reeked of the same thing: Her running away from a situation she didn't want to face.

"I don't even know what's yours and what's not," he said, proving to be much more difficult than Lisa.

"It's a bad idea," Jason continued. "Just come talk to Bennett. You should see him, Jen. He's...broken."

She didn't want to see him like that and know it was her fault. "I'll figure something else out. Thanks, Jason."

She started to hang up when he practically yelled, "Jennie, wait."

"What?" She controlled the sigh she wanted to heave, only letting it leak out in a slow hiss.

"Don't you think you owe him something?"

"You don't get it."

"Of course I don't. It's obvious to me that you're using your art as a wedge—again."

"I have to go."

"Fine."

Jennie hung up, unwilling to have her "older" brother lecture her. Calling him had been a bad idea, but as Jennie contemplated who else she could get to clean out her studio, the only answer was Bennett.

Everything always came back to Bennett.

Even Pepper wouldn't be able to tell what belonged to Jennie and what had come as part of the partially furnished rental, especially as Jennie had spent less time with her friends the more serious she got with Bennett.

She sat in the lobby for a while, unwilling to go upstairs and feeling utterly uninspired to go to the studio. Could she give up her art? Was she using it as a way to end things with Bennett? Was she really that big of a coward?

How did she even feel about him?

So many questions, and very few answers. But just as she'd done when Kyle hadn't shown up at her wedding, Jennie was determined to figure things out.

THANKSGIVING CAME, AND ALONG WITH IT, JASON AND HIS family. The atmosphere between Jennie and her twin was a bit awkward, especially in the small space with four more people. Her mother felt well enough to make a turkey, and Jennie could peel potatoes without starting a fire.

A fire.

She thought of Bennett at every turn, it seemed.

Her father had bought several pies to go with their dinner, and Kaitlyn had brought rolls and volunteered to make the gravy and stuffing. So Jennie retreated a few feet away and sat with her nieces, asking them about school, their friends, and what they wanted for Christmas.

All the smells of roasted meat and buttery bread came from the kitchen, and it seemed like no time had passed before Jennie's mom said, "It's ready. Come eat, girls."

Jennie got up with her nieces and joined everyone at the tiny dining room table. Three more chairs had been crammed around it, and two plates sat at the bar for the kids. Everyone looked at Jennie's dad, and he gazed back at them.

"What a year," he said. "Jennie came home, and we had to leave for a short time." He smiled, but his eyes shone with tears. "I am grateful for each of you." He put his arm around his wife and looked at her with such love, Jennie's heart gave a painful leap.

She wanted that kind of love in her life. Wanted to have someone at her side, helping her make hard decisions, comforting her when things seemed to be going downhill, loving her through the easy times and the difficult ones.

The distinct thought that she could have all of that and more with Bennett came into her mind. And suddenly nothing else mattered. Everything that she'd thought she needed fell away.

"Are you going to sit down?" her mom asked, and Jennie practically collapsed into her seat.

"What's wrong?" Her mom didn't reach for the bowl of creamed corn in front of her, nor did she take the mashed potatoes as Jason tried to pass it to her.

"I've made a big mistake."

Jason scoffed, and then said, "Oh, you're serious." His wife elbowed him, and he glanced at her. "What? Jennie never admits when she's wrong."

Jennie stared at her brother, the sting of his words settling in deep. "Yes, I do," she said.

"Rarely." Jason finally got rid of the potatoes when her

mom took them. But even as she scooped some of the buttery, cheesy food onto her plate, she watched Jennie.

"What kind of mistake?"

"Do you think he'll forgive me?"

"Of course," Jason said. "I told you to just go talk to him."

"Are we talking about Bennett?" her mother asked.

Jennie didn't know how she could even make it through one more meal without talking to him first. But she slid a couple slices of turkey on her plate, added mashed potatoes, and kept the food moving around the table and over to the bar while she thought.

Kaitlyn had moved the conversation to something else, and her dad was currently talking about the possibility of getting a small dog while they were in Seattle.

"So what?" she asked when the conversation finally hit a lull. "I just show up...and what?"

Jason rolled his eyes and looked at his wife. Kaitlyn wore a look of supreme sympathy and put another forkful of potatoes and gravy in her mouth. After she swallowed, she glanced around the table. "Jason acts like everything between us was smooth sailing."

"It was," he said.

"But," Kaitlyn said loudly, covering whatever else Jason might want to say. "We were younger, much more foolish, and he has a bad memory."

"What?" he demanded. "What have I forgotten?"

"That you had no education, for one," she said, finally

locking her eyes onto his. Fire practically shot from her expression. "Remember how we sat on your front steps while you went through a list of possible careers?"

"But that didn't mean our relationship was in danger."

"Yes, it did." She looked at Jennie and gave her half an eyeroll. Jennie leaned forward, not wanting to miss a word of this conversation. It felt like Jason and Kaitlyn had always been a perfect match, and to hear they'd had problems too gave Jennie some hope.

"You actually broke up with me, if you'll remember right," Kaitlyn said, tucking her hair behind her ear. "Something about wanting to provide a good life, have a steady job, that kind of thing."

"Oh, for like a day," Jason said, scoffing again.

"It was actually about six weeks before he figured out what he wanted to do." Kaitlyn put another bite of food in her mouth. "And it was agony for me, and everyone kept telling me to wait, that he'd come around. He finally did."

Jennie looked at her brother, who now carried a healthy dose of redness in his cheeks. "Was it really six weeks?"

"Mm hm." Kaitlyn looked at him fondly. "You showed up on my doorstep with your letter of acceptance into the police academy. I can't believe you don't remember this."

"He's getting old," Jennie said, her spirits starting to lift. No, she wouldn't show up on Bennett's doorstep with a letter of acceptance to the police academy. She didn't have a job at all.

"Very funny." Jason took a drink of his sparkling cider. "So what are you going to do about Bennett?"

"I don't know." Jennie poked at her food. "Can I really just show up and ask him to take me back?" She looked hopefully at the other adults seated at the tiny table with her. "I don't have anything to give him."

"Oh, honey." Her mom patted her hand. "You have you."

Well, she hadn't been good enough in the past.

Different man, she told herself. Everything about her life now was different, right down to the length of her hair.

The only thing that wasn't was her desire to be an artist.

And maybe that was the problem. Her art had separated her and Bennett once before. Was she really going to choose art over him for a second time?

Her heart still hadn't healed completely from Kyle's disappearance from her life. But she knew she'd never be whole if she stayed in Seattle. Which meant she had to figure out what to do and how to get Bennett back—and soon.

After all, they'd broken up two weeks ago, and she wasn't going to let Jason figure things out faster than her.

Bennett picked up the ball and threw it again. The golden retriever raced after it, but Gemma stayed on the grass, her tongue lagging out of her mouth. He probably needed to stop before Patches ran himself right into a heart attack. The dog simply wouldn't quit.

So the next time he brought the ball back and dropped it at Bennett's feet, Bennett gave him a treat and said, "All right, bud. All done."

Patches collapsed next to Gemma, his whole body heaving as he panted. Bennett looked across the park, wishing the sky didn't hold such a dark gray color today. It matched his mood perfectly, and he wished he had a project to work on in his wood shed as the rain fell.

You do, he thought. But he didn't want to work on the headboard he'd designed for Jennie. He'd done it weeks ago, right after finishing the buffet, and he'd planned to give it to her for her birthday.

But it now looked like he wouldn't even get to talk to her on her birthday, let alone see her, hold her, kiss her, and present her with the headboard.

He sighed, picked up the ball, and said, "Let's get a drink, guys. Then we better get home before the sky opens." The last thing he needed was a soaking wet golden retriever to care for. Though he could barely look at Patches sometimes because of the way he reminded Bennett of the woman who'd brought him over, Bennett sure didn't know what he'd do when he had to give the dog back.

The dogs lapped at the water he poured into a big bowl for them, and they jumped into the bed of his truck when he said, "Load up."

He'd just pulled into the carport when the first drops of rain hit the tin roof, and he hurried the dogs inside so everyone would stay dry. He puttered around the kitchen, making coffee and setting bread in the toaster.

He didn't want to be in the house, though. So he filled a thermos with hot coffee and dashed through the rain to his wood shop. Inside, it smelled like wood and wet cement, and Bennett breathed it in, wishing he had Jennie at his side on this melancholy day.

But if he had Jennie at his side, the day wouldn't be melancholy.

He was really tired of thinking about her, but he didn't

know how to stop. Her departure from his life had happened so suddenly, just like last time. Unlike last time, the ache in his heart hadn't lessened with time. True, only three weeks had gone by, but he felt sure she'd call or text on Thanksgiving.

She hadn't.

Now he was holding on for her birthday in just a few short days. He wasn't scheduled to go into work for three more days, and he thought if he started the headboard now, he could get it done in time.

So he turned on the lights, the saws, and the space heater and got to work. The wood felt like butter beneath his hands, and the planes came together quickly. The slats were beautiful and smooth, and he got the whole thing assembled before he took a break.

His back ached, and he'd finished his coffee long ago. A dog barked, and even through the soothing sound of the rain on the roof of the shop, Bennett knew it was Gemma and that someone was at the house.

Done for the day anyway, Bennett left the wood shop after turning everything off, and approached the house. He wasn't sure how long he'd been outside, or what time it was, but it was definitely dark enough to walk slow so he didn't trip over something accidentally.

Not that there's anything to trip over.

He heard the quip about his neatness in his mind, in Jennie's voice. His heart twisted in his chest, as it had been doing with every reminder of Jennie in his life.

And the biggest one of all stood under his carport, out of the rain. Her brother, Jason.

"I thought you might be out in the shed," he said, his hands buried deep in his pockets. "What are you working on?"

He wasn't about to tell Jason about Jennie's gift. "Just puttering around," he said, indicating with his thermos that they should go inside. Jason led the way, and Bennett took a moment to kick off his wet boots.

"Coffee?" It smelled old, so Bennett dumped it down the drain and started a new pot.

"Sure." Jason sat on the couch with Patches' head in his lap. "I miss this dog. He was mine, you know."

"He was not. Your parents got him long after you and Kaitlyn got married."

"No, really." Jason looked up, his eyes so much like Jennie's Bennett couldn't look at him for longer than a few seconds. "I got him and brought him home. It's how we learned that Kaitlyn is allergic. We had him for about a week before I took him to my parents and asked them to keep him for me." He stroked Patches like he'd raised him from a pup, and Patches laid there with a blissful look on his face.

"He's a great dog." Bennett turned and got two mugs down from the cupboard. "So what brings you by? On patrol?"

Jason wore his uniform tonight, and he didn't just stop

by for social calls. "Yeah. Nothing much going on. Was driving by."

"How was Seattle?" Bennett could make small talk if he had to. He didn't much care how Thanksgiving in Seattle was, but at the same time, he was dying to know how it'd gone.

"Good," Jason said, looking at Bennett. "Good."

"Good." Bennett noticed the repetition, the falsely positive look in Jason's eyes. "Cream or sugar?"

"Sugar." Jason groaned as he stood and came into the kitchen. "I can do it." He worked in the kitchen, putting his coffee together. "She's going to come back," he said.

Bennett's gaze flew to him. "She is? When?"

Jason shrugged. "I don't know, Bennett. But she will." The lieutenant met Bennett's eyes and added, "Hang in there," and went back to the couch.

Bennett felt like someone had struck him with lightning. His heart beat irregularly, and as he joined Jason in the living room and switched on a basketball game, he really wanted to take a picture so Jennie would know her brother didn't outwork Bennett just because he was a cop.

BENNETT FINISHED THE HEADBOARD THE NIGHT BEFORE Jennie's birthday. He'd carved birds into it, trees, waves, anything he thought of that reminded him of her. He'd stained the oak a very dark brown, and glossed it until it shone like dark gold.

After swiping on the last brushful of gloss, he stepped back and admired the craftsmanship. He wondered if she'd ever see it. Maybe he'd give it to his mother for Christmas. He'd gone to Bell Hill to visit them for Thanksgiving, and it had gone reasonably well. They were outside the Hawthorne Harbor gossip circles, so they didn't know about the dancing, hand holding, and kissing at the unveiling.

His mother had a way of reading his mood before he'd even said a word, and she'd known something was off, but Bennett had managed to blame his job for the source of his foul energy.

But the job was fine. The dogs were fine. The house was fine. But everything that Bennett had thought was fine in his life before showing up at Jennie's was not actually fine. He did not like coming home to only canines. He didn't like eating cold cereal for dinner. He didn't like that, on his days off from the fire house, he could go a full twenty-four hours without talking to another human.

He didn't like that he couldn't have a long text conversation with a woman who made him smile. He didn't like that he'd gone back to living like a monk. He didn't like that his only source of escape was a woodworking project or throwing a ball to a golden retriever that wasn't even his.

Anger filled him, and he wanted to take out his phone

and call Jennie right now. Tell her that she'd broken his heart, and couldn't she at least call the way she'd promised?

Sadness immediately descended upon him, and then helplessness. He knew that in a few minutes he'd be back to the acceptance phase of this vicious cycle.

She'll come back.

Right. Bennett scoffed at Jason's words from the other night. Jennie had gone to Seattle a month ago. If she was going to come back, she would've by now.

Bennett left the headboard to cure and went inside, where once again, he'd been pushed off his own couch by two huge dogs. Didn't matter. He poured himself a bowl of cereal and sat in the recliner, another basketball game blaring from the TV.

He couldn't believe he'd thought this life was enough. Or even close to what he wanted. But cold cereal and big dogs were all he had at the moment.

The following morning, Bennett got up and ran with the dogs. He didn't have to be to work until mid-afternoon, so he had plenty of time to shower and stew over calling Jennie. "Just to say happy birthday," he said into the hot spray. Everyone deserved a happy birthday, didn't they?

Bennett hated the weakness in himself, but if there was one thing he wanted to be weak about, it was Jennie Zimmerman. So after he showered and shaved and was sitting at the kitchen counter with a couple of fried eggs, he tapped out a simple *Happy birthday, Jennie* text and sent it.

Minutes ticked by. The eggs got eaten. The dogs got fed. The coffee in his mug turned cold. Jennie didn't answer.

Bennett felt like marching out to the wood shop and chopping the headboard into fifty million pieces. His head buzzed and his heart pounded. Was it so hard to simply say *thank you*?

Jennie had never been particularly good at expressing her gratitude.

A knock sounded on his door, and both dogs jumped down from the couch as if whoever stood on the porch had come to see them. Now, if it was Nelly, she probably had. Bennett took a deep breath to drive out his fury and frustration. After all, he couldn't snap at a little girl for coming over to see the dogs.

"Back up," he said to Gemma, who stood an inch from the door. "Go on. Move." He opened the door to find Jennie standing there.

He froze, his heart tangoing in his chest again. He couldn't speak as he stared at her. She wore that pair of blue jeans with a navy hoodie, her hands tucked in the pockets.

"Hey, Bennett," she said, worry coloring her voice and dancing through her eyes. "Can I come in? It's pretty cold out here."

"Sure, yeah." Bennett backed up a step and almost fell

as he tripped over Gemma. "Back up," he growled at the dog, but she didn't listen. She rushed Jennie, and so did Patches.

Jennie laughed, that magical sound that Bennett decided right then and there that he couldn't live without.

"I sent you a happy birthday text," he said as she crouched down and gave Patches a scrub along his neck and back.

"I got it. I was just driving." She straightened and looked right at him. "I was on my way to see you, so I figured I'd wait to respond until I saw you."

Bennett's eyebrows went up. "Oh? And what would your response be?" He couldn't decide if he was angry with her or so dang happy to see her he didn't care she'd left him for a second time.

Because she *had* come back.

She started tapping on her phone, and a few seconds later, she gave one final push and looked up. Three seconds passed before Bennett's phone beeped.

Thank you, Bennett. I miss you. I made a mistake. I'm sorry. I love you.

Bennett's breath stuck in his throat, and his stomach swooped around like it was on a roller coaster without the rest of his body.

I love you.

He loved her too.

Slowly, he lifted his eyes to hers.

Jennie felt like she'd swallowed something dry and sharp. She hadn't wanted to tell Bennett how she felt in a text, but he'd messaged her before she could show up.

Ten minutes. She'd only needed ten more minutes.

"Is this true?" He held up his phone, hope shining in his dark eyes.

"Yes." That was all she could get her voice to say.

"Well, I don't know what to say." Bennett wore a bit of confusion in his expression now.

"You don't have to say anything." Jennie took a deep breath. "I'm the one who needs to do all the talking." She glanced past him, smelling something delicious hanging in the air. "Maybe I'll have some coffee first?"

"Coffee?" Bennett dropped his hand to his side, still gripping his phone. "You don't like coffee."

"Turns out I do." Jennie gave him a smile, realizing that she had so very much to tell him.

"I don't understand." Bennett was so handsome, so strong, and yet so utterly soft too.

Jennie approached him, wanting to touch him to ground herself. She reached up and swept her hand down the side of his face, half-expecting him to slap her hand away.

He flinched, but that was all. His eyes burned into hers, and normally she would've looked away.

"I've been lost for so long," she said. "After I realized that I wanted you in my life, I had to do a bit of soul-searching. It took a little longer than I wanted, but still less than Jason."

Bennett's eyebrows drew down, and Jennie giggled. "Don't worry about that." She stepped past him and moved into the kitchen to pour herself a cup of coffee.

"Seattle has some great coffee shops. I found myself reading a lot in them, or surfing on social media. The apartment my parents have is so small."

She sat at his counter, both dogs settling at her feet. "And one day I decided I needed to figure out if I liked coffee or not, or if I was just being pretentious with the tea." She took a sip of her coffee and stirred in another spoonful of sugar. "I suppose you can figure out the rest."

Bennett crossed the room from where he still stood near the front door. "What else?"

"There's a great gallery—smaller, but still great—that's

willing to look at my stuff once the new year comes." She shrugged. "I don't know if I'll send them anything or not."

She thought of the space she'd rented. She'd managed to do two pieces while there, but she hadn't particularly liked them and had left them with her parents.

"I tried fish I'd never eaten," she said. "I walked in places that scared me. I read books I'd never heard of." She chanced a glance at him and found him listening raptly.

"I learned that I mostly know myself. But I do like coffee...and I couldn't stay in Seattle without you."

Bennett gazed at her, a small smile touching his lips. "I've thought about moving up there," he said.

"Oh, you'd be so unhappy up there." Jennie shook her head. "I thought about asking you for about half a second. But that wouldn't be fair to you."

"Why? I can make furniture anywhere. And the firemen in Seattle might actually go out on the truck every once in a while."

She couldn't tell if he was kidding or not. She shook her head again, appreciating that he'd thought of moving to be with her. He hadn't said he loved her back, and that stung the slightest bit.

"No, I saw you at that restaurant. It was pure torture for you."

"It was really loud in there."

"Exactly." Jennie gave him a grin so he wouldn't take that word personally. "I barely like the city, and I've lived in one before." She glanced around his perfect house. "Plus, you have this place, and you could never give it up."

"I might." He shrugged one shoulder and reached for his coffee cup. He promptly put it down again when he realized it wasn't what he wanted.

"This is your grandmother's home," Jennie said. "I could never ask you to sell it. Or leave it. I knew that. And I knew I wanted to be with you, so the only choice was to come back."

"Sounds like a hard decision." His voice turned hard too.

"It wasn't, not really." Jennie didn't know how to explain. "It wasn't until Thanksgiving that I realized I was in love with you and needed to do something about it."

She watched him, desperately wanting him to proclaim his love for her too.

"I've been miserable," he said. "No one at the fire house would sit by me at meals anymore. The dogs have never been in better shape, because I run them every morning."

"I haven't been happy either." Jennie reached out and cradled his face again. "I'm sorry. I thought I needed something I didn't really need."

"And what was that?"

"A job." Fear laced its icy fingers around her heart and squeezed. But she pushed it away, back down, where she couldn't listen to it. "But I'll figure something out."

She hoped. She'd paint oils and setup a stand on the

pier if she had to. But she had to be in Hawthorne Harbor, she knew that much.

She wrapped both hands around her mug and absorbed the warmth. "So anyway. It's quite a long story, and I'll tell you all about it. Honest, I will. Right now, though, I'm just dying to know how you feel about me."

She abandoned the coffee cup and turned fully toward him.

His expression blazed, and he asked, "Jennie, do you really not know?"

She felt very near tears, and her fingers shook as she shrugged just the slightest bit.

"I'm in love with you," he said. "I have been since I was seventeen years old."

A tear splashed Jennie's cheek, and her whole face felt like it was squished up in the most unattractive way.

"And you don't need a job. I'll take care of you, so you can just throw pots to your heart's desire. And you'll move in with me after we're married, and I'll build you an art studio right beside my wood shop." He gently touched her arm, his skin warm and electric at the same time. "Okay?"

"Is that a proposal?" Jennie sounded like she'd sucked in a lungful of helium, but she didn't care.

"Oh, no," he said, deadly serious. "When I propose, I'll be down on both knees, begging you to be my wife."

Jennie leaned toward him, taking his face in both of her hands. "I'm sorry, Bennett."

"No more apologies," he whispered, his eyes already

closed. They suddenly sprang open again. "I mean, I want to hear all of your stories about why you came back. I do. But I really just want to kiss you now."

Jennie wanted to kiss him too, something she much preferred over talking anyway. So she did, thrilled that it felt like the first time for the third time in her life.

This time, though, it was much, much better, because she was kissing the man she loved.

"OKAY, SO ARE YOUR EYES CLOSED?" BENNETT STOPPED walking, and Jennie squeezed her eyes closed a little tighter.

"All the way."

"Okay, no peeking."

After they'd kissed and made up, he'd leapt to his feet, claiming to have a surprise for her.

She knew he'd taken her out onto the back deck, down the steps, and out toward the wood shed. The anticipation of seeing what he'd built for her when he had no idea if she'd even come back to town had her heart flopping around in her chest.

"Okay, just a sec." He let go of her hand, and she could hear him fumbling with the latch on the wood shop door.

The scent of Bennett—wood and sweat and machinery—hit her, and she startled when his hand slid down her arm to hers. "All right, come with me."

He led her, taking stilted steps, into the shed and turned her slightly. "This way. Go this way." He kept nudging her until he was satisfied with her position.

"Okay, you can open your eyes."

He stood next to a huge piece of carpentry that had been intricately carved. She knew immediately that it was a headboard for a queen bed, and she covered her mouth with her hand.

"Bennett." His name was made mostly of air, and Jennie couldn't take all the details fast enough. "It's beautiful."

"I've obviously never been in your bedroom," he said. "But I thought...." A blush crept into his face, clearly seen even through the dimness in the shed. "I thought I'd like to know that you were being watched over by the things you love most."

He stepped closer to the headboard and pointed. "See the hawthorn trees? You love those. And I know they're not as good as the one you did, but I think they're recognizable."

He looked at her for confirmation, and she pressed her palm over her heartbeat as she nodded. "They're great."

"I know you love watching the birds flying over the ocean. And the beach is one of your favorite places. And these are lilies. And—"

"Okay, Bennett." His nerves were cute, really. "I love it. It's fantastic." She stepped over to him and ran her fingertips along the top, where most of the birds were. "Thank you."

"Happy birthday." He took her into his arms and swayed with her. "I almost didn't make it. I was so mad at you."

"I know." She pressed her forehead to his and closed her eyes. She didn't know how to apologize enough.

He kissed her then, stealing the *I'm sorry* she was about to utter for the third time that morning.

Jennie never wanted to be without this man, and while she may have second-guessed herself on the two-hour drive from Seattle, she knew now that she'd chosen correctly.

No piece of art was as valuable as Bennett Patterson's kiss. His love. And Jennie counted herself lucky to have experienced both.

Bennett couldn't believe his beautiful, stubborn Jennie had come back to him. He hadn't believed her twin brother when he'd stopped by last week, and he could barely believe it now, though they sat across from each other in a quiet restaurant in Bell Hill.

He couldn't help himself as he continued staring at her. Every once in a while, he realized he wore a goofy grin, and he worked to straighten his lips.

She'd been talking for quite a long time, and he enjoyed listening to the sound of her voice as she detailed how she'd gone from gallery to gallery until she'd found the smaller one.

As she told about the studio space she'd rented, but how sterile it was and how she felt stifled there.

As she told him about the tiny apartment, and how

her mom wanted a small dog to comfort her after her treatments.

"So do we get to keep Patches and Gemma?" he asked, hopeful.

"I'm sure my parents will come back to town eventually," she said. "Probably before summer, for sure."

"Yeah, I know." Bennett tried not to sound forlorn, but he sure would miss Patches. "Maybe I'll get Gemma a friend when I have to give up Patches."

Jennie laughed and took a sip of her peach lemonade. "You'll be happy to know I learned I actually like dogs on my little personal exodus."

"That's great news." Bennett sat back as their food came, and he gazed at his pulled pork macaroni and cheese with great appreciation.

He'd like to get a diamond on Jennie's finger as fast as possible, but he was still unsure about her thoughts on marriage. When he'd mentioned it earlier, she hadn't commented.

He didn't want to push her on her first day back in town, but he also wanted to make a plan. Get a date set. Know how much longer he had to wait until he could come home and find her there.

"So talk to me about marriage," he said slowly, spearing a forkful of pork along with a few noodles.

Sure enough, her eyes held anxiety as she lifted them to his. "I want to marry you. I do."

"The I do's come later, sweetheart." Bennett could only

make this as light as possible, hoping to eliminate that panic from her face.

"I've always wanted to get married in the summer," she said, swallowing.

So another seven months. He could wait that long. Maybe.

"And?" he prompted, because she had more to say. "Are you worried I won't show up? Because, Jennie, we can go to City Hall today, if you wanted."

Her face lit up. "Really?"

"I've been married before," he said. "It's a lot of ceremony for a five-minute thing." He shrugged like it was no big deal, but he knew it was. Besides, marrying *Jennie* was something he wanted to savor, enjoy every last moment, and if she wanted to go to City Hall, he'd do it. But the idea of a big wedding at Magleby Mansion also appealed to him.

"What do you want to do?" she asked.

"I want to marry you in Magleby Mansion," he said, leaning forward. "I promise I'll show up. I'm not your ex."

"I know that," she said as she picked up her fork and started stirring her salad. "I do, Bennett. I know that."

He wasn't sure if she was trying to reassure him or herself.

"So what do you want?"

She took a bite of her salad and chewed, obviously thinking about it. "If we get married in the summer, could it be an outdoor ceremony?"

"Sure."

"At the Mansion. In the gardens."

"Or the beach," he said. "Reception at the mansion."

"Oh, I like the way you think."

"So there are options." He was just glad she was discussing the M-word with him. Now he just needed a really great way to ask her to be his wife.

So the following day, he fibbed a little and told her he had to work first thing in the morning. The truth was, he didn't have to go into the fire house that day at all.

Instead, he parked near Wedding Row and started down the street, where two jewelry stores sat across the road from one another.

He didn't think for a single moment that he could pick out a ring for Jennie. She'd want to choose her own, but he could get a very simple wedding band to propose with. Then, once she said yes, he'd take her to pick out the diamond she liked best.

He entered the shop to the sound of a bell, almost cringing and wanting to rush right out again. Four women trained their eyes on him, and he knew all of them.

"Bennett Patterson," Sue Grafton said. "I thought I'd see you in here again one day."

"Is it Jennie Zimmerman?" Nadiya Harris asked. "I heard she was back in town."

"This is confidential, right?" he asked, glancing around. He wasn't sure he'd fare much better across the street. Maybe he should've driven to another town to make this purchase.

"Absolutely," Sue said with authority. "Not a word about anything purchased or said in this shop leaves the shop." She glanced at the other women, and it was clear she'd be handling this sale. They wandered off, where Nadiya started wiping the already clean glass.

"What are you looking for?" Sue asked.

"I just want a band for now," Bennett said. "Then I'll bring Jennie here to pick out her own diamond."

"Smart man." Sue grinned at him and led him to a case with gold and silver bands. Bennett had no idea, and he asked a lot of questions.

In the end, he left with a gold band with ridges around it, and he hurried back to his truck before anyone else could see him with the delicate jewelry store bag.

After all, the last thing he needed was gossip getting back to Jennie that he'd been spotted on Wedding Row without her. That would completely ruin the surprise.

Not that he had a surprise in mind. Or a plan. Nothing. He took the ring out of the black, velvet box and slipped it into his pocket. He'd carry it around until an idea struck, and then—then, he'd ask Jennie to finally be his.

HE DIDN'T COME UP WITH ANYTHING THAT WEEK. SURE, HE walked through the Festival of Trees hand-in-hand with Jennie. They bought a few gifts for their family members, ate more peppermint-flavored foods than was humanly possible, and enjoyed the themed Christmas trees.

But the ring stayed in Bennett's pocket. He took it with him to the fire house, when he ran on the beach with the dogs, or into the wood shop. His brain constantly whirred, and yet all he could think of was pulling it out one day and asking her to marry him.

He wasn't sure what was so hard about the proposal. They'd already talked about marriage. He knew she'd say yes. Somehow, though, he wanted the moment to be special. More than a mutual agreement that they should get married. After all, he knew what a big deal it was for her to commit to wearing that white dress again, and waiting to walk down the aisle, hoping he'd be standing at the altar like he promised.

So the proposal had to be perfect.

Bennett went to the Internet for ideas, but everything seemed trite and something a much younger couple would enjoy. He didn't want to fish the wedding band out of a piece of cake or have her swallow it by putting it in a drink.

He just wanted to ask her to be his wife.

On his days off, he worked in the wood shop, a jewelry box coming to life before his eyes. Suddenly, an idea hit him. He could finish this jewelry box for Jennie and when he gave it to her for Christmas, the ring could be inside.

She was planning another trip up to Seattle for the holidays, and Bennett picked up his phone and called her. She'd been working in her studio, producing a few paintings and a few pots and selling them in an online shop. Mabel had also agreed to house several pieces as a permanent display at the Mansion, and Jennie had sold enough to keep herself in Hawthorne Harbor for another month.

He wouldn't be surprised if she was elbow-deep in clay and couldn't answer. But she did, with "Hey, Bennett."

His whole body turned soft at the sound of her voice. "Hey there, beautiful."

"What's up?"

He straightened, spurred on by the tone of her voice, which said she was busy but had answered anyway. "So when are you going to Seattle?"

"I'm driving up on the twenty-third," she said. "I'll be back on the twenty-seventh."

"So could we celebrate Christmas together on the twenty-second?"

"Yeah, sure. You know I can't cook, right?"

Bennett chuckled. "I'm aware. But let's have dinner at my place. I'll grab something and we can exchange gifts." His throat turned dry at the thought of giving her an engagement ring in just eight days.

"Sounds great. You're not working today, right?"

"Just in the shop."

"So when I finish these pots, let's go get something to eat."

"Just text me." Bennett got back to work after the call ended, determined to have the best early Christmas celebration in history. And that meant a phone call to Mabel to order a dinner for two from her kitchen and to ask about the paintings Jennie had left on display at the Mansion.

"There are several," Mabel said.

"Great, I'll come pick one out later today."

"So you want a dinner for two for the twenty-second. From the wedding menu."

"That's right."

Mabel sighed, but it was filled with all kinds of happiness. "I'm so glad you didn't let her push you away."

Bennett chuckled and watched the dogs roll around on the grass. "I almost did, Mabel. She was gone for a while there."

"But she came back." Sadness touched her words now, and Bennett wondered what was behind them.

"Yes," he said. "She did."

"I'm happy for you two."

"Thank you, Mabel." Bennett hung up and faced the next item that needed to be accomplished before his romantic evening: finishing the jewelry box.

"Jennie," he said under his breath as he measured and made marks on the wood. "Will you marry me?"

He shook his head. "No, gotta say I love you first." He

took a deep breath and took the measured and marked wood over to the table saw. "Jennie, I love you." He looked out the open door of the wood shop to the cloudy sky beyond. "I love you so much. Will you do me the favor of being my wife?"

Yeah, he didn't like the order of those words either, and the shrill shriek of the saw forced him to focus on the task at hand, lest he *lose* a hand.

Maybe presenting her with the gift would be enough. Maybe he didn't have to actually say the words.

He glued and clamped the small pieces together, knowing full well he'd need to say the words. Honestly, they shouldn't be so stressful. He'd said them before.

But not to Jennie, and that was the real difference.

Jennie clutched her present nervously, wishing she'd taken the time to unwrap it and re-do the job so it was prettier. She shouldn't have trusted Marge at the hardware store with her gift-wrapping needs, but it had been a free service. Still, the white paper with black wrenches all over it didn't seem all that festive, and Jennie felt like it was a dead giveaway as to what was inside.

She knocked on Bennett's carport door and went in, admitting defeat. She couldn't change the paper now.

Soft music played from the speakers in the living room, and the scent of roasted meat and something sweet hung in the air.

"Bennett?" she called, glancing around. His house was definitely clean, though it felt lived in too.

"In the bedroom," he called from the hall directly in front of her. "Be out in a sec."

At least she could prolong the moment until he saw the hideously wrapped present.

She walked into the living room, where both dogs wore a festive red and white bandanna around their necks. She put her gift under Bennett's tree, where several more waited. She hoped they weren't all for her, as she only had the one for him.

She turned, her nerves firing through her on all cylinders. She really needed to stop fretting over this. It was Christmas, and there were more important things the two of them could do to build memories.

Her eyes landed on the huge painting—the huge, brand new painting—that now hung on Bennett's wall. It had not been there last week, and it fit like she'd been commissioned to paint it just for that spot.

She stepped around the back of the couch, the front door to her left and the dining room to her right, and admired the painting.

She'd loved this one when she'd swept the bright reds and golds and oranges of the sunset over the ocean.

He came out of the hall and spied her standing there. "Oh, you found my new painting."

Jennie glanced at him, at that little grin on his face, and looked back at the scene she loved so much. "I would've given it to you."

He put his arm around her waist and pulled her right into his body. "Nah. I can afford to buy it, and I needed to see Mabel anyway."

"About what?" she asked, her heart ba-bumping in her chest. Had he scheduled the Mansion for their wedding? Jennie herself had thought about doing it every day since she'd been back in town. Printing off the reservation and putting it in an envelope for his Christmas gift.

She wanted him to know she was ready to try the whole getting married thing again. She wasn't afraid of marriage. No, she was terrified of sending announcements, finding the perfect dress, getting all dolled up, and showing up to find the groom had bolted.

But Bennett wasn't Kyle, and she wanted him to know she trusted him.

She hadn't set the reservation though, somehow wanting a ring on her finger before she did.

"Mabel made our dinner tonight," he said, his lips dangerously close to her earlobe. "Do you know what this painting is called?:

Of course she did. "Romance in Red," she said.

"It fits here, don't you think?"

Jennie did think so, so she nodded. "Should we eat first, or do gifts first?" she asked.

Bennett took a deep breath and turned her toward him. He gazed down at her, all the love and happiness in the world right there in his eyes for her to see.

"I'm starving," he said. "Let's eat first." He laced his fingers through hers and led her over to the kitchen. "So I asked Mabel to make us a Christmas feast for two, with items from her wedding menu." He cut her a quick glance, and Jennie's heart did a little quickstep in her chest.

"So let's see what she sent us." He lifted a piece of paper from its spot next to a tower of foil containers. "Herb-crusted chicken with mashed potatoes, baby carrots, and heir covert."

He put the sheet down. "I don't even know what that means." He laughed, and Jennie thought it was the greatest sound in the world.

"Green beans," she said. "And that sounds divine." She was hungrier than she thought.

Bennett didn't go back to the paper. He got down plates and pulled open a drawer to get silverware.

She started unveiling the food to find one filled with a delicious-looking stuffing that had walnuts and smelled like sage. "Gravy," she said, marveling at the golden color of it. "And this paper says there's cheesecake for dessert."

"Ah, that must be this one." Bennett pulled a rectangular foil pan out of the fridge, and sure enough, when he peeled back the lid, there was an entire cheese-cake, along with strawberry and chocolate sauces, and fresh berries to go with it.

"There's no way we can eat all of this," Jennie said with a smile. "And I didn't think we'd do a whole dinner at our wedding."

That got Bennett's attention, and he set the plates on the table. "No? You just want to do a reception?"

"The menu will be different. I know Mabel does a

crepe bar as one of the choices." Jennie brought over the silverware, napkins, and cups. "It'll be cheaper."

"I don't care how much it costs," Bennett said, his voice low. "Remember how I don't have a mortgage?"

Jennie remembered, but she wasn't sure she needed to feed the whole town as part of their wedding celebration.

"Just don't make a decision based on money," he said, meeting her eye. "Okay?"

"Okay," she said simply. They moved all the food to the table and sat down beside each other. The stillness of this small town hit Jennie like a load of bricks, and she was so grateful to be back where there wasn't so much traffic, so much busyness, so many people.

Being in Bennett's home with just him and the dogs felt as peaceful as anything Jennie had ever done, and after her first bite of creamy, buttery mashed potatoes, she said, "I think we should serve dinner at the wedding."

Bennett nodded and smiled, piling up a carrot, a bit of potato, and a bite of chicken all together on his fork. "So we'll do the ceremony on the beach. Dinner at the Mansion, reception after that."

"Sounds like a lot," Jennie said.

"It's a wedding," Bennett said. "It's the first day of the rest of our lives together. It's meant to be a lot. To celebrate."

Jennie took another bite, the flavor of the stuffing and the chicken together enough to make her moan. "I want to sample all the food at the Mansion before we make a decision."

Bennett chuckled, and said, "I'm sure we can make that happen."

She ate until she was so full she couldn't take another bite. Bennett lit a fire and turned toward her, that romantic music still lilting through the air. He really did know how to put together a fun, flirty evening for the two of them.

"Presents?" he asked, only a sliver of nerves in his expression.

"Sure," she said. "But you go first."

He nodded and turned to the tree, catching sight of the hideous gift she'd brought. Heat filled her face when he laughed and lifted it up. "I can't wait to open this."

She shook her head and smiled too, glad when he presented her with a box that was much bigger than something that might hold a ring.

He sat beside her on the couch and said, "Open it."

Jennie lovingly took off the silver ribbon and slid her fingertips under the flap of paper he'd taped down. As the wrapping came off, she found a stunning jewelry box.

"Oh, Bennett." She traced her fingers along the edges, admiring the beauty of the redwood and the way he'd brought out the natural grain with a light stain.

"It's wonderful."

"I know you don't wear a whole lot of jewelry," he said, practically tearing the box from her hands before she could open it and see the intricate compartments inside. Knowing him, there would be a dozen of them, all perfectly sized for certain pieces.

Before she knew what was happening, he slid to the floor, both knees hitting it as he set the box on the couch beside her and taking the lid off in one motion.

"But I'm hoping you'll wear this." He plucked a ring from the box and held it toward her. "Jennie, I'm madly in love with you, and I want to marry you. What do you say?"

Jennie took in the plainness of the ring, noting that he'd only bought a band and she'd get to pick out her own diamond. She drank in the hopeful sight of him before her, kneeling, begging her to be his.

She wanted to hold onto this moment forever, so she took one more breath before a smile burst onto her face and she said, "Yes."

Bennett grinned too and put the ring in his palm. "It's just a gold band. We can go get a ring in the morning before you go to Seattle. Or when you get back. Whenever." He slipped it onto her finger, sure and shaky at the same time.

She admired it, and then him, and she leaned forward to take his face in her hands and kiss him—kiss her fiancé for the first time.

"I love you," she whispered against his lips, glad she'd found the courage to get out of her own way so she could have this brilliant, beautiful man in her life.

"And I love you." He kissed her again, and she hoped she could distract him from her gift for a while.

But nope. He pulled back quickly and reached for it before re-taking his spot beside her on the couch. "So I'm assuming this is for me."

"I didn't even bring anything for the dogs," she said, foolishness rushing through her.

"Oh, don't worry about them." Bennett cast them a quick glance. "I've got about five things for each of them come Christmas morning."

Of course he did. Jennie giggled and said, "Look, it's the thought that counts, right?"

"Are you kidding?" he asked. "I just proposed. This better be amazing." He shook it, and Jennie loved the playful look on his face.

"Just open it and put me out of my misery."

He laughed and tore the paper off, not even trying to preserve it, because wrapping that ugly should be burned.

"Hey, it's a miter saw," he said, wonder and happiness in his voice. "How did you know I needed a new one?"

"Oh, you know." She shrugged one shoulder. "Intuition."

Bennett cocked one eyebrow. "Who told you at the hardware store? Rusty? Or Walt?"

"Rusty," she said with a laugh. "Apparently, you spend a lot of time in the aisles making wishlists."

"I do not." He gazed down at the saw again. "But I did have my eye on this saw. Thank you, love." He kissed her again, and Jennie felt as if her heart would burst with love for him.

"So," he said, pulling her back onto the couch with him. She tucked her feet up under her body. "What date do you want me to book with Mabel?"

"Let's do early June," she said. "I mean, if you can get that time off."

"It's high fire season in the wild," he said. "But I'm not on the wildfire crew. Sometimes it's a bit tricky to get time off though, as we lose some of our guys." He kneaded her closer, pressed his lips to her forehead. "But I'll talk to the chief right away and put in a request."

Jennie snuggled into him, thinking he was the best present she could ever get. "I love you," she whispered. "I'm so glad you took me back."

"Sweetheart, I'd do it all over again." He sat up and looked at her, right into her eyes. "You know that, right? I'd do whatever I had to in order to be with you."

Warmth filled her from head to toe. "I know."

"I love you." He matched his mouth to hers, and Jennie let herself fall into the love and passion of his kiss, knowing she'd have a wonderful life with Bennett Patterson, the man she'd loved for so long.

Hawthorne Harbor
SECOND CHANCE ROMANCE
the end

"Trent, party of two?"

Trent Baker stood, wondering if he could get out of this date before it really started. Kathy was a brunette—his only requirement for his friends, who had been setting him up on dates for a couple of months now—but she wasn't anything like the kind of woman he wanted to spend more than five minutes with.

He knew, because they'd been waiting for a table at the steakhouse for twenty minutes and he'd stopped talking halfway through.

But he didn't ask Kathy for a raincheck, because he'd never cash that in. And she didn't act like she wanted to leave either. Maybe she just wanted ribs or the killer delicious rolls at Stan's.

Trent thought at least he'd eat well tonight, but he wouldn't be getting a second date.

Kathy carried the conversation, and Trent felt himself loosening up a little bit as drinks came, and then main dishes. He laughed with her when a couple on the dance floor started doing a professional swing and took a long drink from his soda, thinking maybe he just needed to open his mind to women he didn't immediately click with.

Her phone went off, and she said, "Do you mind?"

"Go ahead." He had his phone on the table too, because his six-year-old son, Porter, could need him at any moment.

Of course, his sister who watched the boy had never interrupted one of Trent's dates yet. But Kathy didn't know that, so Trent's phone sat on the table, screen up.

Kathy twittered over something on her device, and she looked up and said, "It's my boyfriend."

Boyfriend.

The word echoed through Trent's head, and he blinked at the woman across from him. Her thumbs flew across the screen and the look of joy on her face couldn't be anything but sincere.

"Boyfriend?" Trent finally asked, employing his police officer voice. Maybe not the one he used on his four German shepherds while he worked on their K9 training, but close.

Very close.

Kathy looked up, surprise on her face. "Yeah, Bruce?"

As if Trent should know who Bruce was. Trent had been back in Hawthorne Harbor for four years, and sure, he worked for the police department. But he certainly didn't know every citizen in town.

"How long have you and Bruce been dating?" Trent put his napkin on the table, ready to flee this disaster. Ready to simply be a single dad for the rest of his life. He could raise Porter. He could. He could find some way to ease the loneliness in his life. He could.

But he wasn't going out with another woman from this town.

"Oh, six or seven months." Kathy put her phone down and beamed at him.

"What did you think this was?" Trent waved between the two of them and leaned his elbows on the table.

She blinked, confusion racing through her eyes. "Oh, no." She covered her mouth with one hand. "Did you think this was a date?"

Trent refrained from rolling his eyes by looking up at the waiter as he arrived. "We're ready to go," he said, already pulling out his wallet.

"So no dessert?"

Trent threw a few twenty-dollar bills on the table and stood. "No dessert." The woman had gotten her steak and salad bar already.

"Trent," she said, but he was already walking toward the front door. He had to drive her home—he wasn't going to be rude or anything—but he didn't have to stay in public for this conversation.

Embarrassment and frustration heated his face, and

though autumn had arrived in Hawthorne Harbor, Trent felt hot from head to toe.

Thankfully, Kathy caught up to him and got in his truck without further incident.

"Georgia said she had a friend who needed a friend."

Trent grunted, not sure how to respond. Friends who went out together paid for their own meals. They didn't dress up in bright pink sundresses, heels, or put on as much makeup as Kathy had.

Of course, he barely knew her. Maybe she did dress like this all the time.

"It's fine," he said, practically jamming his foot to the floor in his haste to get this date over with. "I don't want to talk about it."

The drive to her house took eight minutes. Eight painfully long minutes of silence, and Trent didn't get out to walk her to the door. After all, her *boyfriend* was probably waiting behind the closed door.

"Thank you for dinner," she said, and Trent nodded her right out of the truck. He watched to make sure she got inside, as darkness had fallen and the police officer in him wouldn't let him just drive off.

But then he did pull out of her driveway and head down the highway toward the coast.

He didn't want to go back to Eliza's and explain anything to her, and the date had only lasted one hour and fifteen minutes, including that awkward drive.

His sister would ask a lot of questions and then start scrolling through her phone for more of her single friends. And Trent had already tried with three of them, and nothing had clicked.

"Maybe nothing ever will," he said to himself and the night in front of him. "Maybe Caroline was your click." The very thought of his wife made his heart pinch.

But he'd spent a year in complete mourning, barely alive, barely there for his toddler. And he wasn't going back to that person. Caroline wouldn't want him to anyway.

Maybe coming back to Hawthorne Harbor was a bad idea, he thought.

But his sister lived here, and his parents were just a few minutes away in Bell Hill. He'd needed their help with Porter, and their support in everything after Caroline's death.

He'd been lucky to get a spot on the police force, but his experience from the international airport in Seattle had sealed the job for him.

Cheery, yellow light caught his attention, and he realized he'd driven all the way up to Magleby Mansion. A party was clearly in full swing, and Trent felt like he was living inside a bubble.

Other people had fun. Great first dates. Boyfriends and girlfriends. But he just had his K9 dogs, his son, and his monotonous day-after-day job.

He wanted *more* than that, but at the same time, he was comfortable with the life he had.

Maybe that was why dating stung so much. It reminded him of how far out of his comfort zone he had to get in order to start and maintain a relationship.

He turned into the circular lane to turn around, a truck with a construction rack on it catching his attention.

"Michaels Construction," he read to himself. He eased on the brake and stopped, snapping a quick picture of the side of the truck so he could call and get a quote on what it would take in terms of time and money to build a deck off the back of his house.

If there was anything he loved more than his son and his K9 dogs, it was his back yard. All it was missing at this point, after four years of Trent's hard work, was a deck.

But he wasn't going to call Michael on Friday night. He didn't need to add insult to injury.

HE CALLED THE CONSTRUCTION COMPANY ON MONDAY morning and got a Lauren who scheduled a time for the general contractor to come out to Trent's house to take measurements, talk dimensions, and get the information he needed to provide a quote.

Trent had the whole day off, and with his son in school, he found himself out in the yard with all four German shepherds under his care.

He threw them a ball for about thirty minutes before all of them found the shade from the three giant Washington hawthorn trees he cultivated along the side of his back yard.

All four dogs panted, their huge tongues lolling out of their mouths while Trent pruned and weeded, hopefully for the last time before winter set in.

"Hello?" a woman called, and Trent startled away from the rose bushes. Wilson stood, and Trent held out his hand for the dog to stay.

"In the back," he said, moving toward the fence to unlatch it.

He rounded the corner of the house and came face-to-face with the prettiest woman he'd seen in years. And years.

She had long, dark hair she'd pulled into a ponytail which draped over her shoulder, and she looked at him with sparkly, dark eyes that made his breath catch somewhere behind his lungs.

"I'm Lauren Michaels," she said, extending her hand for him to shake over the chest-high chainlink.

Trent fumbled the latch, his heart also tossing around inside his chest.

"Lauren Michaels," he said, understanding dawning on him as he finally got the fence open. "I'm Trent Baker." He shook her hand, enjoying the zing as their skin met. He had so many questions for her, and none of them were about the deck.

The biggest one—and one he'd really need to know before this woman left his property—was *Do you have a boyfriend?*

"How do you feel about dogs?" he asked, keeping himself between her and the rest of the yard.

"I love dogs," Lauren said, trying not to admire this man quite so much. But he clearly spent time in a gym—and the yard, if the work gloves were any indication—and he had beautiful brown hair and a pair of eyes to match.

He wore a T-shirt that strained across his chest and biceps, and while Lauren had known who Trent was the moment he'd called, it was clear he didn't know who she was.

Or even that she *was* a *she*. It was a common mistake, what with her last name being a common first name for men. Still, it had an S on it, but somehow people overlooked that a lot.

"So I have four German shepherds back here," he said as he finally started walking into the yard. "They're police dogs, and they only respond to me. They shouldn't even approach you. And you can't approach them until I say." He cast her a quick glance that held kindness and apprehension, along with the power and authority in his voice. "Okay?"

"Sounds great," Lauren said, following him and wondering if she could ask him out again. Did she really want to get her heart sliced again by this man?

He doesn't remember, she told herself, but she honestly wasn't sure if that was better or not. His wife had just passed away, and Lauren hadn't known that. No wonder Trent Baker had no recollection of her first, flubbed attempt to get a date with him.

She waited near the back door, which had a few steps leading down to the yard and he definitely needed more for this stunning space. From the dwarf apple trees to the lavender growing along the house, to the grape vines to the stunning hawthorns on the far side of the yard— where the dogs waited—Trent definitely needed a deck to enjoy all of his hard work.

Trent kept walking and he spoke to the dogs in low tones so that Lauren couldn't tell what he was saying. He finally turned and gestured for her to come on over. She did, glad when only one of the shepherds came with him as he approached her. She liked dogs, sure, but maybe not four sixty-pounders at the same time.

"This is Wilson," Trent said, and he yipped at the dog before it came trotting forward to greet Lauren.

Wilson sniffed and she crouched down to give the dog a healthy pat around his jowls and ears. "Oh, you're just a big softie, aren't you? I bet your dad lets you sleep on the bed and everything." She grinned up at Trent, stunned again by his good looks.

So maybe she'd been glad she hadn't run into him in three years, but that didn't mean she couldn't try again. Did it? He was single, she knew that. Not really into dating, from what she'd heard.

But she wasn't in the gossip circles much and could only rely on what she heard from Gillian. And Gillian had a long-time boyfriend and didn't know as much as she used to. Other than her, Lauren spent all of her time with men, and they certainly didn't know the last time Trent had gone out with someone.

One by one, each dog came over and got some love from Lauren, and she caught Trent looking at her with a strange glint in his eye. She couldn't interpret it before she cleared her throat and got back to business.

"So, tell me about this deck." She turned to survey the open area at the back of the house. "How big are you thinking?" She pulled her tape measure from her tool belt and flicked it out.

She was the best general contractor in town, but she didn't work nearly as much as some of the other companies. She didn't want to think it was because of her gender, but she couldn't think of any other reason.

Trent detailed the kind of paradise he wanted, and Lauren could see it come to life in her mind.

She used her tablet and the expensive construction software she'd bought to draw up some quick plans as he took the dogs inside to get them a fresh bowl of water.

Twenty minutes later, Lauren felt confident she could tap "generate" and her tablet would give her a timeline as well as a quote for this dreamy man she really wanted to work with.

She didn't need to ask him out today if she could land this job. And the truth was, she needed another big project once she finished the wing up at Magleby Mansion.

"So where are we at?" he asked, coming down the steps and exhaling heavily. "My son will be done at school soon, and I have to go pick him up."

Lauren's chest squeezed on the word *son*, but she didn't let it show. "I can email this to you." She raised her eyebrows in a silent question.

He joined her at her side, the scent of his skin hitting her like a heavenly punch of cologne and sweat. She kept the swoon under control, but his voice rumbled through her when he said, "I have time. Let me see it." He peered at her tablet, and Lauren reminded herself to get the job done.

"Okay." She cleared her throat, wishing he didn't make her so nervous. Maybe if she'd gone out with anyone whose name she could remember in the past three years, her heart wouldn't be hammering quite so hard right now.

She detailed the project, the hawthorn wood she'd use to mirror the trees, the swing, the benches, the place for the permanent umbrella to be secured so the bay winds wouldn't disrupt his back yard barbeques.

"And what does this cost?" he asked, taking a step back. "It's beautiful. Exactly what I want. I just...." He gave a chuckle that sounded nervous. "I'm on a budget."

"Of course," Lauren said. "We can do three payments. One-third up front. One in the middle. And one at the end once you're one-hundred-percent satisfied with my work."

Their eyes met, and Lauren wasn't sure if she was hallucinating or not, but she felt a quick spark of attraction between them. Fine, it was more like a lightning bolt.

Could he feel it too?

The seconds stretched, and she finally shook herself out of the depths of his eyes. "Here's the price and time-line." She tapped the button and the drawings changed to the quote. She handed him the tablet and stepped back. "I have to finish my great-aunt's place first, so I'm not available until probably the end of October."

And then she had the Festival of Trees after that. She opened her mouth to say she couldn't start until the new year when Trent said, "This looks great," and handed back her tablet. "You're hired."

Happiness flowed through Lauren, and not just because she'd gotten another job to keep her in business for another few months. She'd learned to take things day by day, month by month. Doing that, she'd kept Michaels Construction in business for six years.

"Is your great-aunt Mabel Magleby?"

"That's right." Lauren tapped a few more buttons and added, "I'll get this printed. Do you want to stop by my place to sign it? Or I can bring it over here at your convenience." She was so professional, and while she might want to take Trent to lunch, she also wanted him to recommend her to all of his friends who might need something done, whether it be a bathroom remodel or a new addition to their house.

"I can come to you." He smiled, and honestly, such an action on such a handsome face should be illegal.

"Great." Lauren stood there, though she had no reason to stay for another second. And Trent needed to go get his son, but he didn't move either. Perhaps the lightning had struck him too.

"What's Mabel doing up there?" he asked.

"A complete renovation of the west wing," Lauren said, seizing onto an opportunity and hoping she didn't mess it up. "She's having a big party for the reopening. You should come." She added a smile to her face, thinking her invitation could be interpreted as friendly. Like, *Hey, the whole town is invited, so you should come.*

She started for the corner of the house and the fence, but he said, "Lauren?"

Lauren turned back to him. "Yeah?"

"Have we met before?" He tilted his head, those eyes harboring so much intelligence.

Lauren wanted to deny it, but she also really wanted a second chance with him. So she let herself emit a light laugh—not a giggle. A businesswoman such as herself did *not* giggle—and toss her ponytail over her shoulder.

"I asked you out once," she said with a quick one-shoulder shrug. "I didn't think you remembered that."

Trent looked like she'd thrown a glass of ice water in his face. "I don't remember that. When was it?"

"Oh, I don't know. Three or four years ago."

Something dark crossed his face, and Lauren took it as her cue to leave. "It was no big deal." She rounded the corner and had her hand on the latch when he practically yelled her name.

He came around the corner, almost colliding with her. She blinked at him, all the shadows gone from his eyes. She really hoped her invitation to dinner four years ago wouldn't jeopardize this deck now. She not only needed the job, she really wanted to work on this specific project.

"I'd like to take you up on your offer," he said. "That is, if you don't have a boyfriend." He reached up and rubbed his hand up the back of his neck in the most adorable way.

Lauren's face burst into a smile. "I don't have a boyfriend."

Trent grinned too. "Great. So I'll stop by and sign those papers and we'll chat then. I really am late to get my son."

"I'll be at the Mansion most of the day tomorrow, if you want to stop by up there." Lauren didn't usually feel so shy—as evidenced by her bold move to ask out the new bachelor in town all those years ago—but somehow, in this small patch of lawn, with Trent, she did.

"I'll see if I can get up there," he said. "I'm on duty tomorrow."

Lauren nodded and got her slightly shaky legs to get her off his property and back to her office before she blew her second chance with the deliciously handsome Trent Baker.

Trent sat in the parent pick-up line, his heart thumping in some strange way it hadn't in so long, he couldn't even identify what kind of beat it was.

But he knew it had everything to do with the beautiful Lauren Michaels. Had she really asked him out before? How could he have forgotten a woman like her?

He'd almost texted his sister to find out if she remembered Lauren, but he didn't need her asking questions. And Eliza would. She was as keen as their mother, and the last thing Trent needed was either one of them asking about his love life.

When he'd picked up Porter on Friday night, Eliza had asked, "So?" and all Trent had been able to do was shake his head. He'd tell her about Kathy's *boyfriend* eventually, but Trent didn't need to relive the humiliation right now.

The back door of the SUV opened, and Trent put on his daddy smile. "Hey, bud, how was school?"

Porter climbed into the backseat, his backpack huge and getting stuck on the top of the doorframe. He yanked on it and finally settled in the middle of the bench seat.

"Joey brought a lizard," he said, his voice high and full of excitement. "And Miss Terry chose three people to hold it, and I got to!"

"That's great, bud." Trent eased the truck out of the line and into the drive-through lane. "What was the lizard's name?"

"Chicken."

Trent scoffed. "What?" He glanced in the rear-view mirror and met Porter's eyes. At least they were his and not Savannah's. No, Trent saw her in the shape of his son's face, the roundness of his nose, and the way everything seemed to be made of magic. Including, apparently, lizards named Chicken.

"Yeah, Chicken," Porter said.

"Put your seatbelt on, bud." Trent stopped at the sign before pulling out of the school driveway and waited for his son to click his buckle.

"I guess lizards are born from eggs," Porter said. "And Joey thought that it would be a chicken, so he named it Chicken even after it was hatched."

"Okay, then." Trent turned toward Main Street, wondering if it was too early to grab dinner. Then he wouldn't have to leave the house again that night. He wondered when he'd become an old soul, as a thirty-seven-year-old shouldn't want to eat dinner at three-thirty in the afternoon.

"Are you hungry, Porty?"

"No, it was Baylor's birthday, and his mom brought doughnuts." He just looked out the window, but Trent felt like someone had stabbed a toothpick into his heart.

He hadn't been able to take a treat into Porter's class last year, because he'd been on duty. This year, he'd already put in for a vacation day in March, so he could be Mister Mom and take cupcakes to Porter's classmates.

"Maybe we could grab sandwiches and take the canines to the beach."

"Will you teach me that word for find?" Porter asked.

"Yeah. You can work on it with Tornado. He's still trying to learn it."

"Wilson always takes over."

"Yeah, well, Wilson is the pack leader." Trent turned down Main Street. "Pick a place, and we'll stop and get something and go."

Trent took the dogs everywhere with him. Sometimes he leashed one or two and made them work among pedestrians. Wilson and Pecorino had performed brilliantly at the Lavender Festival a few months ago, and then Trent had paired Wilson with Brutus for the Fall Festival.

Tornado was still a bit excitable, but he'd done really well with Lauren. *That's because Lauren has calm energy,*

Trent thought. As he'd been working with his police dogs —and taking training courses from the K9 Unit in Seattle —he'd learned a lot about a person's energy.

And Tornado hadn't whined once with Lauren, so she definitely possessed an energy that spoke to Tornado's.

"Pizza," Porter said as Trent drove by The Slice. Simple things like that used to frustrate him, but now he just flipped around and parked across the street. If his son wanted pizza, they'd get pizza.

Trent held his son's hand as they crossed the street— properly, in the crosswalk. He didn't need anything getting back to his boss that he wasn't a law-abiding citizen when he wasn't on duty.

They joined the line for family night pizza, and by the time they had their two boxes and were ready to head to the beach, the sun was already sinking fast. Trent sighed. He really disliked winter, and it seemed like the season was nearly upon them.

As he set the pizza boxes on the seat on the passenger side and then turned to move around the front of his truck, his eyes caught a flyer taped to the lamppost.

"Magleby Mansion grand unveiling," he read aloud. He pulled down the paper and searched for the date. It was next weekend, and he heard Lauren's voice saying, "You should come. You should come."

Surely she didn't mean as her date, but when Trent thought about those few charged moments in his back yard, his thoughts turned muddy.

He folded the flyer and put it in his back pocket before he got behind the wheel. He'd simply ask her tomorrow when he went to sign the work contract.

The beach brought relief to his soul in a way that nothing else could. Savannah had loved the sound of the surf, the feel of sand against her bare feet, and watching the sun sink into the waves.

Trent had tolerated the beach while she'd been alive, but now he treasured his time there, especially when he went with Porter. He felt closer to her there than anywhere else, and he often told his son stories about her while they ate or threw a Frisbee for the dogs.

Tonight, Trent felt weary though he hadn't even put on his uniform and gone into work. He sighed as he sank onto the blanket he kept in the back of the truck.

"Wait," he told the dogs, who quivered with anticipation of running out into the waves. Several other canines ran around the sand, but Trent's dogs couldn't go until he released them. And they better come back as soon as he whistled.

Wilson sat, which helped Pecorino and Brutus to do the same. "Tornado," Trent said as if he didn't care at all if the dog sat or not. But he did, and Trent said, "Yep."

All four dogs sprinted toward the ocean, with Tornado barking every other step. Trent shook his head and laughed as they met the water and sent splashes several feet into the air.

"Your mom used to make the best chocolate mint

brownies," he said to Porter as the boy opened the lid on the first pizza box. "And we never came to the beach without them, even though I used to tease her that they'd melt."

Porter picked up a piece of pizza and paused before he took a bite. "Do you know how to make the brownies?"

"I have her recipes, yeah." But Trent hadn't made any of them. He made boxed macaroni and cheese, or spaghetti, or hamburgers and hot dogs. Savannah used to make delicious pasta casseroles and the best soups and stews on the planet. But Trent hadn't been able to bring himself to pull out her binder and look at her handwriting as she made adjustments to the measurements or left herself notes for what to do next time she made the dish.

Because it was too painful of a reminder that there would be no next time.

"We should make them," Porter said. "Maybe for Aunt Eliza's birthday."

"Yeah." Trent ate and kept watch over the dogs while the sun sank. When they had just enough time to get back to the truck before it was too dark to see, he packed up and took his son home.

THE NEXT DAY, TRENT SHOWED UP TO WORK TO FIND ADAM Herrin in a less-than-joyful mood. "What's up with him?"

Trent asked out of the side of his mouth. Sarah, Adam's personal secretary, glared at the Police Chief's door. "Oh, someone called and asked about the security plan for the Festival of Trees, and you know how the Chief feels about that."

Trent did know, and he also understood Adam's frustration. "The Fall Festival ended ten days ago."

"That's exactly what Adam said." Sarah gave Trent's hand a pat. "How's Porter?"

"He's doing great." Trent started to move over to his desk, hoping he didn't have any paperwork to deal with from his day off.

"Didn't you have a date over the weekend?" Sarah asked, and Trent cringed. He'd enlisted almost everyone around him to help him find a girlfriend, and while it had sounded like a good idea at the time, now Trent was really regretting it.

"Yeah, it isn't going to work out."

"I have a neighbor—"

"I think I'm going to try it on my own for a while." Trent gave Sarah a smile he hoped would soften his words. He wasn't sure if he was saying he'd find his own dates or if he'd just like to stop dating for a while.

Until Lauren Michaels had shown up at his house yesterday afternoon, Trent would've chosen never going out again. But she had him reconsidering his decision.

Thankfully, he only had a couple of reports on his

desk, and he flew through them before heading outside to work with his German shepherds.

As he set up a new "bomb" for Tornado to find, Chief Herrin came through the gate. "You got a minute, Trent?" he asked.

"Sure thing, Chief." Trent paused in his prep.

"I'd like you to run point on the Festival of Trees security," Adam said without looking away from Trent. "How do you feel about that?"

Pride swelled in Trent's chest. "Sure thing."

"I need a report by the end of the week." He finally glanced around the dog training arena. "I know it'll take you from this more than you'd like. But with Janey pregnant, I'm not sure I can handle another event right now."

"Janey's pregnant?" Trent rarely knew any town news, and he grinned at his boss and good friend. "That's good news, right?"

"It is, yeah." Adam smiled back. "But she's high-risk, and I'm trying to juggle things at home, and with Jess...." He blew out his breath. "I can't take on the Festival of Trees."

"I've worked it for three years, boss. I can do it." Trent really wanted to do a good job, not just for Adam, but to feel like he was doing something good with his life.

He'd never struggled before Savannah passed away, but now he felt like he really needed to make something of his life. The problem was, he didn't know how, and often simply reverted to keeping Porter fed and bathed, his yard and garden in tip-top shape, and tried to get his dogs to find trace amounts of explosives in pull toys.

He was comfortable in his life, and heading up the team for the Festival of Trees would pull him from that comfort zone.

And so would going out with Lauren Michaels.

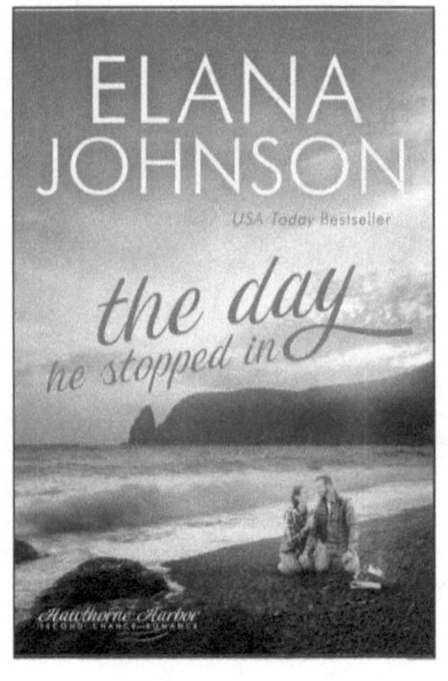

The Day He Stopped In (Hawthorne Harbor Second Chance Romance, Book 2): Janey Germaine is tired of entertaining tourists in Olympic National Park all day and trying to keep her twelve-year-old son occupied at night. When longtime friend and the Chief of Police, Adam Herrin, offers to take the boy on a ride-along one fall evening, Janey starts to see him in a different light. Do they have the courage to take their relationship out of the friend zone?

The Day He Said Hello (Hawthorne Harbor Second Chance Romance, Book 3): Bennett Patterson is content with his boring firefighting job and his big great dane...until he comes face-toface with his high school girlfriend, Jennie Zimmerman, who swore she'd never return to Hawthorne Harbor. Can they rekindle their old flame? Or will their opposite personalities keep them apart?

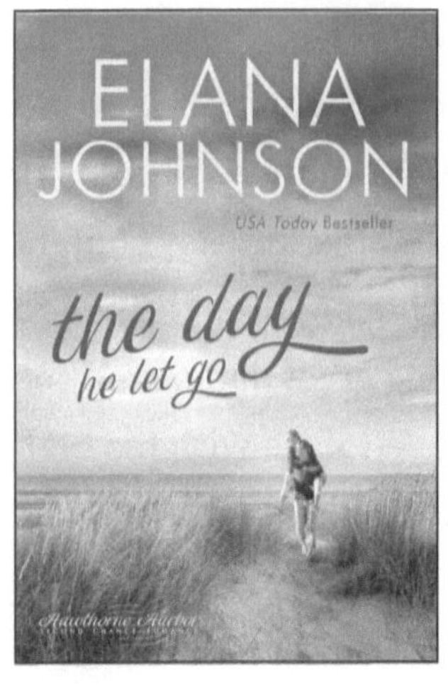

The Day He Let Go (Hawthorne Harbor Second Chance Romance, Book 4): Trent Baker is ready for another relationship, and he's hopeful he can find someone who wants him and to be a mother to his son. Lauren Michaels runs her own general contract company, and she's never thought she has a maternal bone in her body. But when she gets a second chance with the handsome K9 cop who blew her off when she first came to town, she can't say no... Can Trent and Lauren make their differences into strengths and build a family?

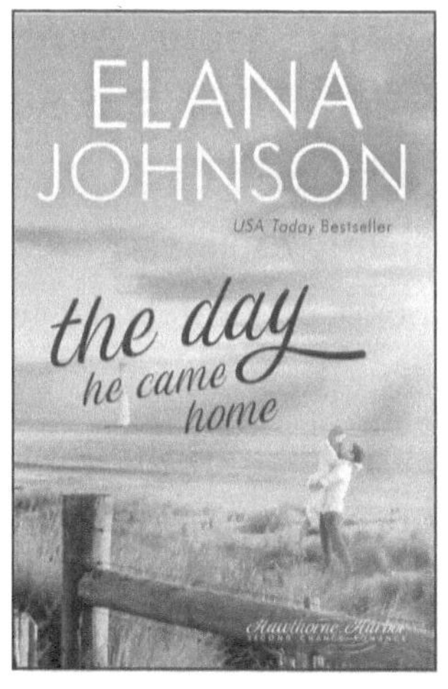

The Day He Came Home (Hawthorne Harbor Second Chance Romance, Book 5): A wounded Marine returns to Hawthorne Harbor years after the woman he was married to for exactly one week before she got an annulment...and then a baby nine months later. Can Hunter and Alice make a family out of past heartache?

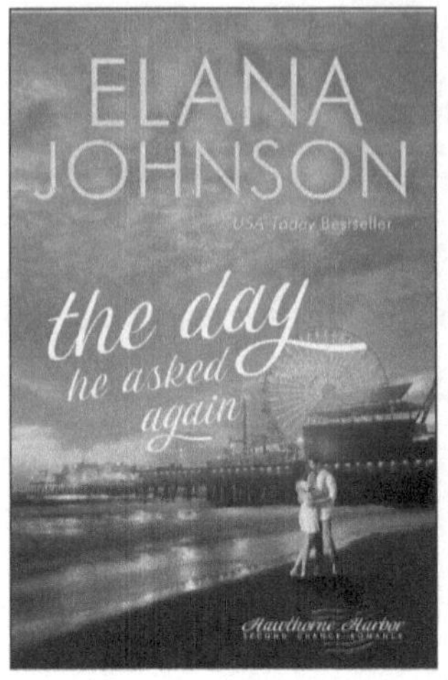

The Day He Asked Again (Hawthorne Harbor Second Chance Romance, Book 6): A Coast Guard captain would rather spend his time on the sea...unless he's with the woman he's been crushing on for months. Can Brooklynn and Dave make their second chance stick?

The Billionaire's Enemy (Book 1): A local island B&B owner hates the swanky high-rise hotel down the beach...but not the billionaire who owns it. Can she deal with strange summer weather, tourists, and falling in love?

The Billionaire's Driver (Book 2): A car service owner who's been driving the billionaire pineapple plantation owner for years finally gives him a birthday gift that opens his eyes to see her, the woman who's literally been right in front of him all this time. Can he open his heart to the possibility of true love?

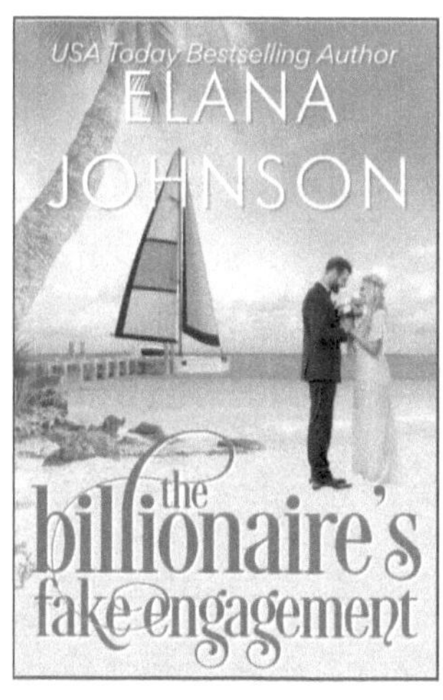

The Billionaire's Fake Engagement (Book 3): A former poker player turned beach bum billionaire needs a date to a hospital gala, so he asks the beach yoga instructor his dog can't seem to stay away from. At the event, they get "engaged" to deter her former boyfriend from pursuing her. Can he move his fake fiancée into a real relationship?

The Billionaire's Cinderella (Book 4): The owner of a beach-side drink stand has taken more bad advice from rich men than humanly possible, which requires her to take a second job cleaning the home of a billionaire and global diamond mine owner. Can she put aside her preconceptions about rich men and make a relationship with him work?

The Billionaire's Bodyguard (Book 5): Women can be rich too...and this female billionaire can usually take care of herself just fine, thank you very much. But she has no defense against her past...or the gorgeous man she hires to protect her from it. He's her bodyguard, not her boyfriend. Will she be able to keep those two B-words separate or will she take her second chance to get her tropical happily-ever-after?

The Billionaire's Boyfriend (Book 6): Can a closet organizer fit herself into a single father's hectic life? Or will this female billionaire choose work over love...again?

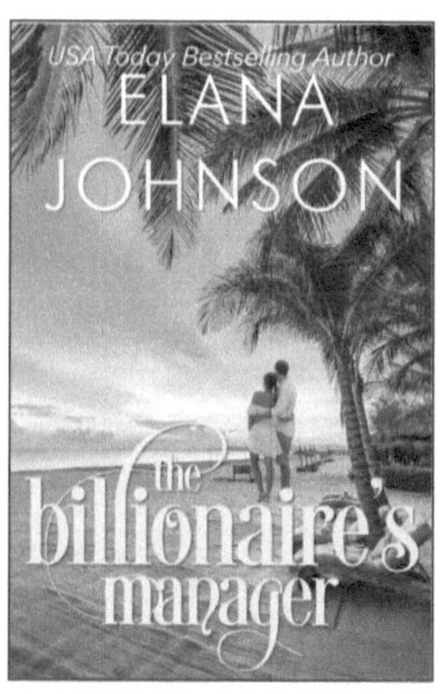 **The Billionaire's Manager (Book 7):** A billionaire who has a love affair with his job, his new bank manager, and how they bravely navigate the island of Getaway Bay...and their own ideas about each other.

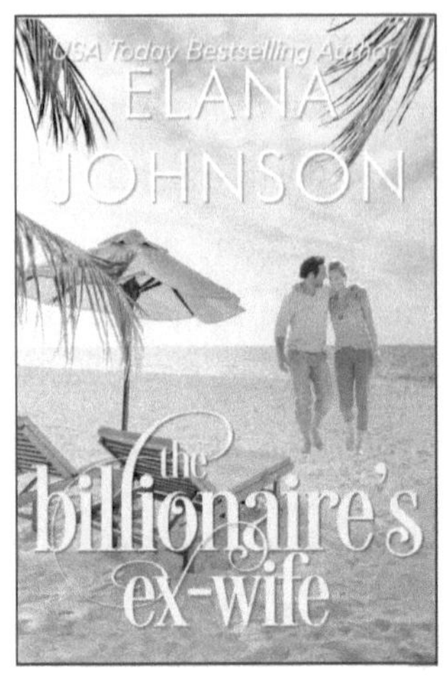

The **Billionaire's Ex-Wife (Book 8):** A silver fox, a dating app, and the mistaken identity that brings this billionaire faceto-face with his ex-wife...

The Helicopter Pilot's Bride (Book 1): Charlotte Madsen's whole world came crashing down six months ago with the words, "I met someone else." Her marriage of eleven years dissolved, and she left one island on the east coast for the island of Getaway Bay. She was not expecting a tall, handsome man to be flat on his back under the kitchen sink when she arrives at the supposedly abandoned house. But former Air Force pilot, Dawson Dane, has a charming devil-may-care personality, and Charlotte could use some happiness in her life.

Can Charlotte navigate the healing process to find love again?

The Billionaire's Bride (Book 2): Two best friends, their hasty agreement, and the fake engagement that has the island of Getaway Bay in a tailspin...

The Prince's Bride (Book 3): She's a synchronized swimmer looking to make some extra cash. He's a prince in hiding. When they meet in the "empty" mansion she's supposed to be housesitting, sparks fly. Can Noah and Zara stop arguing long enough to realize their feelings for each other might be romantic?

The Doctor's Bride (Book 4): A doctor, a wedding planner, and a flat tire... Can Shannon and Jeremiah make a love connection when they work next door to each other?

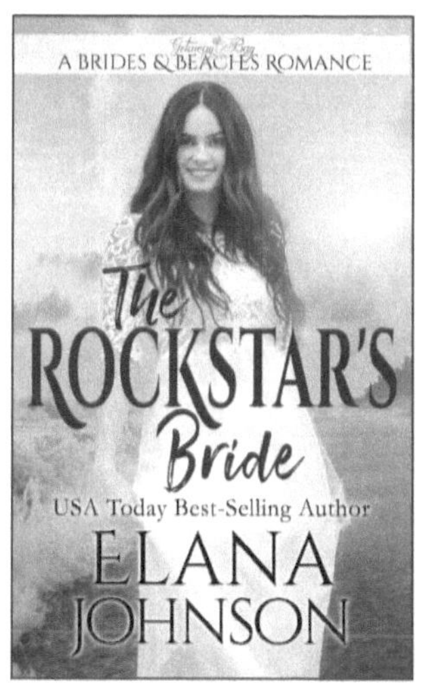

The Rockstar's Bride (Book 5): Riley finds a watch and contacts the owner, only to learn he's the lead singer and guitarist for a hugely popular band. Evan is only on the island of Getaway Bay for a friend's wedding, but he's intrigued by the gorgeous woman who returns his watch. Can they make a relationship work when they're from two different worlds?

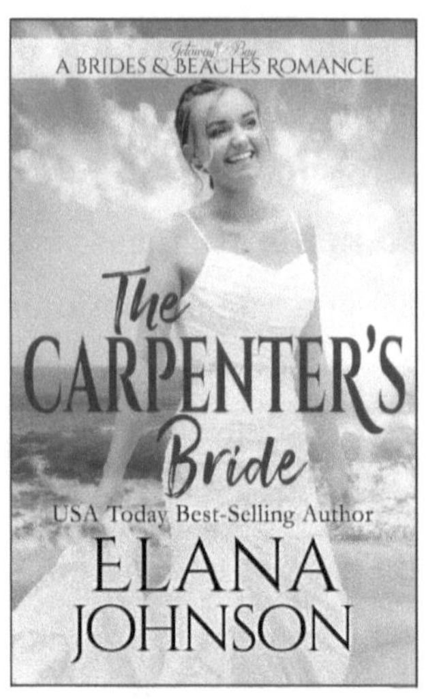

The Carpenter's Bride (Book 6): A wedding planner and the carpenter who's lost his wife... Can Lisa and Cal navigate the mishaps of a relationship in order to find themselves standing at the altar?

The Police Chief's Bride (Book 7): The Chief of Police and a woman with a restraining order against her... Can Wyatt and Deirdre try for their second chance at love? Or will their pasts keep them apart forever?

Love and Landslides (Book 1): A freak storm has her sliding down the mountain...right into the arms of her ex. As Eden and Holden spend time out in the wilds of Hawaii trying to survive, their old flame is rekindled. But with secrets and old feelings in the way, will Holden be able to take all the broken pieces of his life and put them back together in a way that makes sense? Or will he lose his heart and the reputation of his company because of a single landslide?

Kisses and Killer Whales (Book 2): Friends who ditch her. A pod of killer whales. A limping cruise ship. All reasons Iris finds herself stranded on an deserted island with the handsome Navy SEAL...

Storms and Sentiments (Book 3): He can throw a precision pass, but he's dead in the water in matters of the heart...

Crushes and Cowboys (Book 4): Tired of the dating scene, a cowboy billionaire puts up an Internet ad to find a woman to come out to a deserted island with him to see if they can make a love connection...

Accidental Sweetheart (Book 2): She's excited to have a neighbor across the hall. He's got secrets he can never tell her. Will Olympia find a way to leave her past where it belongs so she can have a future with Chet?

Bodyguard not Boyfriend (Book 3): She's got a stalker. He's got a loud bark. Can Sheryl tame her bodyguard into a boyfriend?

Not Her Real Fiancé (Book 4): He needs a reason not to go out with a journalist. She'd like a guaranteed date for the summer. They don't get along, so keeping Brad in the not-her-real-fiancé category should be easy for Celeste. Totally easy.

She Loves Him...Not (Book 5): They've been out before, and now they work in the same kitchen at The Heartwood Inn. Gwen isn't interested in getting anything filleted but fish, because Teagan's broken her heart before... Can Teagan and Gwen manage their professional relationship without letting feelings get in the way?

ABOUT ELANA

Elana Johnson is the USA Today bestselling author of
dozens of clean and wholesome contemporary romance
novels. She lives In Utah, where she mothers two fur
babies, taxis her daughter to theater several times a week,
and eats a lot of Ferrero Rocher while writing. Find her on
her website at elanajohnson.com.